I0682589

SEXTING

GB Hope

Sexting

A work of erotic fiction by GB Hope ©

with graphic sexual content

Published by GB Hope in the United Kingdom 2013

ISBN: 978-0-9570745-5-2

Cover design by Jon Parris

Printed by Lightning Source UK 2013

5 copies of this book have been sent to British Libraries for legal deposit

By the same author:

Who Do You Think *You* Are? You're My Henry Allbones

Queen of Spades

Stranger on Stranger

The Genie-alogy of Nathan Levy

Fighting Out of Mobberley, England

Fighting Out of New Milford, USA

To Joey

Acknowledgements

Many thanks to my alpha readers:
Kay Bolton, Amy Gray and Bernie Morris

SEXTING

PROLOGUE

ELISE: *Have my panties arrived there yet?*

MICHAEL: *Oh, and good evening to you — it's half past five here. Finally talking to me, then? :) I just knew you were sending panties. No, nothing has arrived yet. You know, there's a man in Toxteth, Liverpool, who works at the main Post Office sorting depot, who sits wearing your panties every night while he watches TV. Haha.*

IRENE HANNAH: *Michael, I got the money. Thank you so much. Please stay and be my friend on here. I know I've not deserved your friendship. Please tell me how I can make it up to you.*

CINDY: *Michael, somehow I think how to taste your lips, how to taste your skin, how you sound... LOL #I'm going insane. I read too much romantic erotic novel, hehe. Seriously, my Belgian friend ask to be more than friend. I say I want to him May I back off? He go away upset. I so confused. My family conservative. I can't talk them.*

MICHAEL: *Elise, I'm so good, aren't I? I'm still giggling about the Post Office man. He's sitting there in just your panties. Hahahaha. And his wife is there doing the crossword as if nothing is out of the ordinary! Hahahaha. No, seriously, they'll probably show up tomorrow. Unless you put the wrong address on. I've got a weird neighbour, we call him the Prince of Darkness. Maybe he got them. You didn't put your address in the package, did you? I dread to think what he'll send you back. Hahahaha.*

ELISE: *You're a very bad man, you know.*

1

CINDY

Early in his writing career Michael Lincoln expected he would look up from his word processor, out through his window and be able to take in the flat calm of the Pacific Ocean, or the choppy Atlantic. The North Sea, even, maybe the Thames river. Some body of water, surely. He glanced up from the first draft of his third crime novel and beheld the magnificent vista of Garrand's Scrap Yard in Newton-le-Willows, Merseyside.

Michael's novels sold quite well on Amazon and electronic platforms, but the shabby view seemed to sum up his lack of serious success. Also, Michael was not one of those lucky bastards who wrote one letter to a publisher and were offered a massive deal. He was in the 2,000 rejection slip club, although he was yet to paper his spare room with them, and had long ago given up on finding an agent. Nowadays he got turned down by email. His publisher/editor was a one man band working out of Swindon in Wiltshire, a quiet man who seemed to be terrified of technology, but together they muddled through and somehow made a profit.

Michael wandered across his open plan warehouse conversion flat, heading to the coffee machine. He loved the place; it wasn't the largest space in the building but he had his lounge area with massive plasma TV, his pool table and, on the far wall, a mini-football goal with a heavy curtain hanging behind it to collect his wayward shots; yes, a bizarre thing for an adult to have indoors but a great way to relieve the tension of hours on the keyboard. Michael flicked up one of his mini-footballs and volleyed it into the top left corner of the net. Unfortunately, his Nike mule went with it so he had to go and retrieve it.

His writing wasn't enough to pay for the flat. For that he had his late Uncle Harry's will to thank, and his own success on a BBC game show. Drinking his coffee, Michael looked out of the windows on the front of the building. All he could see from this angle was his junior school, surely not something a mover and shaker should be able to do. At least Michael, now thirty-seven, had not been born in Newton-le-Willows. His parents had escaped to the country from London when he was four. Why the countryside they picked was the Wirral, just across the Mersey from Liverpool, was a mystery to him. Then they had drifted over to this historic town, which Michael loved a great deal. Some friends lived nearby, and a couple of schoolmates were literally nearby as they were called Garrand and ran the scrap yard.

Michael returned to his study area, sat down and turned on his computer. While he waited, he drank his coffee and looked at his daughter's photo on his desk. Hope Lincoln was nine years old, currently living in Manchester with her mother and her mother's new knob head, South African, boyfriend. "Get off my car, kaffir!" Only four months since he was officially divorced, the emotion of the event still troubled Michael. He saw Hope as often as possible, and she was exactly the same happy little girl, considering the upheaval, and he loved her with all his heart. His ex-wife, Sam, was a good-looking woman; he no longer thought of her as beautiful because that would assume she had morals and was beautiful on the inside. No, she was sexy and clever and stupid all rolled into one package. The woman had illogically trashed his life without any meaningful reason or warning (he was 100% sure there had not been another man at the time). He would try to remain civil with the woman only for his daughter's sake. As he sat there, he thought of one unfortunate side-effect of the situation; it had always been a running joke that Hope would eventually attend the Hope Academy school on the edge of town. Not to be, now.

He shook his head and went on to his favourite book website at the moment: *GoodReads*, intending to check the entrants for his latest giveaway. His Recent Updates page flashed up and he was inordinately happy to see the little red sign that meant he had four messages, plus there was some sort of notification. He checked the status of his book first, ten copies of which were on offer. He wasn't convinced that *GoodReads* was the most fruitful way to get a book noticed; most people seemed to simply 'mark as to read' without any intention of buying a copy. There were 902 entrants, with two days to go. Not bad.

He checked the notification. Some man called Gary, from Canada, wanted to be his friend. Gary was no doubt a great guy, but that request would be ignored. It was probably wrong from a professional point of view to be even slightly negative on that kind of thing but it still seemed odd to Michael to make friends with complete strangers. When he saw *GoodReads* members with 3,000+ friends it baffled him; what was the point of it? Michael had seven friends on the site. Not counting his publisher's wife, he had two middle-aged American women who loved crime novels, and who said hello occasionally. There was his real friend in Newton-le-Willows, Tony, a rabid John Grisham fan, who introduced Michael to the site in the first place. He had Beverley in Leicester, who he chatted with from time to time; eighteen-year-old Irene Hannah in the Philippines, who had a very pretty face in her profile picture but never said two words to him and, oh, there was twenty-three-year-old Cindy in Indonesia. Cindy who would just not shut up, and the fact that her English was so appalling made Michael at one stage consider the rude option of barring her. But she seemed harmless enough so he battled through, even giving her

English lessons now and again.

Speak of the devil, one of the messages was from her, of course. Michael blew out his cheeks and opened the message. Fuck me, he thought; at the first impression, it was even more incomprehensible than normal.

CINDY: *Hello, kekke. Wotcha. Enter you giveway, thnks giving to Indonesia aswell usual place.*

Yes, thought Michael, opening up the giveaway to Indonesia because of Cindy would surely mean one of her compatriots would win a copy and that he would incur about £10 in postage. Michael came off Cindy's message for a moment. Instead, he checked his email. Just the one from his publisher, Henry, asking if he had wished the entrants good luck, as they had agreed on. He quickly fired off a reply saying he had done so for each and every one of the 902 entrants so far. Then, for the hell of it, he decided to send a few anyway. He went into the list of entrants and picked a woman called Janet who, from her profile image photo, looked quite normal. She came from Birmingham. He sent her a message wishing her the best of luck in the giveaway. Then he chose a male called Ivan, who he found came from Chicago, and gave him the same message. Next, he stumbled across a lovely Asian woman in a red blouse, by the name of Elise. Looking at her profile, he craned forward and paid more attention. She was nineteen years old and lived in Singapore. Singapore was a new one on him; all he knew was that it was an island in the Far East, lost to the Japanese in World War Two, Raffles hotel and Changi prison camp. Interesting name though, he felt, for an Asian: Elise McHugh.

MICHAEL: *Hi Elise, I just wanted to wish you the best of luck in my giveaway.*
Kind Regards,

Michael Lincoln

A large truck banged into Garrand's scrap yard down below. Michael watched Stephen Garrand hopping from a portacabin to wave it in, then rush to close the gate with a nervous glance left and right. Michael smiled at his shady neighbours' activities. The older of the two Garrand brothers was definitely a complete rogue. A few months ago when virtually all the manhole covers and grids in nearby Warrington had been stolen, Michael had suspected the Garrand brothers.

Alfie Garrand came into view. Both he and his brother were built like middleweight boxers. A heated conversation ensued with the wagon driver. Michael left them to it and returned his attention to *GoodReads*. That girl, Elise, certainly was cute. He looked closer at her profile page. She had the ubiquitous *Tumblr* thing, and expressed her love for

Young Adult, Dystopian and Crime books. Only seven friends like himself – clearly she was quite sane.

It was getting late in Indonesia so he decided to bite the bullet and attempt to translate Cindy's message.

CINDY: *Hello, kekke. Wotcha. Enter your giveway. Thnks giving to Indonesia aswell usual place. Bad day here, kekke. My mood very low, change profile picture many time. Want life to go fast so life is over.*

Good grief, thought Michael, she's really on one today. He checked her profile picture; indeed new, but still sexy and with her brunette hair coming forward to her eyes. Probably if she was ugly he would have already dumped her.

MICHAEL: *Hi, Cindy, I see your English is coming along :p*
What's upset you?

2

ALFIE

Most of the consignment on the truck was, in fact, legal, but there was a quantity of copper wire, stripped from the railways, tucked in there as well and, because the driver had been late, it prompted a few heated words. Alfie Garrand was more overtly aggressive than his brother, so it was Stephen who brought the matter to a close, putting an arm around the driver's shoulder and calling over the young lads who worked for him to get on with the unloading.

'I'm sorry I was late, Stephen,' said the driver. 'There was a crash on the East Lancs road.'

'It's all right, Frank. Don't mind Alfie there, his missus is giving him jip again.'

'Fuck off!' called Alfie, overhearing them.

Stephen laughed. 'Come and have a cup of tea, Frank.'

Loud banging on the metal gate stopped them dead. Surely it wasn't another police and council officials spot-check. Britain had gone metal theft mad recently and the authorities were cracking down on it. But then a woman's voice broke the tension.

'Alfie, open the frigging gate!'

Stephen laughed again. 'I rest my case. The delightful Shirley Garrand.'

'Fuck off again,' said Alfie, going towards his wife's dulcet tones.

Alfie opened the heavy gate and found his blonde wife in an agitated state, her black Porsche Cayenne standing there, which was a surprise as they only lived thirty seconds walk away. 'What's wrong, babe?'

'The fucking Dibble stopped me over the tinted side windows on the Cayenne,' said Shirley Garrand in her strong Liverpudlian accent. 'Made me rip one off and ordered me to remove the others.'

Alfie examined the ruined tints to the driver's side window.

'They were right sarcastic bastards, as well,' continued Shirley. 'Nothing better to do. Damaged my nails doing it.'

'Babe,' whispered Alfie, embracing his designer-clad wife. 'Don't let it upset you. You just go home, put your feet up and forget it. I'll put a new tint on.'

Shirley's rage subsided; her world was back in equilibrium. She kissed Alfie.

'What do you want for lunch?' she asked.

'Can I have you?'

She giggled, pushed hair out of her right eye, and patted his chest. 'Don't be naughty.'

She kissed him again before retrieving her handbag from the vehicle and tottering off on her huge platform shoes. How does she drive in those? thought Alfie. He didn't immediately drive the Porsche into the yard, as a man was approaching. The man was in his sixties, scruffily dressed, shambling along, but he also got a kiss from a passing Shirley Garrand. Alfie jumped into the Porsche and moved it onto their property.

'All right, Rimski?' called Alfie, jumping out and clicking the Porsche locked.

The man entered the yard and Alfie closed up the gate behind him. His name was Lionel Rimmer, a member of the Garrand's staff, who answered to Rimski even though it wasn't an appropriate nickname for his age any more.

'Look at this,' said Rimski, offering up a plastic oval cup, similar to half a pair of flying goggles.

'What am I looking at?' asked Alfie, puzzled.

'I've had my first cataract done. I've got to wear this bloody thing at night so I don't scratch myself.'

'Oh, of course, your operation. Did it go well?'

'It's fantastic! Everything's so clear, straightaway. The green of the gate stands out. Shirley's car there is shiny, when it was dull to me yesterday. I tell you, that...'

'Yeah, yeah, okay, Rimski. Don't go overboard. I'll look forward to my own operation one day. What brings you in?'

'The doctor says I can go to work as normal, but no heavy lifting or bending for a month.'

Alfie looked at the older man as if he had just called his mother a whore.

'So, basically what you're saying is, you're no use to man nor beast for a month?'

Rimski pulled a face that suggested he was only following doctor's orders. Alfie laughed.

'Come on,' said Alfie. 'I think the kettle's on. I've got an easy job for you that your great eyesight is perfect for. Putting a tint back on that car window.'

'But I'm not working today, Alfie.'

'I think you are.'

Michael needed another cup of coffee after reading Cindy's reply:

CINDY: *Michael, although when I was eighteen I'm feel so old. Being old is nothing, age is only age :p. I always hope I will face my old age faster, die faster, as soon as leave this world is better.*

Back to his desk, he watched Shirley Garrand walking from the scrap yard. Whenever he saw her, he was always flashed back to his teenage years: the hottest girl in school. Never gave him a second glance. Bitch. He grinned to himself and sat back down, starting to type.

MICHAEL: *Cindy, what's all this talk about death? You want to live fast and die young? Don't be upset, there's always an answer to the thing that's upsetting you. Hey, listen, if I base a character on you she'll be cute, sexy, intelligent (though her English won't be very good :p)*

He could see she was online at that very moment. He decided to stay with it in case she responded immediately.

CINDY: *Michael, base of my character. OMG. Sorry I disturb you work. I feel down, that's all. Don't worry. Don't make character silly bitch. Kekke. I travel to other side of country soon. Miss me?*

Michael drank more coffee and set down his cup.

MICHAEL: *Cindy, what's on the other side of the country?*

She was still online, but was taking a long time getting back to him, so he delved into the chapter of his manuscript that was causing him trouble. No correct path to take jumped out at him, so he returned to Cindy, as she had appeared again.

CINDY: *Michael, thanks for attention. I tell you when get there. Sorry for dramatical words, heh. I need to calm myself, this situation normal for me. I know I can handle it myself, your message arrives on the edge of my upset.*

Haaaaaaa, thank for everythink. :D

Speak you tomorrow.

Aww, he thought, sipping his coffee. He checked Cindy's profile image, sweet with her brown hair in a fringe just above her eyes. He wished he could be there to give her a hug, and maybe travel with her.

3

SINGAPORE

Nineteen-year-old Tricia Kin asked her daddy for a Ferrari 430 for passing her driving test. The man had laughed in her face. A Porsche 911 had been her compromise option. He laughed again, kissed her on the forehead, and told her he loved her very much, but he had a meeting to get to. An Audi, then?

So she was having her first drive in her brand new Audi A3 sportback around the Queenstown area of Singapore. Her daddy had eventually agreed to the smaller A1, but it was a done deal.

She turned into the underground car-park of a new apartment condominium and parked alongside Mr McHugh's Kia Sportage. She liked being alongside Alexander McHugh in any way, shape or form. She didn't know exactly what the man did for a living, a bit like her father, but this was one of his latest developments – fingers in many pies, so to speak.

There were only a few other vehicles in the car-park, as most of the residents had yet to take possession of their properties.

Tricia made her way up to the condominium's swimming pool area, guided by the playful squeals of children. She came out into the blue oasis just as little Lewis McHugh bombed into the deep end. His laughing older brother, Peter, avoided the splash, as did Tricia with a little skip. Mrs McHugh, a petite Singaporean woman, spotted Tricia's arrival, took her by the hand and led her towards the bar where the very handsome Caucasian, Mr McHugh, was playing at being a cocktail bartender. His face lit up on seeing Tricia: a new customer.

'No, no,' she protested, laughing. 'Hello, Mr McHugh. I'm driving. Just something soft, please.'

'I don't do anything soft, Tricia,' he replied, looking straight at her with his piercing blue eyes.

Tricia blushed. She was pleased that Mrs McHugh hadn't seemed to notice.

'Sit down, dear,' said Mrs McHugh. 'You don't like to swim, do you?'

'Not in the slightest, Mrs McHugh. Unlike Elise. Where is she, by the way?'

Mr McHugh pressed a small cocktail on Tricia. 'No worries with that, I promise, Tricia.' He winked at her.

Tricia felt herself absolutely burning. 'Thank you, Mr McHugh.'

Elise McHugh put in an appearance, looking sultry and

stunning in a skimpy black bikini, her jet black hair pulled back into a ponytail. She wasn't particularly tall, but quite toned. Tricia exchanged waves with her best friend, as ever coveting her gorgeous figure, before Elise dived head first into the pool. She swam almost the entire length underwater before emerging to wrestle her two kid brothers.

Mr McHugh came from behind the bar and sat near to Tricia. Tricia fancied Western men in general, but the suave Alexander McHugh really floated her boat. She sipped her cocktail and expressed her delight to him. He turned away pleased, and missed her secret grimace to a smiling Mrs McHugh.

'Elise says you might be leaving us,' said Mrs McHugh.

'Yes, I'm thinking of studying abroad. Seattle or London.'

'Well, I don't know about Seattle, but I've been to London with Alex. Perhaps his English relatives could help you if you choose there.'

'Thank you, that would be wonderful, Mrs McHugh.'

They watched Elise and the boys swim for a while, before Elise hauled herself from the pool, squeezed her hair down over her left shoulder and joined them, towelling herself down. Mr McHugh fetched his daughter a drink, before settling back down beside Tricia. Elise sat on the other side of her friend to hear all about the Audi. Mid-description about the climate control, Tricia's phone beeped with a message, the tenth that day; there was a new boyfriend on the scene, as well as a new car. Tricia read it, then ignored it. Naturally the two girls discussed the boyfriend, a handsome Singaporean who worked in the banking industry. Elise had already heard intimate details of Tricia's new relationship. She herself was single. There had been boyfriends, but surprisingly for such a beauty, Elise McHugh was still a virgin. Not that she was shy, just well brought up in a loving family. She was interested in sex, saw enough of it on *Tumblr*, and liked the *Fifty Shades of Grey* style books in her love of reading.

The two girls left the condominium soon after, Elise in a tracksuit and baseball cap, intending to bathe once home to the apartment she and Tricia shared. Tricia drove joyously and Elise agreed that the car felt very sporty. Nowhere took very long on the small island of Singapore and they were soon at their apartment block in the exclusive Mandarin Gallery, on Orchard Road.

While Tricia prepared some dinner, Elise went for her bath. It had been a busy day; although on holiday from school she had endured the dentist, cheered herself with some retail therapy, then joining her family for the swim before the condo was officially handed over.

Amid the detritus of a quick noodle dish (Tricia being a poor cook) the two girls lounged around on their laptops; Tricia making contact with her boyfriend, Elise checking Facebook, then on to *GoodReads* to find a new book. It was nice to have a few new messages; Janelea in San Francisco, and, ooh, Danny in Melbourne. Elise felt herself blush a little. The final message wished her good luck in the giveaway she had entered. It pleasantly surprised her. 'Gosh, how nice,' she said, but Tricia was too engrossed to hear. Elise immediately checked the profile of this author, Michael Lincoln. She didn't actually remember entering the giveaway, but she probably went in it because so few of them are open to more than the US, UK and Canada. His profile photo was black and white, but he looked okay. Quite sexy and distinguished, in fact. She liked older guys, especially Englishmen, and Australians.

ELISE: *Dear Mr Lincoln, thank you so much for your good luck message. I hope I win, but will definitely get the book regardless.*

Dylan Wang wanted more than anything to be a classical guitarist. He took his guitar everywhere with him, he played on the bus and in the park, entertained work colleagues and delighted some, but not all, of his girlfriends; not that he had many girlfriends. His work was in the uninspiring hotel trade, as a porter, and when he did find a girlfriend, she was invariably a receptionist or a waitress he met there.

He was a good-looking guy, though a bit shy and very morally upstanding, with a genuine personality. He was liked by everyone, and in the hotel staff room it was a fun thing, while resting between shifts, to listen to him play. Nobody thought he used his talent to make friends or to get female attention; he was just Dylan.

Dylan was keen to improve himself, if not by becoming a professional musician, then by training to be a doctor. It was such an extraordinary ambition for his family that he rarely mentioned it, especially to his father. He had applied to attend the Lee Kong Chian School of Medicine in the autumn, already having passed two tests and begun the interview procedure. He was prepared for the long haul of studying; perhaps he would get his musical break in the meantime.

Dylan drove an old Honda Civic, when he could get it to start. He shared an apartment with two other porters. But they were night porters, so as long as he didn't wake them with his music, it seemed like he lived alone.

He had six older brothers, possibly one of the reasons why he felt secure enough to be happy with the world. They all watched his back and encouraged his music. He also had a younger sister, whom he doted on.

Currently he was between girlfriends; that was how he thought of it (a bit like Michael Lincoln being between wives). But he was talking with a specific barmaid at work and hoped to persuade her to go out on a date with him soon.

4

PLASTIC BOBBY

Michael Lincoln had not really dated since the collapse of his marriage. He was on good terms with a couple of local women in the pub, and there had been a little action there, but he wasn't interested in anything serious. Of course, his friends had tried to fix him up with someone, and his best mate's sister, Keira, was the latest to be linked with him. She was a thirty-year-old divorcee herself, with a son the same age as Hope. Always a willowy blonde, she was now still sexy, if a little drawn in the face and her hair a little less lustrous. Michael supposed he would have been happy to get together with her, if his head had been in the right place. Keira lived towards the train station end of the town, in one of those new-build rabbit hutches where you can drive the car into the garage, as long as you don't intend to get out of it.

Michael took a walk onto the High Street, glancing to the bend in the road where the imposing St Peter's church stood, past the Old Forge which best friend, Tony, said had once belonged to his ancestors, and was now someone's nice home. A couple of people acknowledged him in passing. He took his time, mulling over the description of a murder in his new book. Often, he would wander the town, having a good think, sometimes riding on his bike. He certainly wasn't one of those writers who sat at their laptop in a pub or café.

'Michael, hi!'

The police never used to greet him with "Michael, hi!" but this was a female Police Community Support Officer, one of those low-paid, plastic, police officers with limited powers of arrest (or no powers of arrest, he wasn't sure) who walked aimlessly around the streets, pretending to be real police. Michael smiled because this particular PCSO was in fact, Keira. He allowed himself to imagine that her wide smile was for more than just friendship. She looked remarkably sexy in her stern uniform, with her hair up in a ponytail, underneath a cap with a blue band.

'Hi, yourself, Keira. I thought I was bang in trouble there for a minute.'

'You might just be,' she teased.

'You're a bit off your normal beat, aren't you?'

'I'm covering for a colleague's illness. Have I caught you having one of your plot walkabouts? Sorry, Tony said that's what you do sometimes.'

'Keira, you shouldn't say caught you, you'll have me fixating on the powers of your uniform.'

'Oh, I'm just me, Michael.' She paused, moved from one Doc Martin to the other. He thought she was going to pepper spray him for a moment. 'I was wondering...'

A loud disruption outside the Post Office grabbed their attention. With a watching crowd, two teenage women seemed to be fighting.

Michael laughed. 'Wey-hey, must be Thursday in Newton le Willows.'

Keira headed straight to the disturbance. Michael watched on, highly amused. The fight was more hair wrestling and poor attempts at eye gouging, until Keira tried to break it up and then fists started flying. Michael thought about stepping in; after all, if he started dating Keira, he didn't want her to have false front teeth, but some of the watching women pulled their own friends away, and it dissolved as quickly as it had started. Keira came back to Michael, adjusting her uniform as she did so. Michael refrained from stating the obvious, that she had no powers of arrest anyway.

Michael and Keira chatted for a little longer before the uniform seemed to get the better of her and she felt she should move along. It was only later, after getting his milk and bread, that Michael realised that she had not got round to asking her question of him.

He returned to his apartment and made a nice Thursday brunch of bacon and egg muffin with coffee. Then he had a brief phone chat with his parents, who had retired to sunny North Wales, just checking they were all right, and enjoying their view of the Irish Sea. Just as he was considering his mood for getting down to some serious writing, the phone disturbed him. He was surprised to hear his daughter's voice and immediately asked why she wasn't in school. She put on a croakier tone and said she was too ill to go in that day. He sat at his desk and they happily talked for a good twenty minutes. Not once did he ask about her mother, although he did enjoy thinking about her phone bill.

After Hope had rung off, he threw himself into work on the book. There was nothing at all moving outside the window, either that or he really put in a concentrated effort. He was pleased when he eventually sat back and had a good yawn and stretch. Football, he thought. Football was the order of the day. He went across and put in some startling midfield skills before curling the ball into the top corner. Next, he was playing for Manchester City in the FA Cup Final, collecting the ball. Can he turn? It's a good chance. Goal!

He'd gone a day too long without shaving, putting it down to being single again. Determined not to let himself slide, he showered and shaved and put on clean casual clothes. With a fresh cup of coffee, he drifted back over to his desk. Outside, it looked like it was going to snow again. The Garrands' staff appeared busy all of a sudden but there was no sign of either brother. He went onto his publisher's special Kindle site where they both followed the sales. He had a few new ones, but that month he was being outsold ten to one by another writer in the stable who churned out motorcycle travelogues.

Good for him, thought Michael, with a snarl, switching to *GoodReads*. He ignored Cindy's daily message, instead reading that Beverley in Leicester had won her tenth book in a giveaway. Michael had only ever won once, and that turned out to be about teenage vampires. Then he read the replies to the good luck messages he had sent out. The man in Chicago, Ivan, said thanks, and that beauty in Singapore said thank you and that she would be sure to get the book regardless of whether she won. That made Michael purse his lips – he hadn't intended to prompt her to buy the thing with his little good luck message. He clicked onto her profile. Her photo showed a cute smile with small, whiter than white teeth. Her face was delicate, so she was clearly a slender, petite, young woman. Again he perused her interests, which stated that she liked reading, of course, movies and swimming. He clicked on her *Tumblr* site. There were the usual images of beautiful interior design, beautiful people, artistic bookshelves, movie clips with actors he didn't know, fashion items, quotes about love, yet more beautiful people. Then a section titled Me, which brought up about a dozen different shots of the girl in various clothing or hairstyles, one doing the v-sign, which Cindy had once said was called the *Twist* in the Far East. Michael realised how incredibly gorgeous this Elise was. He found something called gifs, which he figured were brief mobile phone images that kept repeating themselves. One in particular had her making a gesture of not being able to understand something, scrunching up her pretty face and touching her head above her left temple.

He went back onto *GoodReads* and sent Elise a message.

MICHAEL: *Elise, it was great to hear from you. Listen, it wasn't my intention to encourage you to buy the book. If you are happy to give me an address I will post a copy out to you immediately.*

Best wishes

Then he went back to that gifs thing and watched it over and over again.

5

MINNESOTA FATS

Michael's local pub in Newton-le-Willows was very sports orientated, leaning towards football, golf and pool. There were six pool tables in the back. He took part in the golf days, but drew the line at turning out for the football team after once breaking an ankle. Every six months or so they held a pool competition. Despite having no serious practice, just messing around on his own table as usual, Michael found out through friends that his good showing last time had made him one of the favourites to win.

It was a raucous crowd for the evening's competition. Michael entered the pub in the company of his best pal, Tony, who couldn't pot a plant, never mind a pool ball. They bought themselves pints of lager before checking the strategically placed blackboard on which was scrawled the draw. Tony laughed as he found the name of Michael's first round opponent.

'It's a fix,' pronounced Michael.

He was up against last year's winner, Alfie Garrand. Michael felt a slap on his back, spun about to find the man himself standing there. 'Alfie, good to see you, mate.'

'Are you ready, man?'

'Let's do this thing.'

Shirley Garrand found herself pulled forward by her husband away from a girly chat. Michael looked her straight in the face, yet she still failed to notice him. Michael grinned and started to open his cue-case. Shirley drank from her large glass of wine as she moved into the crowded pool table area. Her expression suggested she was seeing the place for the first time. Tony blatantly admired Shirley's rear, until Michael nudged him.

Games were underway all around them. Stephen Garrand was about to lose to a middle-aged lady player, so transferred his attention to his brother's game. He acknowledged Michael when their eyes met.

Michael watched with amusement as Shirley made the effort of getting up on a bar stool seem like the sexiest action in the world. He then saw Tony place down his pint pot and take up station where he could watch Shirley's bare shoulders and the pool table at the same time.

Michael's match was interrupted by the boisterous reaction to Stephen Garrand's defeat. The man took it in good spirits, saluting the lady with his whisky glass, then he joined the group watching Alfie's game.

It didn't last long – Alfie was on fire; he was Minnesota Fats, he was the Cincinatti Kid. Michael played some good shots when he got the chance but the writing was on the wall. He watched the winning ball disappear with a plastic plunk, then shook Alfie's hand. Shirley jumped off her stool, clapping her hands as if Alfie had won the World Snooker Championships. She threw her arms around her husband's neck and started kissing him. Michael ignored the show of affection, glanced at a goggle-eyed Tony, then his eyes alighted on Keira, watching him from the main bar. Done with the pool competition, Michael picked up his cue case and his beer and headed towards her.

'Hey, I'm on now,' protested Tony.

'I'll be back, mate.'

Keira looked different out of uniform, wearing jeans and a flowery blouse, her hair loose to her shoulders. She smiled. Her conversation had been with a general crowd, so she could swivel on her chair at Michael's approach. 'I take it you lost,' she said, 'judging by Shirley Birley's reaction.'

Michael smiled. 'Oh, of course, Shirley Birley, as it was in school. The curse of a mother remarrying. I see you've already got a drink.' He winked. 'Save me from bothering.'

She sipped her drink.

'Come to support your brother?' he asked.

'No, actually, I'm entered myself. I'm quite into ball games.'

'I'll be sure to watch closely.'

'Do. I'm very adept.'

'I hope you manage to go deep into the tournament.'

Michael was buffeted by a passing group and had to politely acknowledge one of his recent one night stands. Keira tried not to grin, and went back to sipping her drink, but Michael had noticed it; of course, her brother must have told her about his philandering.

'Tony's playing now,' he said. 'Shall we offer support?'

Keira nodded, letting him help her down from the stool. Michael noted the unfolding of the long legs, and the wedged sandals, very much a change from the work boots. He had to take her hand through the crush, but they managed to squeeze in tight together with a view of Tony playing.

'He's useless,' she pointed out, making them both laugh and get even closer.

In Singapore, Elise and Tricia were at the Hard Rock Hotel on Sentosa island, having drinks with Tricia's cousin, Helen, before the woman moved to San Francisco with her new husband.

In truth, Elise didn't know why she was there, as she and Helen had never really got on. The sooner she went to California the better. Elise smirked to herself at her nasty thought, and looked around the bar to take herself out of the conversation. There was a mixture of people in there, both Caucasian and local. There was also a handsome guy with a guitar strapped to his back. He was doing that thing often seen in hotels or restaurants, of off-duty staff engaging in social chat with on-duty staff, while making sure the management didn't see them. He finished his conversation, kissed the barmaid he was talking to and then headed out. Elise watched him go, liking the way the guitar seemed to make him walk with a bounce.

It was time for the emotional goodbyes. Elise shared a genuine air kiss with Helen before stepping back to let the cousins embrace. The new Caucasian/American husband bounded into the bar and picked up Tricia with a bear hug, although he had only met her twice before. He was a little more reserved with Elise, exchanging waves. The family gathering drifted out of the bar, with Elise gesturing to Tricia that she would be fine there until she got back. She sat back down and took out her iPhone, keyed in the password and went on the *GoodReads* app. She found two messages. One from Danny in Melbourne, which she would read later, and one from that writer man in England. She read his offer to send a copy of his book, and thought how nice that was. She mulled it over for a moment, decided there was no harm in it, but decided to give her parents' address, just to be on the safe side.

She had just finished when Tricia skipped back into the bar.

'Shall we go?' asked Tricia. 'Movie tonight?'

'Sure,' answered Elise, as they walked out together.

They discussed possible movies on the way to Tricia's Audi. It was a very humid day so they were glad to get the air conditioning on as they left the car-park. In fact, Tricia was still adjusting the climate control when she pulled onto the exit road and collided with a car leaving from the staff car-park. While Elise just made a silent O with her mouth, Tricia swore loudly, before hopping out of the car. Elise saw that the Audi had hit the side of a Honda. She watched through the window as Tricia attempted to talk to the other driver – attempted, because he was in the back seat checking to see if there was any harm done back there. Oh God, Elise hoped no small children had been shaken up by the little prang, then looked on in amazement as the man she had seen in the bar climbed out of the Honda, cradling his guitar. It was only the instrument he had been concerned for. Once he was sure everything was fine, he smiled warmly at Tricia, and was clearly waving off any interest in damage to his car. Tricia was trying to apologise and gesture that details should be exchanged, but he wasn't interested in any blame being apportioned. Finally, they shook hands and Tricia got back into the Audi. Elise watched the man wave cheerfully to them, lifted her own hand automatically, then listened to Tricia's account.

'What a great guy! He said not to worry about insurance. He even offered to pay for my repairs, even though I was clearly at fault. Wow, I hope all my future accidents are as smooth as that.'

'Future accidents?'

The girls laughed, then drove on. Elise knew that Tricia would make one phone call to her father and the Audi would be taken care of. They returned to the topic of what film to catch that night, but all the while Elise continued to think back to the handsome man with the guitar.

6

HUMP AHEAD

GoodReads review posted by Cindy:

Finally finished reading The Peking and Bombay Murders by Michael Lincoln. The issue storyline is probably not my style, anyway, yes because I am soft lovers of romance, and the same anti-kill murder, but the novel is different anyway, who knows what kept me reading until the end, in addition and not too long that I think there is something interesting and setting decision. I enjoyed the heck. All the time I like this book. Well done, Michael.

One of the joys of Michael's life involved waiting for Hope to appear at the door to her classroom, in amongst her friends and usually identified easily by her silly hat or pink bubble jacket. She would look to the agreed place where he or Samantha stood, her face would light up and she would run across, divesting herself of her bag or violin case to be caught up and swung round. The face lighting up and being swung round was just with him, of course: Samantha would already be walking towards the gate, telling her to carry her own violin case and that she shouldn't even think about the ice cream van. Or maybe that was divorce speaking in Michael's head.

He still had the fun of swinging her around under the armpits, but it didn't have the same emotions now that she was in the grimmest school in South Manchester. She didn't seem to mind, however, still wittering on about her day, and she found her juice drink ready in the glove compartment as they drove the half hour down the motorway to Newton-le-Willows.

At his apartment there was the regular coat joke, where he pretended to help her off with her coat while really keeping it on her shoulders. They always had a good laugh about that. Then there followed the hour of *Good Luck, Charlie* and *Shake It Up, Chicago* (episodes which he had already seen) before he prepared her tea. He didn't mind when she asked him to get her a drink, or the ketchup. Afterwards there was the playful argument between more television or homework – she ended up doing both. Later they played ball, and played horsey, which was always terrible on Michael's knees.

He never tried to write when his daughter was staying. This visit they wrapped a birthday present for one of her friends; at one stage he tried to put some Sellotape across the bridge of her nose, saying it would get some of the dirt out of her pores, but she playfully screamed and refused all his attempts, making him put it on his own nose instead. When removed, the little strip seemed to have half the dirt of Newton-le-Willows on it.

After reading his daughter a bedtime story and settling her down in her room, he would have a beer and watch some sport or a US drama. *GoodReads* called to him once he had settled on the sofa. The view was all quiet outside as he waited for the computer to warm up. Then he re-read Cindy's review of his second crime novel. *I enjoyed the heck*, made him smile. He fired off a quick message to her. She really was a darling; he would have to get back to chatting properly with her, despite the language barrier.

Michael loved that little envelope logo at the top of the page, which today had the figure one in the top right corner, indicating one message. He clicked on it in anticipation of Elise, and got her. He read the message sent from the *Hard Rock Hotel*. There were copies of his books lying all over the place. He found a padded envelope and copied her Singapore address onto it. Then he Googled the place. It took a while for Google street maps to bring up the house. What it showed was a cross between a Chinese restaurant and a mansion, standing well back behind ornate gates. The extraordinary building was white and pale green with dozens of long vertical windows and a grey tiled roof. There was a bright red post box just inside the gate, and what looked like a gold Buddha up near the front door. Michael assumed then that Elise lived at home, with wealthy parents. He did a 360 degree turn in the map, to discover all the neighbours were similarly loaded. He then made the camera take a tour down the street, immediately noticing the smoothness of the road surface. Parts of Newton-le-Willows were like a Himalayan track to drive along. He had recently passed workmen patching up a stretch of patched-up road. Then he saw something that made him laugh out loud. Painted on the road in big letters was the word HUMP, quickly followed by AHEAD to warn of a speed bump.

'Hump ahead,' he laughed. 'Brilliant.'

He went back to look at Elise's home. He assumed all of Singapore wasn't as rich as that. Would she ever Google his building, he wondered? Could he pretend he owned it all? He considered a new message.

MICHAEL: *Elise, greetings from cold, cold England. I feel very exotic talking to Singapore. It was lovely to hear from you. I'll get the book in the post very soon. Maybe I can have a new character in my latest novel who comes from Singapore.*

Have a great day.

The following day was a Saturday. Michael dropped Hope at the house of one of her friends in the town, from where some of the mums were taking a gaggle of girls 'skiing'at the *Chill Factor* in Manchester; he assumed they would be going down the indoor slope on rubber inner tubes or something, before a visit to McDonald's or Frankie&Benny's and a sleepover. It was a wrench to give her up for the whole day, but he had to let her be with her friends.

Michael picked up a pint of milk and a newspaper. Back in his apartment, he turned on the computer. It seemed a strange day for the Garrand crew, down below. The brothers, old Rimski and three other men all piled into two vans and left the compound at high speed. Michael smiled to himself and shook his head, wondering what they were up to.

GoodReads called to him first, while his coffee brewed. Cindy was there, of course. In his mind he pretended that he couldn't wait for her cross-country trip, for some peace and quiet, before remembering that the girl could message from anywhere on the go. He loved her, really. And there was one from Elise, which excited him, maybe just because she was new, he told himself, but nevertheless he enjoyed the feeling.

ELISE: *Mr Lincoln, hello from humid, humid Singapore. What I would give to be in a cold climate for a while. I think it's so cool that you're a writer. I'll look forward to reading your book. I've added you as a friend, I hope that's all right. Speak to you soon.*

Michael sipped his coffee as he thought about that. He

looked at Cindy's message, before even considering a reply to Elise.

CINDY: *Michael, on train now speak. Going to Medan in the north to see where father born was. Many hours in train station, but listen music and have my guitar with me. Don't play just touch, heh. Lots people talk nice with me. Hehe. Get back to you soon.*

MICHAEL: *Cindy, are you travelling alone ? Are you safe? Have you enough money with you?*

Impotently worried for Cindy, 9,000 miles away, he clicked back on Elise's image. His new friend was online, according to the notice in red alongside her name, but he wasn't anticipating a conversation.

MICHAEL: *Elise, please don't call me Mr Lincoln. Sir will do just fine. :p*
Your house looks amazing on Google maps, and I've had a look around the local area; very impressive looking place. I have to admit I don't know much about Singapore, apart from the war and Raffles hotel. I'm here writing, so it will be nice to be interrupted any time for a chat.

The phone rang. Michael talked with his friend, Tony, for a minute or two. Mainly it was to find out if he wanted a ticket

45

to the annual cricket club dinner. Despite not really liking cricket, Michael was easily persuaded with descriptions of great food and debauched revelry. Near the end of the conversation, he noticed that the number one had popped up above the message envelope sign. With childish anticipation he bid goodbye to Tony and clicked it open.

ELISE: *Sir, I have a confession to make. I'm actually seventy years old, with greying hair and bad teeth. Hehe. No, don't worry. I just wanted to say that's my family home. I have an apartment I share with a girlfriend, but I thought it better go there. The book won't get misplaced, I have a spot on the counter where the maid will put my post.*

Well, I'll get on with my exercises, then bath. It's night time here, of course. Raining, but very humid. I might go for a run, nice in the rain.

Speak soon, I hope

Wow, thought Michael, re-reading the message. He quickly responded.

MICHAEL: *Your family has a maid? Is it safe to run at night? I couldn't imagine a woman running here at night.*

ELISE: *Very safe here in Singapore. It's the best time to run at night. My family has four maids.*

Michael burst out laughing.

MICHAEL: *Four maids!? Are you kidding me? Your parents must be millionaires. Sorry, I'm holding you up from your exercise. I hope to speak soon.*

ELISE: *Sir, I look forward to it myself. Goodnight.*

He didn't go back on to insist she call him Michael. He sat there with his arms crossed, thinking that was a nice way to start a friendship.

7

RIMSKI

Lionel John Rimmer, aka Rimski, was delighted with the results of his first cataract operation. The initial discomfort of the surgery had faded and everything was just great, apart from his wife, the blind bat, missing the target with the eye drops twice a day. His blurry left eye still interfered with his vision, but if he closed that one, then he felt like a teenager again. Roll on his next appointment; that's what he thought. He could see the open fields behind his terraced house in Newton-le-Willows, he could read the newspaper, the television was much better, and driving at night, though he wasn't supposed to be driving yet, was less of a terrifying experience for all involved as he could see the white lines on the motorway.

He walked onto the High Street to buy his usual Daily Mirror newspaper and put a bet on the gee-gees. Rimski, at sixty-four, had never lived anywhere else but Newton-le-

Willows, and knew everything and everybody. He waved to the girls in the chip shop, and acknowledged a neighbour who was heading to the dentist. Beryl came by on her regular walk from her flat to her mother's house, and right on cue she stopped mid-stride, turned 360 degrees, had a little conversation with her invisible companion and carried on.

The traffic was busier these days; every bugger seemed to have a car, despite the extortionate petrol prices and insurance costs. He disliked seeing foreign number plates, convinced those people never paid their speeding fines or parking tickets, and he hated those snotty women who owned massive 4x4s which they could neither drive nor park. There was one outside the Spar convenience store as he approached, trying to back a BMW X6 into a space, holding up fifteen to twenty other cars. He stopped for a moment to watch the show in mild despair, and it was a good thing because that few seconds saved him having to talk to Mrs Garrand, as she ran out of the shop towards her brand new Mini Cooper. It was Joanne Garrand, Stephen's wife – not Alfie's darling missus, Shirley, who had a soft spot for him and always gave him a kiss when she saw him. No, it was the horrid, older woman who never came anywhere near the yard, just lived the high-life off Stephen's toil and sweat. Rimski watched her as she put her shopping on the roof of the car and took a phone call, in her jeans with ludicrously big turn-ups, white sandals, some kind of multi-coloured poncho and big sunglasses on top of her groomed, blonde head. There was another reason he disliked Joanne Garrand. Twenty years earlier when she was plain Joanne Hailwood from Widnes, dating Stephen Garrand, she had been a small-time glamour model; local advertising campaigns for car parts and double glazing and making a fool of herself accompanying darts players on stage for exhibition matches. Rimski still had images of her somewhere at home, when her hair was lustrous and her face fuller and free of laughter lines. The thing that ruined his opinion of Joanne Hailwood was her breasts. At some stage she had been advised to go ahead with surgery to make them much larger, not massive, but clearly unnatural. But she had moved away from, in Rimski's opinion, the perfect breasts she already had. Because she was a minor local celebrity he had quite intimate knowledge of her body. He never thought about it these days; it just lay in his subconscious whenever he saw her, but her breasts had been wonderful and she had ruined them. He couldn't describe them properly, what man could; they were just lovely and a bit pointy and different from all those tits he used to look at on page three of The Sun. They were fascinating, unique breasts, and the silly bitch had thought it right to blow them up to twice their size.

Joanne Garrand had driven off and he was still standing there thinking about her breasts twenty years earlier. He giggled to himself, shook his head and stepped towards the shop doorway. In a flash he was nearly wiped out by a cyclist coming along the pavement. 'Oi!' shouted Rimski, 'You dickhead!'

It wasn't a youth on the bike, which slowed rapidly at the screamed abuse, but a man in his thirties, his face screwed up with rage at the thought of someone having the temerity to shout at him in the street. The cyclist turned and came back towards Rimski.

'You were fucking daydreaming!' snarled the man, coming to a stop.

'This, if you haven't noticed, is the pavement, dickhead.'

'Call me a dickhead again and I'll forget you're an old man.'

'You're a dickhead.'

The man went red in the face. As he started to lift his left leg over the bike, Rimski stepped in with a left hook and a right cross to the man's head. It was almost comical, the cycle lout tangled by his own machine as this old man laid into him. Rimski finished with a fabulous head-butt and the man went down in a clatter of metal and a spurt of claret. Apparently nobody witnessed the incident, either to cheer the vigilante or to gasp with shock. Rimski decided to buy his paper somewhere else and headed off around the nearest corner.

Stephen and Joanne Garrand lived in one of those state-of-the-art wooden German houses that was put up on the concrete basement in about six hours, on a plot of land on the road to Haydock racecourse and the M6 motorway. It wasn't a Grand Design worth two million pounds; really it was a posh, eco-friendly bungalow with gardens in the process of being landscaped to the sides and rear, and an underground garage for the Mini Cooper and Stephen's Audi Q7. The nearest neighbour was the Autotrader building five hundred yards away which of course lay empty in the evenings, and the noise from the motorway was almost unnoticeable, so apart from that, Joanne was happy there. She had her bespoke kitchen and her walk-in wardrobe. She had her little south-facing studio for her new pottery hobby, surrounded with images of her past glory days as a model, plus one or two of the children, Henry and Olivia. The kids went to the Byrchall school in nearby Wigan. They could have walked to the Hope Academy, but Joanne thought they looked better in maroon than grey.

Joanne showered and, while wrapped in a towel, went to the master bedroom to do her hair. Through the window she watched the arrival of the landscape gardeners: two teenage men in dungarees. Because they were handsome and flirted with her she hadn't complained about their painfully slow work. Stephen would come home at night and moan about the lack of progress, but she just kissed him, handed him a glass of wine and changed the subject. In expectation, she chose black lacy underwear from Victoria's Secret, a flimsy white blouse with short black skirt and black socks up to the middle of her thighs.

With perfect precision she heard the 4x4 crunch onto the drive at the front of the house. Then the car door slammed. He was going around the side. Joanne checked her appearance in the mirror above the living-room fireplace. She could hear him calling instructions to the gardeners down at the trees which marked the boundary. She was at the open front door when he came back to the front.

His dungarees were the same as the gardeners, but he had on underneath a sleeveless white tee-shirt which showed off his impressive physique. He was about thirty. Of course, owning a landscape gardening business he was sunburned, his hair a close crew cut. He smiled a very white smile out of his bronzed face. 'Afternoon, Mrs Garrand.' There was a slight hint of his Irish roots in his voice. He threw a discarded brush into the back of his Mitsubishi, making it into a show of great physical prowess.

'Hello, Mr Kelly.'

Joanne wasn't quite leaning on the door with her head cocked at a coquettish angle. Mr Kelly stepped over to her in his muddy boots. 'I wanted to ask you, Mrs Garrand, are you satisfied with the standard of work, so far?'

'Quite satisfied, I suppose. It could take place with more urgency.'

'I'll be right on to that, Mrs Garrand.'

They began kissing in the porch, with him pressing home his advantage. 'Boots!' she managed to remind him.

'I know the house rules, Mrs Garrand.'

Her blouse was instantly open and he was devouring her right breast through the lingerie. He thought her breasts were fabulous. As they kissed, she decided that she no longer liked the dungarees – they were too awkward to undo. They didn't even attempt to go anywhere more comfortable. He had her on the sturdy hall table with her knees up in the air and her lacy panties pulled aside.

8

CRISPY FRIED KANG KONG

ELISE: *Michael, I've taken the liberty of using your first name. Forgive my impudence? Wow, terribly humid here in Singapore today. I'm eating out with my family. I'm having Crispy Fried Kang Kong with Cuttlefish. Haha.*

MICHAEL: *Elise, crispy fried what!? I'm considering which kind of boring sandwich to have for lunch. Either Cheshire or Cheddar cheese. You must be eight hours ahead there.*

Forgive my ignorance of Singapore, but is English your second language? What do you do, may I ask? Are you a student?

Michael had been mid-exercise when he saw Elise's message pop up on the computer screen. Wearing just tracksuit bottoms, he was back, prostrate on his floor, throwing a ball up above him, volleying it and trying to then save the shot from going into the goal. He would be sectioned if anyone saw his childish game, but it did work him aerobically, as well as toning his stomach muscles. He tipped his latest shot onto the bar. Flat-out, panting, he strained to see his monitor; was that a number one above the envelope symbol? Not yet.

While still sweaty, he moved his dirty laundry nearer to the washing machine, and left it there, then vacuumed the living area after the previous evening's filmfest with Tony, who had a very scattergun approach to his snacking. Next, he drank plenty of water and took a long shower.

He made coffee before deciding on the Cheshire cheese for his sandwich, with a mini pork pie. He sat looking out through the front windows of his apartment, scanning across the quiet school, watching people going about their daily business on the street. He gave consideration to a useless window cleaner at one of the nearby houses. It was a day when he couldn't get into the mood to write. He no longer felt guilty when that kind of mood came over him, knowing he would flow incessantly on another occasion. He thought about that evening's cricket club dinner. He was fixed up with Keira. She was a lovely woman, very attractive. But did he want to get involved just yet? He tore into his sandwich and gave the window cleaner three out of ten.

In the middle of the afternoon a message came through from Cindy in Indonesia.

CINDY: *Heya, I'm in Depok. I stay with nice people. Thanks for offering money. No need, took plenti of money. I argues bigtime with step mom, she say I selfish. I wanted to be away for a while and see where my people come from. Everythink fine, I look round here for a few days. You are daebak!*

Don't worry.

Michael had a little smile, sitting there at his desk. What a girl! Daebak meant great. At least that was what she had once told him it meant.

MICHAEL: *Cindy, you keep safe. I look forward to speaking with you when you have done what you need to do.*

Love

In the end, Keira stood Michael up. Tony apologised for his sister, saying it was something to do with her son being unwell. Michael was neither relieved nor disappointed. He fancied a session on the booze and some of that promised revelry. The cricket club's bar was packed out and noisy. Michael knew most faces; he'd kissed several and punched a few over the years. He and Tony drank with a small group of male friends. Occasionally, a raucous laugh would have Michael look at one group or another. It just happened that the Garrand clan were at tables within his range of vision. Several of the scrap yard staff were there with wives and girlfriends, with Rimski and his quiet little wife, gathered around Stephen and Alfie and their better halves. Michael continually checked out Shirley, who seemed to be enjoying herself, and Joanne, who seemed to be there for the sake of showing face. Shirley's multi-coloured dress was strapless, showing bare shoulders and Marie Antoinette cleavage. Her hair was down by her ears and clipped up in a very cute manner at the front. Joanne appeared more conservatively, in a dark dress over jeans and high leather boots. Stephen looked at her and she immediately made an effort to talk to the woman next to her. Michael saw Stephen as a bit of a control freak: the Ronnie Kray to Alfie's Reggie.

Alfie was already on the shorts, and laughing jovially with people on another table. Michael wondered what the odds were on a good barney by the end of the night. He thought through his own mood. He would stay for the meal, because it was paid for, and some of the speeches and presentations, but would probably slink away before any partying got underway. Tony was smiling at him, so he put an arm around his friend's shoulder and drank deeply.

The function room held a panoramic view over the cricket field. For some reason everything was green in there: carpet, tablecloths, chairs, balloons. As Michael followed Tony, who seemed to know where they had to be in the melee of people, he remembered that the club's logo was green. He sat down, saying hello to an elderly couple on their table whom he vaguely recognised. He wondered why he felt so out of place. Why was he feeling down? Did he attend last year's function, with his wife, perhaps? Surely that couldn't be the reason for his blues.

A passing bottom nudged his shoulder. He glanced up at Joanne Garrand. She looked at him in a not unfriendly fashion, but didn't offer an apology. She sat down just out of slapping distance from him at the next table. Michael didn't intend to stare at her, he just happened to be angled her way, and didn't want to shuffle his chair so that he wasn't facing her. She continued to glance at him, between sipping her wine and chatting with the women on her table. Michael's imagination began to take hold of him. Was she suggesting with her eyes that they should blow this place and go off together, as they were both clearly uncomfortable with being there? He didn't grow up with Joanne, as he had Shirley. Stephen Garrand had picked her up in a Widnes nightclub, apparently. He couldn't even remember speaking to her before. Now here they were acting like kindred spirits, desiring a one-night stand behind the groundsman's hut. Right on cue, Joanne shuffled her own chair to unknowingly shatter his imagination, giving him a profile shot of her drinking and talking. Ruefully, Michael sought conversation from Tony, who had just finished a little catching up with old friends.

Elise had been to the movies with a group of friends, then for a meal afterwards. Once home and bathed and lounging on her bed in shorts and tee-shirt, she opened her laptop and went on *Tumblr*. Then another friend phoned her, so that chat took her into the early hours.

She padded to the kitchen for a glass of milk. She was very awake, and (because she had finally got around to reading *Fifty Shades of Grey*) started thinking about England, about the author EL James, and Shakespeare, and Dickens, and Hammersmith (where some of her cousins lived), and King Henry the Eighth, and Eccles Cakes (eaten for the first time when last in England), and finally about her author friend, Michael. She went on *GoodReads* determined to give him a meaningful message.

ELISE: *Michael, Kang Kong is a vegetable base for the main meal to sit in, which was Cuttlefish that time. Yes, English is my first language. I'm half English and half Singaporean. My dad was born in Sutton Coldfield, do you know it? I'm of Chinese descent on my mother's side.*

I was in a restaurant tonight with my friends, and this boy I didn't know asked me out. It was such a shock because Singaporeans are normally more reserved. I was so rude I just laughed at him.

Oh, I attend Temasek Polytechnic, studying F&B Management, but I haven't a clue what I really want to do.

Back on *Tumblr*, still wide awake, she sought out some naughtiness. The censors were all over pornography in

Singapore, but *Tumblr* seemed to have escaped them so far, and Elise enjoyed watching some beautiful people making love. It didn't matter if it was two beautiful men; it was the magnificent, erect penises that she found fascinating. She had touched her previous boyfriend's cock, and even performed oral sex for a while, but that was it. The moving images of massive shafts coming out from hard abdomens, going in and out of orifices, made her almost sigh audibly. Not that she was desperate to lose her virginity. She just had a normal, healthy interest in those kind of things. Wow, there was a gif of a big cock being roughly handled, the main vein standing out very big. Elise's right hand shot down the front of her shorts.

9

THE BELGIAN

On *GoodReads*, Michael had just spent half an hour correcting the spelling in Cindy's last message. She had asked him to do it, as she was feeling annoyed with her lack of progress with English. He clicked send and sat back in his chair. As sometimes happened, a new, red number one waited for him above the envelope logo. It turned out to be from Dianne, one of his middle-aged American friends. Dianne lived in South Dakota with her husband and a small menagerie of animals. He realised he was disappointed that it had not been from Elise.

DIANNE: *Michael, hi, how are you? I'm reading a novel set in England at the moment. Could you please tell me what "winning the pools" means?*
Thank you,

MICHAEL: Dianne, many years ago, before the national lottery, many people in England gambled on The Pools, trying to guess football match scores.

Enjoy the book.

Next, a new notification message faced him. Clicking on it revealed a woman called Glenie had asked to be his friend. He took a quick look at her profile. Early twenties, lived in the Philippines; another one who lived in the Philippines. Well, he thought, he'd refused Gary in Canada, so he should accept this stranger.

Cindy was back on to him.

CINDY: Michael, Kekekke. That first word there means giggle, remember. You are jjang! Might be going to Korea soon to visit relatives. Wanna come?

MICHAEL: Cindy, you get around a lot. Korea? After a great deal of thought I've decided to pass on that, thank you. :p

CINDY: Michael, next week my Belgian boyfriend comes to my home town. I don't know what he does the rest of year, but God brings him to me for one month only.

MICHAEL: Cindy, I thought I was your boyfriend? :p Enjoy Belgian boy, and enjoy Korea. You're so funny. I love hearing from you.

He waited for a few minutes, but apparently she was gone again. He thought of some ugly Belgian bastard, probably married, flying into Indonesia specially to be with *his* beloved Cindy. But she wasn't his beloved Cindy. Coffee time and then back to the novel.

It was a brand-new, white Land Rover Evoque, stationary in the queue for McDonald's drive-thru in Wythenshawe, Manchester. The driver was a big man, seeming to fill the front of the cabin, while in the passenger seat sat a sleek, blonde woman, checking her messages on her phone. Almost hidden away in the back was Hope Lincoln, playing on her Nintendo DS, so she didn't have to talk to her mother or her mother's new boyfriend.

Dale de Lange ordered at the speaker machine, speaking slowly with his South African accent; he and Samantha had conferred over their meals, but Hope got the same as always. Dale paid, accepted their order through his window, and then drove the five minutes to their rented property in Moss Nook, a nice little suburban area just outside Manchester airport. Dale put the US golf on the television while he popped to the kitchen to dispense with his hated gherkin. He didn't say anything to Hope for turning it to the Disney channel while he was out of the room. He put his considerable frame into an

64

armchair and talked business with Samantha while they munched their burgers.

Hope sat there with her happy meal, looking at her Monster High doll school, set out near the fireplace, but knowing she wouldn't want to play there while they talked boring business. When they started discussing importing and exporting 'units' she tried to watch television, but finished her food quickly and went to her room. Climbing the stairs she heard the stupid applause and whistles for some idiot hitting a little white ball up a field, before climbing into her den to play with her dolls and have some serious discussions in there. Her den was great, made of overturned armchairs, with real green and black army netting over the top. Her mother's boyfriend had made it for her; at least he was good for something. She was soon lost in her own world, quite happy in herself, actually.

It was very rare for Michael's inner doorbell to ring – usually it was the intercom which buzzed. He opened the door to David, the Prince of Darkness, who lived in the next unit. 'David?'

'Michael. My friend. How are you?'

The Prince of Darkness, as the locals had dubbed him, made the enquiry sound as if Michael had just survived cancer and also lost his parents in a road crash. He was such a gentle, lovely man, but completely weird. Only in his late twenties, he always dressed in black, usually with a long, leather coat. His face was totally pale, deathly, from the fact that he only ever left his apartment to buy food. He was usually passed on the stairs with a takeaway in his hands, or Tesco bags. On this occasion he carried a platter of sandwiches, as if he had raided a buffet at a funeral. It was such a strange thing to be carrying that Michael gave the tray a double-take.

'Are you well?' asked the Prince of Darkness again.

'Very well, thank you, David.'

'I'm so, so sorry to bother you... oh, would you like a sandwich?'

Michael desperately wanted to ask where they were from. He was desperate to know. 'No, thank you.'

'I just wanted to ask whether you ever hear that random banging in the building? It's so strange, there doesn't seem to be any running water when it happens, and no set time. I've been studying it, you see, making notes.'

Michael wondered if his puzzled expression was doing the job, while in his peripheral vision sat one of his mini-footballs. 'No, David. Is it really bad?'

'Not really bad. Just very puzzling. I'm going to take it up with the powers that be. I just wanted to ask all the neighbours first.'

'Sorry I can't be more help. I'll listen out for it.'

'Oh, would you?' Again, made to sound as if Michael had just offered to shoot the man if he was ever too badly wounded to complete the raid into Japanese-held territory. 'That's so kind of you. I must go now.'

And with that, his leather coat levitated away, together with the platter of sandwiches.

Michael returned to his desk. He had a new message on *GoodReads*, and to his surprise it was from the friend in the Philippines who never spoke to him.

IRENE HANNAH: *Michael, my dearest pen pal. How are you? I'm so sorry for neglecting you. I've been busy with my work placement from college. I have an internship at the resort of Boracay. Please look it up, it is the most beautiful place. Also busy times with family. I have relatives staying at the moment. My uncle says he used to live in Shrewsbury. Is that near to you?*

I hope to speak again soon.

Michael tried to imagine Irene Hannah's uncle living in Shrewsbury. Then he Googled Boracay, and indeed found an island paradise. He saw that Irene Hannah was online, so replied, of course with no guarantee that she would still be there by the time he had typed his message.

MICHAEL: *Irene Hannah, great to hear from you. Better late than never. :p I'm moving to Boracay! What a place? What were you doing there?*

Shrewsbury isn't too far from me, maybe thirty miles.

How bizarre that your uncle was there. Speak to me any time, I'm just here writing away.

Michael pottered about with the latest chapter of his book. Irene Hannah replied almost immediately.

IRENE HANNAH: *Michael, I want to be a chef. I was on one of the ships there. Great fun but hard work. I'm so excited that you are a writer. I can't wait to read your work.*

Oh, Christ, more Royal Mail postage, thought Michael. Then he giggled to himself.

MICHAEL: *Irene Hannah, please give me an address and I will send copies of my books.*

IRENE HANNAH: *Michael, I have them already. I will start the first one tonight after finishing my project. But thank you so much.*

MICHAEL: *Irene Hannah, how do you read? Do you have an electronic reader?*

IRENE HANNAH: *Michael, my family's too poor for one of those. Haha, never mind. How do you read? Have you got one of those things and do you like it?*

Michael sat there thinking.

MICHAEL: *Irene Hannah, the postal service is riddled with thieves, but I'm very happy to get you a Kindle and send it out. I hope you won't be offended by the offer.*

Fucking hell, thought Michael; that gesture was a bit over the top. No immediate response sent him over to make coffee. He wandered slowly back, glancing out at his view, as he sipped his drink.

IRENE HANNAH: *Michael, OMG. No, I couldn't ask you to do that. I'm fine, honestly. Tell me what you are up to. Tell me what you are wearing, I imagine you in a crisp white shirt and slacks.*

MICHAEL: *Irene Hannah, at the moment I'm in a gold lamé basque and fishnet stockings. I find I write best in these.*
Listen, at the very least let me send you some other novels. I'll check your "to-read" list.

10

RODRIGO

Michael "counted them all out, and counted them all back in again", to use the famous Falklands War reporter's phrase. Looking through his office window, he had watched the Garrand crew set off on a mission in their trucks, then return ninety minutes later with booty to unload. How legal it all was didn't concern him particularly.

He was delighted with his morning's work on the novel. Even though it wasn't even half completed, he considered firing off a couple of submission emails to London agents, just for the futile hell of it. Instead, he drank coffee in his kitchen and came to the conclusion that he should do a food shop immediately. His buzzer rang; – were Waitrose pre-empting him with a home delivery?

He didn't bother answering via the machine, just jogged down the stairs and opened the communal door. Hope stood there with a suitcase, looking like a Second World War evacuee. Michael smiled at her and joked, 'Hello, sweetheart. Have you come on the train by yourself?'

'Mum's over there,' she said, pulling a face and gesturing just out of view.

Michael looked around the door jamb. The white Land Rover seemed to fill the street like a spaceship; the ex-wife was pacing back and forth on her mobile, while the South African boyfriend stood at the open tailgate.

'Yes?' called Michael, in his most condescending tone.

The South African smiled, then slammed the boot shut. 'Hello, Michael,' he called over. 'How are you, my friend?'

Michael didn't bother to reply, instead kneeling down to embrace his daughter.

'They have to go to London,' she explained, unbuttoning her coat because it was a warmish day.

Michael helped her with the coat by keeping it on her and they both giggled. Samantha appeared like a vision in the brightness of the doorway. 'Michael,' she said, exasperated, 'we've got an important business thing that can't wait. My mother's in Harrogate and my sister's insane, as you know, so we had to bring her here.'

Hope was already heading up the stairs, lugging her suitcase. Michael noticed it was one of those new ones, the type children are supposed to be pulled along on in airport terminals. It made him think of Samantha taking Hope to live abroad.

'No worries,' he said, more to Hope than Samantha. 'I love

seeing my little sweetheart.'

'Thank you, Michael,' said Samantha.

'Yes, thank you,' added the South African, taking away all the light.

Michael thought the man could have stayed at the car, and so did Samantha, judging by her furtive eyes. Still, Michael took the opportunity to appraise his ex-wife's nice cleavage above a purplish tee-shirt.

'Just until tomorrow morning,' she said.

Michael nodded. He didn't bother asking what was happening in London.

'See you, darling!' called Samantha after Hope.

Michael leant on the door frame and watched them walk back to the ostentatious vehicle. It might have been his imagination, but Samantha seemed to be telling the man off. They drove away slowly past the school.

After a snack, Hope seemed quite happy to settle down on the sofa to read the book she had brought with her. As a writer, Michael thought better than to disturb her while she was doing that. He went on the computer to try to find inspiration for his sister's upcoming birthday. He tried Amazon, John Lewis and a few other sites. Quickly stumped, he disturbed his daughter after all, 'Hope, what do you think we should get Auntie Cathy for her birthday?'

'You could pay for a man to tile her kitchen.'

Michael laughed. 'Good one. It's only been in that state for two years. Hey, do you want to ring your friend, Ellie, see what she's doing?'

'She'll be having her horse riding lesson now.'

'Oh, right you are. Shall we go cycling? To the park?'

'Nah, I'm good here, dad.'

'Hope, I've asked this before, but are you happy with mummy? You know, the living situation.'

'Of course, mister. Why?'

'No, that's okay.'

Going back on the Amazon site, Michael went on the books section. He had copied down a random list of books from Irene Hannah's "to-read" list in her profile. He then ordered half a dozen of them and clicked to pay with his credit card.

He then opened *GoodReads* up, to find nine messages. Six were from English winners of his giveaway, thanking him for their copies. Paying postage at the Post Office had felt like extortion, but at least they had all got through; he just had to wait longer for news of the overseas ones. Cindy was there, and Elise, and one from that Glenie in the Philippines whose friendship he had recently accepted. He opened that one.

GLENIE: *Michael, how old are you, please?*

Wow, thought Michael, how shallow. Sitting there, at thirty-seven years of age, he felt a bit silly with the whole *GoodReads* thing. But, then again, he hadn't sought out

Glenie.

MICHAEL: *Glenie, I'm 22. Goodbye.*

As soon as he had finished removing Glenie from his friend list, the phone rang beside him. He almost answered with "Glenie?" but then Hope was watching him so he answered, 'You rang?' as if he was in *The Munsters*. Hope giggled on the sofa. Michael spoke for a few minutes, before hanging up. 'Hope,' he called, 'we're going to the park, after all.'

'Oh, okay.'

Elise was out with Tricia and two other girlfriends, Eilynn and Silvia, enjoying the open-mike spot at Wala Wala Café Bar in Holland village. It was dark and noisy and crowded on the second floor, their table festooned with their drinks and snacks. Elise was dressed in a new, maroon, strapless dress, perhaps a little over the top for that venue but she felt great in it, and had been pleased to attract a few glances. The other girls were flirting with some guys nearby, but Elise was happy just to chill out and listen to the music.

It had been a lovely evening. Maybe they could go on somewhere, as she felt like dancing – felt like dancing with some boys coming up behind and dancing close to her. She gradually became aware of the room settling down, and of the girls looking towards the stage, and then she heard the sound of a classical guitar. The tune was Rodrigo, vaguely familiar to her; it was just so beautiful and haunting. She glanced over her left shoulder, saw the young man in the leather jacket, hunched intently over his guitar. His hair was forward, but she still recognised him as the man Tricia had crashed into. She shot her friend a look, but apparently Tricia had not recognised him. Elise returned her attention to the performance. She found it a very moving and entertaining experience and, as the tune carried on, her heart made her wonder if she would ever be able to speak to the young man at some stage in the evening.

Newton-le-Willows' main park was called Mesnes Park. Michael knew there must be great social history to it, but he just disliked the name. He and Hope went there on their bikes. At one of the adventure play areas they slowed and he pointed out Keira and her son waiting for them.

'Hope, there's your future husband.'

'Stop it, mister.'

Michael squealed to a stop. Hope took off her bike helmet. Keira, dressed in a blue Timberland coat and jeans, waved and smiled.

'Michael, hello,' said Keira. 'I'm sorry about the other night.'

Michael dismissed that with a smile and a gesture.

Introductions took place: "Lovely to meet you, Hope" – "All right, chief?" – that sort of thing, then the two children got straight on with playing together, and the two adults sighed down onto a bench in the sunshine.

'Your boy's a handsome little devil,' pointed out Michael.

Keira smiled ruefully. 'Let's hope he doesn't turn out like his father. Another handsome little devil.'

'And where's he, if you don't mind me asking?'

'Fracking.'

'I beg your pardon?'

'His last known movement had him working for one of those fracking companies on the coast near Blackpool. You know, where they shake the earth to release the gas?'

'Oh, right.'

'And Hope's mother?'

'She's down in London today on some kind of business. She was always more of a go-getter than me, but since she's hooked up with this South African businessman boyfriend she seems obsessed with money. She's all right, I suppose. It could have been a lot worse.'

'Sorry again about standing you up.'

They paused, with Hope demanding that her new friend push her along the zip wire.

'She's terrible,' laughed Michael. 'She's got him now, you know. He has to play on her terms.'

Keira smiled. 'How's the book coming along?'

'Very good. I've based a character on Tony again.'

'Not one on me?'

'I might have.'

'Is it a bit raunchy?'

'Well, it has its moments.'

'I ask that, because they say that's where the money is. *Fifty Shades* and all that.'

'My next one will be like that.'

'Good, I'll buy it.'

'Nice one, that's just doubled the sales.'

11

DON'T GOOGLE SHEFFIELD

A couple of days went by without Michael hearing from Cindy. He hoped she was all right on her solo trip; he had tried to look at Indonesia on Google maps, but found it to be not comprehensively covered. He would have to make an effort to find out more about Cindy's country. What would he do if she invited him for a holiday?

He spoke on the phone with his publisher, Henry, in Swindon, and then to his parents; apparently, his sister wanted Marks & Spencer vouchers for her birthday. In the pub the previous evening, as a high point in the conversation, Tony had told him about a relative who had a home-made wooden box with a flip-up panel over their door-bell, intended to keep the weather off. It was hilariously naff, and Tony had earnestly asked the man to make him one, which he would then give as a joke present to someone. Michael's sister had been lined up as another potential customer for the part-time carpenter.

Another friend request came out of the blue on *GoodReads*, again from the Philippines, a twenty-year-old girl called Mary Louise. As her profile image depicted an artistic stack of books instead of a pretty face, he felt okay accepting her. Maybe she wouldn't only care about what age he was. Plus, it said she was #7 most followed, which must be a good thing, whatever it meant.

Michael did some gentle exercise in his games area, with the stormy weather putting a stop to his planned bike ride. Then he made cheese on toast, eating it at his desk because he had suddenly come up with a good line for one of his characters. Whilst there, he checked *GoodReads*. Oh, new message: Cindy.

CINDY: *Michael, I take train as my transportation. I take the cheapest one, cheapest means not reliable :) Fortunately I sit with nice old couple, like my grandparents. 18 hours before I arrive in destination of Pasar Senin station, since it early morning I decide to take a rest in mosque and wait time to pray. In 8am I leave mosque and take bus to Jakarta and going to Depok. Unfortunately because of new rule of transportation bus service not running from Jakarta to Depok. Some people surround me, know I not from there, I feel frighten. Some people are nicer and ask if I go to Depok, say I should use KRL (this is the electric train). The ticket very expensive but train very good. I spend two hours sleep in train and arrive in Depok. I don't remember day one, I too tired, hungry, exhausted and confused. Again I take mosque, house of God, to think. I cry a little, but in the darkest days the Lord puts good people in your life and I meet Nurani, a local girl. She originally from Surabaya like me, takes me to her dorm. She is a student at Universitas Indonesia. Nurani help me so much. Next day I find the places I go to see, and much happier.*

MICHAEL: Cindy, you are amazing. I hope you are safely back in Surabaya now. I did my family tree once. I got the same reaction that you did when I arrived in the city of Sheffield. Whatever you do, don't Google Sheffield.

Still digesting Cindy's message, Michael was presented with one from Elise.

ELISE: Michael, WAKE UP, TEMPERAMENTAL ARTIST!

Haha. Hello from Singapore. How is the writing going? You know, you haven't formally introduced yourself. But I'll excuse you.

I'm having a Nando's with my friends. So nice. Have you realised yet that I am 70 years old with grey hair and no teeth, using my granddaughter's photo for my profile image?

MICHAEL: *Elise, 19 or 70, I'm not fussed. Do you eat out every night? It seems a good life.*

ELISE: *Come to Singapore and I'll show you a good time. Haha, that came out wrong. I'll take you to the best places.*

MICHAEL: *It's a long way to come if you're 70 with grey hair and bad teeth.*

ELISE: *Michael, I thought you weren't bothered? Naughty man. Shall I send you a photo right this minute?*

MICHAEL: *A nude photo? Sorry, did I actually write that down? :p It still doesn't prove it's you. Send one with you touching your ear or something.*

Michael added his email address, then stood up for a walk around his apartment. Cindy and Elise, both were very important to him, he realised. He smiled, scratching his head, wondering if there was any future in it all. He could imagine flying into Singapore, but getting to Cindy felt more like a backpacking adventure. He fired in a shot at the goal and hit the left hand post, excellent, then decided it was coffee time.

Then Elise's image was in his email inbox. She was smiling while touching her right ear.

MICHAEL: *Elise, you might have asked your*

granddaughter to pose like that. But, never mind, I'll live dangerously. What do you like to talk about?

He waited. He considered the fact that he was ignoring his book. She replied soon after.

ELISE: *Michael, can I ask you something? Are you married?*

MICHAEL: *No, I'm not married. I'm between illogical females at the moment. Are you with someone? A boyfriend?*

ELISE: *Michael, I'm a single girl. I've had a couple of boyfriends. I'm very innocent, you know. Hehe. Can I ask you a rude question? If you're not married any more, are you still having sex?*

Innocent, my arse, thought Michael, shaking his head and grinning.

MICHAEL: *I'm okay on that score at the moment, thank you. What about you? Seeing as you say you are single.*

ELISE: *Me? I'm still a virgin. Yep, nothing has gone up there.*

Michael sat looking at his screen, his mouth making silent

shapes and his brows knitted, as he took that information on board. She definitely said, "Yep, nothing has gone up there". She came back straight away with another message.

ELISE: *I have late classes. Must go. I hope you will be able to talk tomorrow.*

Dylan Wang's old Honda had finally decided to die on him, and at the worst possible moment. In a highly agitated state, which was unusual for him, he covered up his guitar on the back seat with a blanket, locked the damn vehicle and started running through the evening streets of the Chinatown district. Actually, his route had him running two minutes behind where Elise's bus to school had just passed; not really that much of a coincidence, but they had been close, nevertheless.

He was heading to one particular office building. Passers-by stared at him; people jogged in Singapore, but he wasn't exactly dressed for it. On the office steps, he caught his breath, seeing the concierge stand up from behind his desk and take note of his sweating, dishevelled arrival. Once he had gathered his strength, he stormed through the rotating door, ignored the concierge's alarmed shouts and bounded up the stairs. His destination was the first floor. He banged through the main door, seeing office workers turn their heads to stare at him. He strode to the left, passing little office cubicles, some occupied, some not, on his right was a rest area where people looked at him from beside the water cooler and palm plants. Then he found his sister, trying to work at her desk, despite looking completely downcast and teary-eyed. She looked shocked to see him, calling, 'Dylan, no!' as she realised her recent, complaining, text message had forced his hand. Dylan kept moving, and walked straight into his quarry, a middle-aged Indian man in a white shirt. Dylan realised the man had about six multi-coloured pens in his top pocket (a strange fact that he would reflect on later) as he landed a tremendous right hand punch on the man's jaw. The Indian vanished from Dylan's radar. As he stabilised his footing, Dylan had to look around to find the man crumpled at his feet, bloodied and disorientated. There were only gobsmacked women employees around to witness the assault, no males to attempt to restrain him, so Dylan pushed his hair back and retraced his steps to his sister, who was by then on her feet.

'Gather your things, my sister,' Dylan ordered her, calmly. 'It is the last time he will insult you by suggesting such things.'

His sister, Susan, quickly put some private things into her bag and was ready to leave. Dylan took her hand and they walked to the lift, not the stairs. They waited in silence, rode the lift down the one floor, then walked out through the puzzled glare of the concierge.

12

WE'VE GOT THE MONKS IN

MICHAEL: *Cindy, who is this Belgian boyfriend? I'm puzzled. Didn't you say you had a local boyfriend?*

At the same time that Dylan Wang was taking action in Singapore, the Garrand brothers set out on their own personal mission. This departure wasn't overlooked by Michael Lincoln in his apartment; instead they left by the small door on the other side of the yard, stepping into Stephen's waiting Audi Q7. Both brothers carried metal baseball bats (Alfie had said "This will really go Ting!") Stephen had a screwdriver down his pants and Alfie a box cutter in his coat pocket, but they were only for emergency use; it was the baseball bats which they focussed their minds on.

Stephen, calm within himself, drove perfectly normally through Newton-le-Willows, down past the church and headed out towards Golborne village. It was Alfie who was a bit steamed up. They both knew exactly where they were going.

In Golborne, Stephen pulled into a side road just off the High Street and parked up. There was a patch of waste ground laid out in front of them, before a solitary industrial premises presented itself to the general public. A couple of Mitsubishi 4x4s sat outside. Stephen and Alfie left the Q7 with the engine running, and the doors open, and marched straight into the concrete-floored, open-plan business. A young lad in dungarees froze on seeing them. They ignored him and moved on, heading to the office. Music played from somebody's radio, Stephen subconsciously giving a slight wiggle to his walk, being the better dancer of the two. They met nobody else apart from the man they wanted to see, which was convenient. He was leaning with his backside against his desk, on the phone. Ting! Alfie played a kind of cricket shot and caught the man around his left knee-cap. The scream hit the ceiling along with the phone. Ting! Stephen had made room for a more conventional baseball swing and connected with the man's defensive left arm, breaking it just above the wrist. The man collapsed in terrible, screaming agony. Ting! Alfie went for the kneecap again, connecting. He wondered whether he had dislocated it, when, Ting! Stephen cracked against the man's left ankle.

As if working telepathically, both brothers departed the scene, seeing nobody except the young man, still in the same place. Outside, they laid into all the glass on the two 4x4s, ting, ting, ting, ting, ting! Alfie gave an extra whack to the side door of one vehicle, right on top of KELLY'S GARDEN LANDSCAPES, before getting back into the Audi as Stephen calmly drove it away.

ELISE: Michael, are you free to talk? I'm so tired from college, I had to tell my friends I wasn't going out. I have two very different questions for you. How do you like to read, electronically or do you like to have the feel of a real book in your hands? And, how tall are you, if you don't mind me asking? I'm 5ft 4.

MICHAEL: Elise, 5ft 4? Are you in the circus? I didn't know anyone could be 5ft 4. :p Only joking, I'm in a cheeky mood. I'm 5ft 9, I think. Our height difference seems perfect, doesn't it? I never wanted to be 6ft anyway. ;) Talk to me any time. Oh, I like the feel of a book in the hand. It's better than two in the bush.

ELISE: *Eh? Your height is perfect for me. I like a man I can look up to. Not that I have many men to look up to. I'm at my parents' house tonight. We've got the monks in in the morning, and my mother wants me here.*

Got the monks in? puzzled Michael.

MICHAEL: *You've got the monks in? Errrm, could I ask you something, perhaps at the risk of missing out on a monk explanation? Were you serious, about saying you were a virgin, if you don't mind me asking?*

ELISE: *Michael, oh, my brother has finally freed up my bathroom. I have to go bath. I'll come back to you. Oh, yeah, nothing has gone up there.*

'She said it again,' Michael said to himself, shaking his head.

He switched over to his novel, but couldn't think straight. A bit of indoor football was decided upon, then a packet of Burger Bites, which he had rediscovered recently in the Spar convenience store on the High street.

Her bath lasted exactly thirty minutes.

ELISE: *Michael, I'm back. Did you miss me? :)*

CINDY: *Michael, sorry, said boyfriend when meant friend, Belgian boy comes over for a month. Nothing happens, he just nice person. Brought to me by God.*

Juggling two women, thought Michael, grinning. He wondered if it was of any importance who he felt like choosing to stick with for a conversation; both were adorable and sexy, both from interesting places in the world. Elise spoke more intelligently, of course, but being half-English was a big advantage on being Indonesian trying to communicate.

MICHAEL: *Elise, go on, explain why you've got the monks in tomorrow. I presume it's a Buddhist ceremony.*

ELISE: *Michael, hehe. You're right. One of the monks who came last year has since died, so the monks will throw the crystals from the dead monk ashes at my family and relatives.*

Michael rocked back in his chair, laughing his head off.

Alfie Garrand threw both baseball bats into Newton Lake on their way back to the scrap yard. Stephen stopped the Audi at the gate and checked that Rimski would lock up, then drove away. Rimski turned to a puzzled, young lad by the name of Darren who worked there occasionally. 'Nothing to worry about, Dazza,' said Rimski. 'They just had to sort someone out. Mrs Garrand has been playing away with an Irish gardener.' He laughed heartily, before saying, 'But you didn't hear that from me.'

Stephen pulled up outside Alfie's house. They briefly connected fists before Alfie jumped out and Stephen gunned the Audi away. Shirley met Alfie in the hallway. Clearly she knew something was badly wrong. She shut the door after her husband, then as she turned she found him right there in her face, having not moved off into the house as expected. She jumped a little bit, then bit her lower lip. He had never, ever laid a finger on her, but right then he looked like he wanted to hit her, pin her to the wall by the neck, at least. 'Alfie?'

He did then turn and walk into the kitchen. She followed, in time to see the beer bottle he had taken from the fridge sail into the far wall and shatter all over the stone floor.

'Do you think I'm fucking stupid, Shirley? That I wouldn't hear about the gardener man?'

She bit her lip again. 'Alfie, it was nothing. Just talk.'

'Fuck just talk! Stop insulting me.' Shirley was distraught, clenching her fists together in a very feminine fashion, feminine as in not about to punch anything. She was crying even before he raised his voice again. 'Tell me what's gone on, Shirley!'

'Nothing's gone on! I swear, Alfie. He's just... I've known him a long time. He's always been cheeky with me. We got a bit physical when he was fixing the rockery. But I swear we didn't have sex. I swear it, Alfie!'

Alfie fetched himself another beer, but this time he started to drink it, while he eye-balled his unfaithful wife.

Stephen Garrand got home and went straight for his twelve-year-old bottle of Glenfiddich. The fact that his whisky was kept in the kitchen cupboard below the work surface where Joanne Garrand happened to be preparing dinner, and she had to move aside, prompted her to ask what was wrong. Stephen found a glass and poured himself a couple of fingers. He looked straight into his wife's eyes while savouring the flavour of the malt. She was prepared to wait for him.

'Me and Alfie took care of something tonight.'

She was used to his shenanigans. 'Will there be any comeback?'

'No, I doubt it.'

'Go on, tell me, then.'

'First, you tell me about the landscape gardener we've been having come round here. The Irish fella.'

Joanne knew her facial expression had remained constant, even as her mind whirled in a panic.

'What do you mean?' she asked. 'We've had four Irish lads working out there.'

'The boss man. Has he tried any funny business with you?'

Joanne cackled. She was happy with the way the cackle came out. 'No, of course not.'

'He did some work at our Alfie's. Shirley was seen getting off with the guy.'

Joanne could finally let some emotion show. 'Shit, Stephen! That's really bad. Are you sure?'

He poured more whisky. 'Pretty sure.'

'Poor Alfie. How's he taking it?'

'He's with her now.'

'Shit.'

Stephen perused what was for dinner. He embraced and kissed Joanne. As she tasted the whisky, she gauged how normal his behaviour was with her. Satisfied, she got on with the food preparation, watching him go through to see the children.

13

THE UPPER HAND

Irene Hannah, in the Philippines, had given in to Michael's request to send her some books, and told him an address in Baguio City. He Googled the place, seeing a crowded city, but up in beautiful mountains. The three chick-lit titles he had chosen from her *GoodReads* wish list had just arrived from Amazon, so he re-addressed them, sealed them tight, wrote on that they were just printed material (for customs) and went for a walk to the Post Office.

It was a cold day. He always blamed Liverpool for letting cold days come across from the Irish sea. He found the Post Office to be full of loud, teenage chavs (blame Liverpool again?) topping up their phone cards and suchlike.

Michael did a brief shop in the Spar convenience store while he was out, chatting to someone he knew in there. On the way back, he saw the Prince of Darkness on the move, leather coat flowing in the cold wind, but there was no opportunity to talk to the man. At the corner of his building, he was passed by Stephen Garrand in a noisy truck. Stephen beeped his horn and Michael waved.

Michael realised that he was keen to get onto *GoodReads* and speak with Elise. Instead, he controlled himself and had some lunch first. When he eventually logged on, there were no messages – not even from Cindy. All his friends, apart from the Americans, were marked as being online, though.

MICHAEL: *Elise, have the monks been and gone?*

ELISE: *Michael, hello, I was just thinking about you. Yes, the monks have gone. We're eating soon, lots of fatty good stuff, my cheeks will get so big. I might shop later, for new clothes. And I need some underwear. I love Victoria's Secret, do you?*

MICHAEL: *Yes, I love their stuff. I'm always buying it for myself. Would you like my opinion on things before you buy?*

ELISE: *That would be great. Nothing too sexy, though, I'm not that kind of girl. :p Oh, bath now, then eat. We can shop a little later if you're free.*

MICHAEL: *Elise, woman, you're never out of the bath! Okay, I'll be here.*

Michael worked on his novel into the early afternoon, before sitting back with his hands behind his head, pleased with his efforts. There was nothing to see outside his window except torrential rain. He flipped over to *GoodReads* and saw a message waiting for him. But first, he air-punched his way to the kitchen to loosen his back up, made coffee and returned to his workstation. Then he went back again for one of those amazing, chocolate, *HobNob* flapjack biscuits. He munched away happily as he looked at the message. It had come in from Cindy.

CINDY: *Michael, I'm home now you lik to know.*

MICHAEL: *Cindy, I'm very pleased to hear it. I hope the trip was everything you wanted it to be. The new book is coming along great. I still can't find a place to introduce a character based on you, though. Hehe.*

Coming off that, a fresh message awaited him.

ELISE: *Michael, I've bought something from Victoria's Secret. See the link, please give me your Englishman's opinion.*

Michael checked out the thing she had just bought which looked fairly standard lingerie to him. He did his own research and found something better for her to consider: a black and white baby doll and matching g-string set.

MICHAEL: *Elise, look at the enclosed link for an Englishman's opinion.*

A few minutes passed. He sat there in limbo, wondering if he had gone too far.

ELISE: *Michael, hahahahahaha. No! I couldn't wear anything like that. I'm so boring and conservative. Did I not tell you I'm a shy girl? Did you believe me when I said I was a virgin? Because it's true.*

MICHAEL: *I did wonder if you were kidding when you said you were a virgin. I know England is void of morals; it just seems a little unusual, that's all. I hope I didn't offend you.*

ELISE: *Michael, not offended. I am a virgin. I can't see the situation changing any time soon. I'm so looking forward to the big O.*

Now he knew she was playing him, but he wasn't bothered in the slightest.

MICHAEL: *No big O? Surely you could go in search of*

that? I can't imagine an English woman not seeking that out, virgin or not.

ELISE: *No, I swear. I want you to know I'm not a loose and easy girl. I may not be a prude but I'm not a loose girl. You would be surprised with my little experience. You have the upper hand, Mr Lincoln.*

Michael turned around on his leather chair a few times. He spotted some bubble wrap under the desk and popped quite a lot of it. He took his scissors out of his skull mug, which also held pens and printer ink, and tidied up a rogue fingernail. What did he, a thirty-seven-year-old Englishman, want with this nineteen-year-old Elise McHugh in Singapore? Where could it all go?

She was back with a new message.

ELISE: *Do you have children?*

MICHAEL: *My daughter, Hope. Need I say she's adorable?*

ELISE: *Oh! You have a daughter? I must see pictures of her. I must! Such a lovely name.*

MICHAEL: *Thank you. You will see pictures.*

ELISE: *My auntie has stopped by. I love talking to you, don't think I'm being rude if I go quiet for an hour.*
love

MICHAEL: *I love speaking to you, too. I'll be here. I'll be formulating advice on the big O for you.*

In his spare hour, Michael showered, and had a go at the sudden appearance of hairs in his 37-year-old ears. He made the decision not to talk to Elise about orgasms, unless she returned to the subject. So, back at his desk, eating an apple, he replied to her latest message, that she was free to talk again.

MICHAEL: *Elise, I find you fascinating, vivacious and possibly a little naughty. The word I'm looking for is sassy. I want another personal image of you. Nude, not rude, but artistic, lying on your bed with your grey hair splayed out and just a fraction of saggy buttock exposed. Ring your grandmother and say, "Granny, I need you to do me a favour..." Hehe.*

ELISE: *Michael, I'll send you many images, no worries. I want a nude shot of you, though.*

MICHAEL: *Elise, you're asking for a nude photo of me after knowing each other for such a short time. That's creepy! That's highly offensive! Where's my camera? Do you want artistic or in your face crude?*

14

COINCIDENCE

'I'll be very pissed off if you rip the cloth.'

Michael sat on his sofa, eating a ham salad sandwich, watching Tony trying to play trick shots on the pool table.

'Don't worry,' replied Tony. 'This one is simple.' He raised the butt of the cue vertical to his right cheek, before laughing, and going over to take a seat, the cue swinging like a sword.

'Tony, you're my best mate. You can tell me, come on, have you split up with your girlfriend again?'

'What? Oh, coming round here like this? No, Wendy's fine. It's my sister. Look, Keira's not sent me, she's not like that. But she's thinking of dating this knob who works in a B&Q warehouse. I was wondering, mate, what's your effing problem? Apart from just coming out of a divorce, that is.'

Michael finished his sandwich, then brushed away some of Tony's crumbs from the man's own scattergun lunch onto the floor. 'You're right. I think Keira's great. I'll call her. Today.'

Tony clapped his hands together and stood up, the cue clattering to the floor. 'Oh, sorry,' he said, retrieving the cue and placing it gently on the pool table. 'I'll get going, Wendy's doing a roast for lunch. Thanks for the appetiser.'

Michael saw Tony downstairs. They high-fived and he watched his friend jog off down the street.

Dylan readied himself to sit down and work on his current chemistry project for school. He had his study area in the corner of the living room of his apartment, although he wasn't expecting serious concentration, due to his sister staying with him, and his night porter flatmates were suddenly less inclined towards sleep and more towards chatting with Susan Wang.

Susan had been temporarily thrown out of the family home by their father for losing her job, but Dylan and she both knew the man would calm down soon and take her back. She was frantically looking for a new position. Dylan glanced over protectively to his sister and the older men, but it was innocent flirting, so he let her be.

Dylan's phone went off with a text. Checking it put him in a dilemma. His barmaid "girlfriend" requested his company, at a café in Plaza Singapura. Could he postpone his project? Could he leave his sister unchaperoned?

Elise was eating out with Tricia, prior to catching a movie. Tucking into fried chicken, she thought she really must get back on with her exercise routine. More swimming, perhaps. The two girls had been chatting incessantly since leaving their apartment, but now over their food, they were independently on their phones. Elise was excited to be contacting England. She had quickly become attached to her special Englishman. They had exchanged normal images; his a head and shoulders one, her a more posed shot, which she examined again as she sat there: leaning forward to the camera, wisps of hair falling beside both ears, flushed cheeks, slight cleavage from her disappointing bosom. Her fingers began to type.

ELISE: *Michael, I meant to ask, sorry. How old is your daughter, Hope?*

Oh, he's online, Elise realised.

MICHAEL: *Elise, she's ten going on twenty.*

ELISE: *Oh, she can marry one of my brothers. Guess where I am? Eating out again. You are not going to like what I look like if we ever meet. I'll be a big girl. Oh, one last question, please. Are you dating?*

MICHAEL: *Elise, I'm sure I would find you very attractive in real life. I'm sort of dating, early days with a woman in the town, round the corner in fact.*

ELISE: *Oh, a woman at your beck and call. I'm so jealous. If it gets serious will you have time for me? :(*

MICHAEL: *Of course I'll have time for you. I'm fascinated by you. I could ask the same thing of you when you start dating. Maybe we should let the conversation flow, and avoid unimportant talk of the weather and food and work.*

ELISE: *What would you like to talk about? This is a critical moment, sir. Choose wisely. Don't bore me.*

Elise slurped her drink up through her straw. She was amused, waiting as a couple of minutes passed, imagining Michael stressing and struggling over how to respond. Then she looked up and saw *him*, car-crash man, guitar boy, sitting at a far-off table with a girl. Elise couldn't believe it. Was he stalking her? Singapore was a small island, but this was getting ridiculous. She grinned into her straw; he could stalk her any time with her happy approval. The girl he was with had nice hair, that was all she could see of her. He had nice hair, and lovely eyes. She determined to discover his name. But then again, these brief sightings of him might be all she was ever going to get; they might both live out their lives in Singapore and never set eyes on one another again. Why didn't she speak to him when Tricia crashed into his car? Madly, she imagined forcing Tricia to go over there and dumbly mention the crash, somehow get his name. But then she controlled herself. If she was fated to be with him, then they would meet again.

MICHAEL: *Elise, what do you wear to bed?*

In Newton-le-Willows, Michael smashed a football in the general direction of the goal. 'What do you wear to bed? Fucking hell, Michael, is that the best you can do? You're a writer, for Christ's sake.'

His eyes hurt from sleeping badly last night. His coffee wasn't the best today. He had telephoned Keira but got only her answer phone.

ELISE: *Michael, loose-fitting tee-shirt and shorts. I don't like to be confined in bed. And you?*

MICHAEL: *Me? I don't wear anything in bed.*

ELISE: *Michael, nothing? Naked in cold England?*

MICHAEL: Sure, naked. I'm hard.

ELISE: *Hard?*

MICHAEL: *Hard as in tough.*

ELISE: *Oh! Hey, leaving café. My friend is shouting at her boyfriend down the phone. So funny. Give me a few minutes, please.*

Elise delayed, and delayed, and got to smile at the guitar boy as she followed an upset Tricia from the café. He looked dumbstruck, and had no time to acknowledge her before she was gone.

Outside in the mall, Tricia was ranting at her boyfriend over some failure or misdemeanour of his. But then, off the phone, she was her normal, happy self, linked arms with Elise and headed to the movie.

But Elise didn't get to see much of the Jason Statham film, as she was engaged in surreptitious texting to Michael.

ELISE: *Michael, did you like my photos? Sorry about the cleavage. Small boobies, you know.*

MICHAEL: *I love small breasts. I have a bad childhood memory about football sized boobs.*

ELISE: *Haha, please tell me about it. Have you had lots of lovers?*

MICHAEL: *Good God. Lots of lovers? Errrm, about eleven. Shall I go through them all, alphabetically? Hehe.*

ELISE: *Go on, write me little stories about what you got up to with them. You're a writer, after all.*

MICHAEL: *Well, one of them would end with her slashing me with a kitchen knife, others end badly, as well. Some are still friends. I would prefer to write a story about being with you.*

Elise caught some of the movie at that stage. She let Michael stew a little.

ELISE: *Michael, a story about me? You mean an intimate story? That would be amazing.*

MICHAEL: *Are you sure? It might get a bit explicit when I get going. Say now if you don't want that kind of thing.*

ELISE: *I won't be offended. You have my permission to do your best. I'm signing off now. I'll see what arrives for the morning.*

In Newton-le-Willows, Michael opened a can of coke. There wasn't much planning to do, so he sat down and wrote something personal just for Elise.

MICHAEL: *I thought you looked incredibly cute as you came out of the bathroom, wearing the white hotel robe. There seemed a slight nervousness about the way you pushed hair behind your ears.*

I was sitting in an armchair, sipping champagne, in just my shorts, still amazed at the ridiculous humidity of Singapore, but grateful for the air-con. You came near to me in the gloom and I saw your flushed cheeks. You explained that you were hot, but I had the feeling that this was a first for you, being in an hotel room with a man. It was then that you slowly started to open the robe, and my anticipation rose, keen to see your beautiful, nubile body.

Then to be faced instead with your pyjamas had us both laughing, and that broke the ice, relaxed us both. You took some more champagne, thanking me again for the wonderful meal. I joked that I had never seen a girl eat so much and you playfully smacked my chest. I stood and we kissed properly for the first time. I could feel you smiling beneath my mouth, before you let my tongue search inside for your own.

We kissed and caressed for quite a while, somehow moving to the bed where I eased you gently down. I found you so absolutely gorgeous, with your little panting breaths. I kissed your neck and around the top of your chest, so aroused by you but careful to keep my massive erection from touching any part of your body. You offered to remove

107

your pyjama top, which I helped you with. You were so determined to be free of the clothing and slipped out of your shorts at the same time.

I cupped both your small, excited breasts and brought my lips to move over their nipples. Then I began an exploration down your body; your delicate ribcage, flat stomach, into your pencil thin pubic hair despite your shy move of a hand to half stop me. I feigned going there, instead moving to your thighs which opened like magic to my approach. I kissed and fondled your inner thighs, and sensed your first arch of the back from the bed.

You suddenly remembered that you weren't completely new to all this and tried to bring me up so you could kiss my chest and mouth again, but I was determined to stay with your soft thighs.

Ever so slowly I made my way to your sex, and you begged me to touch you there. I could see moisture down there on your lips. Not able to resist, I ran my tongue down your pussy from top to bottom, feeling you lift your body from the mattress. I found your clit and rubbed gently with my fingers as my tongue continued to explore you. You were saying something but it didn't seem to be in English.

With extreme effort you squirmed free and brought me back level with you, kissing me with ferocious gratitude. You were reaching for my groin. I asked what you wanted and you told me in no uncertain terms.

I slipped out of my shorts and took hold of myself,

guiding my tip against you, moving up and down, side to side. You were moving so much that the bed sheet was everywhere already. You begged me to put it in you. Normally I would have pulled away, started something else on you, but you looked achingly cute, your hair all tousled, your tongue moving across your upper teeth, so I ran my cock up and down the full length of the outside of your pussy before I pushed in a little way. You arched your body again to receive me, then swore. I recognised that English word.

I pushed in deeper and began to move slowly inside your tight pussy. Your body was wonderful. You started to gasp. Perhaps you were already coming because I could see so much of your juice on my shaft when it came out of you. You were begging me not to stop. I had no intention of stopping, pushing deeper than you thought possible, moving, deeper and faster, fucking you hard, then relaxing and taking it slow again. Somehow you took yourself off me and hurried down to take hold of my cock. You said something about its huge size, then it was in your mouth, being sucked hard. You were very good at that. I stroked your hair and your moist back as you continued. You were so lovely I just wanted to come in your mouth, but I stopped myself. You turned over onto your hands and knees and I mounted you from behind. I fucked you for several more minutes before finally pouring myself into you. We collapsed onto the bed in a sweaty mess.

We found ourselves giggling. I needed a drink badly. We only had champagne so I got up and drank some of that. I watched you roll over onto your back. Right, you said, smiling, that's the foreplay out of the way. What's next?

15

WOMEN OF ST HELENS

Michael sat back and finished his can of coke. He let out a loud, satisfying burp and then, as he looked through the message he had just sent to a virtual stranger in Singapore, mimed a "wow". It wasn't completely naff, he thought, standing to stretch, for something just off the cuff like that. Still, he had shocked himself. It was one thing to write an erotic scene in a chapter of a book, and completely another to send it to a young woman.

Elise read the message while on the bus to school the following morning. Despite flushing bright red with embarrassment and thinking all the people around her could see the screen of her phone, she thought it a brilliant message and the most amazing thing anyone had ever sent to her. It stayed with her all through her few classes that morning, reading it over and over, whenever she could. She considered showing it to her girlfriends, then made the definite decision that it was something to remain private.

It wasn't until she got home that she worded a reply to her Englishman.

ELISE: *Michael, thank you for the best morning message I have ever received. I'm stunned that someone would put me in a story like that. Sorry to be crude but did your writing turn you on?*

Massive shaft huh! Mr Lincoln, is that true or fictional hahaha? But you are an incredible writer, detailed and funny and sexy. Thank you. However I don't think I could ever write something so sexy back, and I can probably never turn you on. Haha!

MICHAEL: *Elise, I'm glad you liked your story. The next one will be set in a women's prison. :)*

Of course it turned me on, imagining your body and soul. And I don't think of you as a loose woman. I think of you as sassy. I think you could turn me on.

Massive shaft: you'll probably never know. I hope I've done enough not to get cruelly dropped, if you do that sort of thing. Haha.

ELISE: *I'm so pleased you're online right now. I really enjoy our conversations. You have done enough and I hope I don't get dropped too, honestly.*

A women's prison huh? I can handle it. Did you really like my photos?

MICHAEL: *It's snowing here and it's as beautiful as you.*

ELISE: *Ahhhh. Keep that up and I'll develop a wee little crush on you. Right, I must bath. I'm going dancing tonight. Can we speak before I go out?*

MICHAEL: *Dancing? Has disco reached Singapore? Very nice. Hopefully you'll meet a nice Singaporean boy to take you off my hands. I'll be here. Go bath.*

Michael went out himself that evening, though no dancing was involved. He took Keira for a meal at a posh restaurant. When she asked where he was taking her, he had joked, St Helens, and she had almost jumped from the moving car. Then, to break the ice even further, he had remembered that joke by Liverpool comedian, John Bishop, something along the lines of "I've never met a woman with hairy ears, and I've been to St Helens".

They had a lovely time. He got her home at a reasonable hour and, as her son was staying at his grandmother's, she invited him in.

Michael immediately saw Keira's naked body in the

kitchen. It was one of those artistic nude images (sitting with knee raised, arms crossed over breasts), holding her son when he was a baby, and it was in amongst the plethora of family images in a montage on the wall. The kettle at least got filled for the coffee, but they found themselves kissing, and soon he saw her body unclothed for real in the bedroom. He found her extremely sexy; her body just as he had imagined. Of course, she wasn't young any more, but there was no cellulite or unattractive belly. Very briefly, his mind wandered to Elise in Singapore, before he focussed entirely on Keira. As he roamed her with his mouth, there was a little butterfly tattoo on her right thigh, but that was a relief, considering some of the multi-coloured full-arm mutilations done by women these days.

Their lovemaking was very nice (perhaps she was a touch more frantic than him) and they lay together in a relaxed and happy manner afterwards, which was surely a good sign for a possible relationship. Michael compared the situation favourably with his recent one-night stands.

He didn't stay the night, the unspoken idea being that her son would be returned home quite early the next morning. They kissed at her front door, he manhandled the lapels of her dressing gown over her breasts, they kissed some more, and he jogged off to the car.

In Singapore, Elise got up early, even though there was no school. She had a driving lesson booked, then would spend the day with her family, to see what her kid brothers were up to. They would all go out for a meal in the evening, no doubt. Mooching around in her pyjamas, eating toast, she checked her messages. A girlfriend, Eilynn, amused her with a story about her crazy boyfriend. One of her schoolmates, Lucy, reminded her when a project was due in, and an old school pal called Philip had dropped her a line. Biting on the toast, Elise wondered what it was he wanted. She was a little disappointed not to have a message from England. Maybe Michael was busy. If they got into serious conversation, perhaps they would have to come up with a codeword for when it was impossible to talk all of a sudden; relatives arriving unexpectedly, that sort of thing. She shook her head; she was thinking too much into it. But then she kept on thinking, and looked at Michael's naughty message again. She didn't think she could possibly match him story for story, or even produce one at all, and it worried her that he would lose interest.

She went through to shower and get ready for her driving lesson. As she sat on the bathroom floor, drying her hair, worry over Michael filled her consciousness again. She padded to her bedroom, throwing off her towel. She appraised herself in the full-length wall mirror. Looking through her underwear drawer, she decided she would have to pick up her clean laundry from home, she was down to her yellow bra set with the message Cute As Can Bee! and a bumblebee on the back of the panties. She put the underwear on. Suddenly emboldened, she reached for her phone and lined herself up for a headless shot in the mirror. Then, after making sure there was no fabric sagginess around her bottom, she took some pictures over her shoulder. The silly panties were a start, she supposed; maybe Michael would prove to be worthy of something sexier? She giggled, and continued getting dressed.

Michael was wide awake, so took a beer from the fridge and checked *GoodReads*. He realised he was addicted to the site. Once, when it was down, he read hundreds of messages online from fellow members, distraught to be denied it. He was delighted to see a message from Cindy. It turned out to be her shortest ever communication, simply saying she wanted him to hear her sing and play the guitar, adding the information of where he could access it. He typed in the details, turned up his speakers, and was instantly blown away by the hauntingly beautiful voice and guitar playing which came through. She was singing in her own language, but that didn't detract from how wonderful it was. He sat there in his darkened apartment, entranced for the full six and a half minutes. Then he played it again. Cindy, what an amazing girl you are.

16

LUCID HAS LEFT THE BUILDING

CINDY: *Michael, I'm ready to have Hope for six months.*

MICHAEL: *Cindy, are you? Haha! I'll give her the news. Note, I didn't say good news. Make sure you've got a lot of food in, she eats for England.*

CINDY: *Eats for England, whaaat?*

MICHAEL: *Never mind. Wait a minute, please, there's someone at the door.*

Once again, Michael was surprised by the ringing of his inner doorbell. This time he had a delegation standing in the hallway, if two people could comprise a delegation. It was David, the Prince of Darkness, accompanied by an American lady, called Gloria, who rented the apartment directly under

Michael's. They both seemed quite happy, so apparently, it wasn't about his noisy football playing.

'Hello, Michael,' said Gloria, giving him a smile.

Michael loved her accent. It could have been from anywhere in the States, as far as he could tell, but it was very cool. 'Hi.'

'We've come about that music last night,' continued Gloria.

'Oh, I'm sorry, was it a bit loud?'

'No, no,' she said. 'David and I, talking just now, realised we both heard it and both thought it remarkably beautiful.'

The Prince of Darkness was seriously nodding. Michael realised the man was holding his Tesco shopping bags.

'Right,' said Michael.

'Could you tell us who it was?' asked the Prince.

'Sure, I'll write it down. Please come in.'

Michael realised how anti-social he was at the moment, having never invited his neighbours in to his apartment before. Suddenly remembering his football goal, he knew why he had never done so. The Prince seemed too embarrassed to enter someone else's home, gesturing that they would wait there. Michael jogged over to his desk, where there was no reply from Cindy yet, jotted down the information she had given him and hurried back to the door.

'There you are. It's a friend of mine, actually. An amateur singer, but very good.'

'More than good, I'd say,' smiled Gloria.

'Michael,' said Prince, earnestly, and there was quite a pause, 'thank you for that. You are a good man.'

'No worries at all.'

Michael bid them good day, and retuned to Cindy. She was being quite lucid, so he didn't want to miss a minute of it. He had already thanked her for the music and expressed how beautiful he thought it was.

CINDY: *Michael, for you asking, I love Led Zeppelin, Black Sabbath, all rock classic, but I'm not a hater of other genre. I want to go to Atlantis. Lol :p kidding. I thought I was a dolphin always around the sea in a past life :p I want to see all the places from the books I read. I want to go to another galaxy. Forget what I say. :)*

Ooh, thought Michael, lucid has left the building.

CINDY: *Michael, sound borring indeed. I just ordinary girl.*

You are anything but ordinary, thought Michael.

Alfie Garrand had not invited Michael, or Tony, or Keira, for that matter, to his monster BBQ party, but they all knew something was happening, with the smoke billowing around Newton-le-Willows, as well as hearing the raucous music and seeing the side streets clogged with parked cars.

There were countless bottles of lager and Alcopops sticking out of bins of ice, extra wooden benches brought in specially and a bouncy castle down the end of the garden for the kids. The professional DJ and his massive speakers were just inside the sliding, full-wall, patio door. All the Garrands' family, friends and associates were there, having a good time, with the weather finally taking a turn for the better.

Alfie wasn't actually in charge of the BBQ; that was left to an enthusiastic Stephen Garrand, helped by a friend called Ryan, who had some catering experience. Alfie and Shirley moved around their guests, occasionally docking with each other to smile and kiss like the perfect couple, which they were, as her recent indiscretion with the landscape gardener had genuinely been forgiven and forgotten by Alfie. Alfie wore three-quarter length black trousers with a white shirt, and a lot of gold bling on show. Shirley was dressed in pale jeans, designer ones of course, and a strapless, white top. She was the best-looking woman there, without even making much effort.

Alfie stopped by the chefs, perusing the sausages.

'Patience,' said Stephen to his brother. He was in a good mood.

Alfie saluted him with his bottle of *Smirnoff Ice* and moved away.

There were a handful of men in the lounge, watching an England friendly on the massive plasma TV. Rimski was amongst them. He had come without his wife, who thought barbecued food was the work of the devil. Personally, he thought the way she boiled everything to death on the stove was quite satanic. He looked up as Alfie came in, smiling and slapping men on the shoulder, then he pretended to despair of them.

'Fellas, it's a lovely day out there. My garden's full of beautiful clunge. No, boys, I'll tell you the truth, my brother's calling for customers. Get there before the rush.'

The men laughed, and drifted outside. Alfie was carrying a bottle of Heineken in the same hand as his *Smirnoff*. He handed it to Rimski.

'Rimski,' whispered Alfie, 'while we've got a second. We might want you to go in on a job soon.'

'Oh, aye?'

'Yeah, a little reconnaissance work.'

'Being the inside man, you mean?'

'That's the phrase I was looking for. I just thought I'd give you a heads-up. Me and Stephen will fill you in soon.'

Rimski nodded, before they stepped into the garden. Stephen, who had magically found a tall chef's hat, made a big fuss of bringing Rimski to the front of the queue to take his order.

Joanne Garrand looked over her wine glass at her husband making an exhibition of himself. Good God, she thought, he thinks he's in *Goodfellas*, or something. She glanced at her children down at the bouncy castle, then looked sister-in-law,

Shirley, up and down. Shirley noticed the look and smiled. Joanne smiled back. Her friends alongside her were still talking about the latest measles outbreak, so Joanne kept her attention on the gathering. Once her garden was completed she would put on a bigger and better function than this, she was sure.

That evening, in Singapore, Dylan was out at Changi beach, at the east of the island, with his girlfriend, his friends and some of her friends, picnicking and generally having a nice time. Swimming had taken place, some of the boys had failed miserably at fishing, and the BBQ had been a superb success. Now the sun was setting. Dylan reached for his guitar and started to play *Romanza*. The nearest people happily paid attention, some of those further away cocked an ear, knowing it was Dylan, and his girlfriend leant in closer to his side. He hadn't quite mastered the piece, but it was beyond anything anybody there could possibly create, so it was a lovely way to round off the day.

Michael shut the window, due to the smell of barbecue smoke, and sat back down at his desk. He switched across from his novel to his email, for the umpteenth time. Elise's images of her in her underwear sat there, for him to scroll along, back and forth, back and forth. On one of them he could almost make out the shape of her sex. As for the others, well, what a curvy bottom she had on her. The bumblebee stuff puzzled him, but that was a minor annoyance in his enjoyment of it all.

17

BATTERIES NOT INCLUDED

Michael got home from a busy day out. There had been lunch with Keira, in, of all places, the restaurant inside IKEA, Warrington, as that was where she happened to be when he phoned her. Recently, they had become relaxed and happy together, although there was still no talk of them officially dating.

From there he headed across to Manchester to collect his daughter from school. She ran to him and he spun her around, in front of about eight new friends; so the relocation was not all bad. Then on to the pictures at the Trafford Centre for the new movie Hope was dying to see, followed by a meal in Nando's. He finally dropped Hope off at her mother's place near the airport. The South African wasn't there, so he and Samantha managed to have quite a long, civilised chat.

Michael switched his computer on, then went and made coffee, looking at his watch. It was too late in the Far East to talk to anybody live, although Cindy was occasionally known to keep strange hours. He settled down to check his messages. There were three on *GoodReads*: Tony, Cindy and Irene Hannah. Nothing from Elise. Probably she was patiently waiting for his response to her images. He should have done it that morning, he realised. Hopefully, she hadn't gone to bed feeling he was ignoring her. Tony's message was to recommend a new Tudor novel that had just come out, as he was known to like that era. It looked a good possibility. Cindy told him she had just taken up a position in an oil company, and would be living in a place called Sidoarjo for her training. He was too tired to even contemplate Cindy in the oil business. Irene Hannah spoke politely but about nothing in particular.

He set to thinking about Elise, and right on cue she popped up in red, as being online.

MICHAEL: *Elise, you're up late. You don't have to chat now but I wanted to thank you for the photos. They are fantastic! Horny, even. I'd return the compliment but I'm sure you don't want to see me in my pants. :p*

He sat, drinking his coffee, waiting patiently to see if she would choose to answer him.

ELISE: *Michael, hi. I've been trying to finish a project. My girlfriends have just gone. I'm having a little wine, trying to relax my mind. What pants do you wear?*

MICHAEL: *Calvin Kleins.*

ELISE: *What makes you think I wouldn't want to see your bulge through your Calvins?*

MICHAEL: *Bulge?*

ELISE: *From the massive shaft. Hehe. Only joking, you don't have to. Do me another story, if you like, when you have the time.*

MICHAEL: *The women's prison one? We'll see. Do all your panties have writing on them?*

ELISE: *Ohhhh, so embarrassing. That was a laundry issue. I do have various types of underwear, some very sexy, although I don't know why I need those. No, no prison! A nice story.*

MICHAEL: *Will there be other photos, in exchange for a story? Elise, I've stared at the cursor for two minutes wondering whether to say this, but what the hell. Will there be images without underwear? Artistic ones, of course ;)*

ELISE: *You show me yours and I'll show you mine. :)))*

MICHAEL: *Is that a promise?*

ELISE: *I don't know. I'm not a loose girl, remember. We'll have to see what you come up with (no pun intended). Oh boy, my lids won't stay open. I must sign off. Is that okay with you?*

MICHAEL: *Of course. Goodnight.*

After a few minutes it was clear she had gone.

MICHAEL: *Cindy, what on earth are you doing in the oil industry? :{) Look, see what I've done? I've treated you to a moustache there.*

Tony had once told Michael a funny Christmas story. All the family were gathered, both sets of grandparents still alive, aunties and uncles galore. The Christmas meal was over and they were all settled down with drinks and snacks to either play monopoly or watch the big BBC film. Tony's young nephew had the SKY remote control. There was ten minutes to go until the film started, so he said he would find some music in the meantime. But instead of hitting channel 342 or 341, for example, he inadvertently started on 942, straight onto three models on an adult channel, simulating having sex. Luckily it was still early, so they had their bras on as well as their panties, but there was a great deal of arse-wiggling going on. The boy had panicked and tried to get the channel off, but only managed to run the full gamut of what was available; blonde, black, pretending to give head, ankles flailing around, policewoman uniforms, fake redhead in the soapy bath, all the way down to channel 900, before he realised he would have to type in something else. Those few seconds to find Sky News, with no escape from the images, must have been excruciating for the young man.

Well after ten o'clock, with the girls on the sex channels down to their panties, Michael settled down on his sofa. A quick search earlier had found his Fuji camera. He had considered bulge shots, and quickly dismissed them as ridiculous. He would hit Elise with The Full Monty. Then she would do the same, and all would be well in the world.

The first few channels provided tattooed slappers with zero sex appeal. The next lot were a bit better; there was a blonde with small breasts and not an ounce of fat on her. Michael moved on, hurried past the deliberately gross ones, and settled on a very attractive brunette who looked East European. There was the full arm tattoo, but he ignored that and focussed on her rear as she pretended she was getting screwed. It was interesting viewing, but Michael found that he was not getting particularly aroused. He checked his camera, remembering how it worked. The weak-battery sign was on the screen but he wasn't planning on a long photo-shoot.

The brunette had the most beautifully miserable face he had ever seen. She knew she was so fit that all facial expression was unnecessary. Michael would love to have been with her in real life, but right there and then he was still only vaguely stirred. He used his hand to encourage life in the little fella. He had failed to get an erection only once in his life, and that was caused by the guilt of cheating on a girlfriend. This time he knew it was because he was planning the bizarre act of photographing himself. He was beginning to get a little distressed, annoyed, even. The manual stimulation had brought some firmness but it was not what he considered an erection. Relax, he told himself. You're just tired. He thought of postponing the event for an hour, watch something else, come back to it. Damn it, why won't you get hard? Brunette had failed, he switched channels, they were giving a taster of the harder stuff to follow, if you paid for it. That was better; he live-paused on a woman, on her back, in the act of copulating roughly. Only her breasts were on show, but at least it was erotic and worked on his imagination. His cock was finally behaving properly; not enormous, but acceptable for a first photo. He switched on the camera, and it promptly proceeded to die because of the batteries. Fuck! Michael quickly swapped the batteries for the ones in the remote control. He found he was sweating and quite embarrassed. He managed to take some shots of his erect cock from various angles, then threw the camera across the sofa.

18

EL PASO

CINDY: Hi, Michael, can't talk for a few days now, training busy. I in team inspec facilities. Boy, methane smell make me ill. Oh, want take my mind off this. So tired. Please forgive for being boring.

MICHAEL: *Cindy, I think I love you. :) Do what you have to do, I'll be here waiting.*

IRENE HANNAH: *Michael, my uncle says English people always tell mother-in-law jokes. Is that true? Please tell me a mother-in-law joke. Oh, please!*

'Mother-in-law jokes,' Michael said to himself, going across to play football. 'Mother-in-law jokes?' He did a few skills, took a few shots. 'What's that famous one? Jamaica? No, she went of her own accord.' That made him smile. Then one came to him, from the genius of the late comedian, Les Dawson.

MICHAEL: *I saw my mother-in-law being beaten up in the street by six men. A neighbour asked me, "Aren't you going to help?" "No," I said, "six should be enough".*

Elise had woken to the images from Michael. It's so big and pale, she had thought, giggling, lying with her laptop on her bed. So different to what she was used to. Haha! She had laughed at how incorrect and silly that last thought had been – she wasn't used to anything.

There was no school, but she was busy minding her two brothers all day at the family home, while her parents attended a function. Whenever she got a moment to herself she checked out the photos, deciding what to say to the man, for whenever he got out of bed on the other side of the world.

Elise loved her brothers to death, but they sometimes exhausted her. She was glad when her parents finally got home at around 8pm, so she could withdraw to her room on the top floor, with the sparkling view of Singapore spread out below, to sit on her window couch and do her own thing. She spoke on the phone with Tricia for a while, then checked Facebook. She ignored other things she wanted to do, as she realised how keen she was to tell Michael her thoughts on his images. She guessed it was about noon or 1pm in England, he would have had a few hours to reflect on his crimes, so she went onto *GoodReads*. He was there, online, waiting for her.

ELISE: *Hello, big boy!*

MICHAEL: *Oh, God, it's you again. :p*

ELISE: *Thank you so much for the photos. Wow! I didn't think you would do it. More! I want more! Haha.*

MICHAEL: *Who do you think you are, Oliver Twist? Anyway, it's your turn. What are you up to tonight?*

ELISE: *I've had my brothers all day. Now they've just come into my room and suggested a film night. Sorry, no images for you today. I'll try tomorrow, but I'm very shy, remember.*

MICHAEL: *Oh, you're teasing me now.*

ELISE: *I'm not. Trust me. There's nothing to stop you writing me another story, or sending more images of you.*

MICHAEL: *I'll think about it. Are you sure your boyfriend won't mind?*

ELISE: *Naughty you. You know I haven't got a boyfriend.*

On that subject, how are things with this local woman of yours?

MICHAEL: *No boyfriend, okay, I accept that. It's developing all right, thank you.*

ELISE: *I'm suddenly insanely jealous. Have you slept with her?*

MICHAEL: *Of course I've slept with her.*

ELISE: *Grrrrr. That's me grinding my teeth. I'm sorry I asked now. Hey, I'm cool, really. Lewis has just freed up my bathroom, so I'm going to bath before the film. Are you free tomorrow? We can really talk tomorrow, yeah?*

MICHAEL: *For a moment then I had to think who Lewis was. One of your brothers, of course. I'll be here tomorrow. I'm imagining you in the bath. Do you shave your... legs? I'd so like a photo of that. Goodnight for now.*

ELISE: *Of course I shave my... legs. Bathroom photos would be so weird. You should show me how they're done. Goodnight. Mwah!*

Michael felt he needed some proper exercise, something more

than just kicking a ball around his living space, so he called Tony, and they ended up kicking a ball around the local park. It was great fun, out on a pleasant day, feeling like teenagers again. When they realised they were completely shattered, they collapsed onto a grassy hillock with a can of Lucozade each and watched some lads in a BMX playground.

They talked books, sport, and relationships; Tony was just fine and dandy with his girlfriend, while Michael assured him that all was well with Keira. In fact, it was her extra shifts as a Special Constable which were interfering with the start of their relationship. Michael didn't mention Elise to Tony.

When he got home, Michael felt refreshed, although he knew he would be hurting the following day. After a long shower, he felt like sending a few *GoodReads* messages to the friends he didn't speak to very often. None of the Americans were online to respond. He let Cindy be, as she had her oil industry training (still that made him giggle and shake his head). Then he tried to send a message to Irene Hannah in the Philippines, but he found himself blocked. 'Odd,' he said to himself. He tried again, then sat there puzzling as to why he was no longer allowed to message the woman. The only reason he could come up with was that she had dumped him, so to speak. 'Oh. Maybe she didn't like the mother-in-law joke,' he said, and gave Irene Hannah no more thought.

MICHAEL: *In El Paso, New Mexico, you find yourself in a small mesh cage. You are very upset and confused. You are wearing an orange prison shirt and your white panties; all your proper clothes were taken by the female prison guard after your interview about smuggling cocaine into the US from Mexico.*

Cocaine smuggling? You don't understand. And where are your girlfriends who you are travelling with. You just want to cry.

Then two shadows move across the hot, smelly, holding pen area. Two big men in guard uniforms approach. They let themselves into your little cell, although one of them stays at the door. The one to come near you is very scary. He starts talking at you, something about your luggage, your court appearance, your situation; it's all a terrifying blur to you. Then he says perhaps they can work something out. You grasp at that chance. It's all a big mistake, you try to explain.

The guard is opening your orange shirt. You are too shocked to protest more than a few scared words and whimpers. He tells you to do what he says and he might get you released. You are naked except for your panties and he is fondling your breasts in turn. The other man watches on, clearly enjoying the show. The first guard then has his hand in your panties, groping for your pussy. You try to pull away but he slaps you hard across the face with his other hand. Now you understand your situation fully. He pulls down your panties and makes you step out of them. Next he orders you to kneel down. You can do nothing but obey him.

He is in complete control of you. Your hands are tied behind your back and then you are tethered to the cage wall. He brings his cock out of his trousers, and you stare at it, growing massive. Your heart is beating with such panic that you don't hear his order to go down on him.

Then you are gagging on the huge member, feeling it pushing down the back of your throat, pumping in and out of your mouth, tight to the lips, with you dribbling saliva down your chin. While he does this to you he is roughly feeling your breasts again.

Then he withdraws and you gasp for breath. He tells you to get your attitude right for when they come back for you. For maybe an hour you remain in that position, tasting his cock, crying your eyes out.

They come back, untie you, and take you into an office. Both men strip naked and you have to kneel between them, alternating your mouth and your hand on their cocks. You are lifted onto a desk and they take turns licking you out. Then you are picked up by one of the brutes and made to lie on him. He pushes his cock up your arse and starts raping you. While this horrible thing is happening the other man moves around the front of you. He puts his cock into your pussy and starts raping you as well. So there you are, completely at the mercy of these two, being double penetrated. They fuck you until you are exhausted and weak with orgasms despite the horror. Both men groan almost simultaneously as they cum into your delicate, abused body.

19

DANNY

CINDY: *Michael, thanks for my story. You are daebak! I know I ask for it, but not enjoy that theme, kekke. Good writing, but not like ideas. Sorry.*

In Sidoarjo, Cindy had found herself lodged in a poxy little hotel room, feeling unwell due to the methane gases she was smelling all day out on inspections, with nothing to do in the evening but talk online to friends, read her books and play her guitar. So she had spoken to Michael in the early hours of the morning, had been her most open and emotional ever, told him all her hopes and desires, that she read all the racy novels from the writers in the west, how she wanted her first time to be with her husband, of eventually being a good wife and mother.

MICHAEL: *Cindy, back up a minute. Forgive me for*

being nosey, but are you saying that you are a virgin?

CINDY: *Yes, Michael. I virgin. Don't mocking me, Michael. Don't mock.*

MICHAEL: *I'm not mocking you, Cindy. Aww, baby, I think it's beautiful.*

Michael had let slip that he was contemplating a naughty story for another friend, without naming Elise. Cindy had begged him to write one for her, as a novelty. Virgin and traditional she might be, but she still, she reminded him, read all the erotic stuff that came out. So he had relented and churned out the cocaine tale.

CINDY: *I like some of it. But not again, Michael. Okay?*

MICHAEL: *No, never again. We'll just talk nice.*

CINDY: *Fighting! :) You are my special friend, Michael.*

Then she had signed off, happy, to try to get some sleep.

MICHAEL: *Elise, I hope you don't mind, but I noticed your handsome, Australian friend, Danny, in your GoodReads friends list. Me and Daniel have been bad-*

mouthing each other for a while, because we are jealous of the other's friendship with you. Anyway, we agreed to meet to sort things out. We got together in a bar in Singapore, and it turns out he's a great bloke and we have a lot of things in common, not least our love for you.

Will you meet us in my hotel so we can both explain how much we care for you?

MICHAEL: *So, the three of us went out for a meal and had a great time. It seems natural for Danny and me to share you, and you seem keen to be serviced by two men. You are showering in my hotel room, while we are drinking Fosters lager (his little Aussie joke). We're not talking, just waiting for you, both of us knowing we want to pleasure you as best we can.*

The lovemaking starts the moment you join us, kissing and fondling, your towel lost, you very excited to be between two men. Danny manages to get his hand between your legs first, so I take hold of your right breast and devour it with my mouth. There is a frenzy of stripping from Danny and I, then you are working our erect cocks with both hands. You are moved to the bed, on your hands and knees. Danny is before you and his cock immediately has your tongue running up and down it. I move in behind. Danny smiles at me and we both mime "spit-roast". We then proceed to skewer you with our cocks, me in your pussy and he in your mouth. You take it as if it were the most natural thing in the world, trying to suck him off while experiencing my full length going deep inside you.

Michael re-read Elise's new story and thought it was dreadful, almost deleting it immediately. But then he saw the new images she had emailed him, and decided to send the message anyway; he would do better with the next one.

The shots from Elise, three of them, pictured her on her bed (from the neck down), naked but for a towel. The towel was draped from between her open thighs, up her stomach, to cover her breasts. Like most thirty-something men, Michael was fairly bored out of his tree with pornographic photographs, but this was amazingly sexy, simply because she had gone to the trouble to do it specially for him. Nearer the camera, her spread thighs were shockingly sexy, the shadow between towel and private place intriguing, and the general freshness of her skin gave him a semi-erection. One arm was palm-side up on the mattress, almost abandoned to the eroticism of what she was doing. Her other hand held the out-of-shot camera, and here was her shaved armpit, and beginnings of her bosom. So, the three shots were virtually the same, and yet totally different in their naughtiness; slight differences in angle of leg-spread, the towel coiled tighter in one shot as if she were desperate to go the whole way and expose herself. He loved them, and he loved her for having the nerve to do it.

'Fucking batteries!'

Michael came out of the bathroom, soaking, soapy, livid, and carrying his camera. He padded across to his desk, dripping everywhere, feeling suddenly chilly, to rummage in a drawer for new batteries. He ripped them free with his teeth, ejected the useless ones from his camera onto the floor as if they were the used shell casings of a gun, and inserted the new ones, as he hurried back to his shower.

Before the steam damaged the camera (which he wanted to throw through the window, anyway) he took some shots of his soaped-up body. Then he placed the camera on the bathroom floor while he focussed on "washing" his genitals. Keira flashed into his mind, but he quickly dismissed her. For some bizarre reason a sexy aunt from his youth joined him as he quickly got big, but then he decided to focus on imagining Elise in there with him, soaping his balls as they kiss passionately, her breasts pressed firmly to his chest. He was massive before he could even begin to fantasise about her slipping to her knees, searching for the camera outside the door, then taking shots from various angles as he made a lot of lather with his free hand.

The camera was discarded again. He was left with the two options; deal with the erection, or let it subside and have a proper wash. He chose the latter one.

Elise was round at an auntie's crowded house for a meal, when she checked her phone. She found she had messages from three men. She was sitting in the living room, near where her mother and a female cousin were chatting. Then her brothers came in with two male cousins and settled down in front of the television. Elise waited until some order descended on the room before beginning to read. Danny in Melbourne talked about surfing, about his friends, and again mentioned that his family would be in Hong Kong in two months time and would she meet up with him there? She replied cheerfully and as non-committally as usual. The next message was from old school friend, Philip, again asking her out on a date. She ignored that for the time being, instead looking at what Michael had sent her. Her eyes widened at the shower images, but she managed not to gasp or say anything to herself. His cock looked so angry, with soap cascading all around. Oh my, she thought, squeezing her thighs together.

She watched the television while deciding how best to respond to Michael.

20

PRAWNING

MICHAEL: *Elise, of course I took care of matters.*

ELISE: *Where? In your hand?*

MICHAEL: No, all the way up the shower wall. Haha. You're so bad, you know. How did we get to this so quickly?

ELISE: *You led me astray.*

MICHAEL: *Am I to see you naked in the shower? Or anywhere else, for that matter?*

ELISE: *I do want to, Michael, but I find it so hard to do that fully. I am a shy girl, really.*

MICHAEL: *Tell me how you play with yourself.*

ELISE: *Me time? Hehe. I like to watch something on screen, and rub my clit. Not too hard, just the right pressure. I'm always very wet during that.*

MICHAEL: *Oh, God! You're driving me crazy here.*

ELISE: *Oh, why? Are you big again? Is Michael Junior excited?*

MICHAEL: *Michael Junior is very excited. I wish you were here.*

ELISE: *I wish I was there. :(My dad might stop me travelling, though. What would you need from me right this minute?*

MICHAEL: *Elise, please don't mention your father during our conversations. He would want to kill me, I'm sure. Right now? I want you to kneel down and put me in your mouth.*

ELISE: *Will you come to Singapore?*

MICHAEL: *Right this minute? Could you concentrate on the matter in hand, baby? Can I cum in your mouth?*

ELISE: *I'd love to show you the city. Er, I suppose so.*

MICHAEL: *Never a good thing to say Er to a man on that topic. :p Will you swallow?*

ELISE: *Michael, may I ask you something? A boy from school has asked me to go prawning with him. There's nothing romantic in it. I wanted to ask your permission.*

MICHAEL: *Prawning?? What the hell is prawning? Elise, you don't have to ask my permission. I'll enjoy the rest. :p Go and have fun on this date. I'll want to hear all about it. Prawning?*

ELISE: *Prawning. Collecting prawns at the beach and then cooking them. Getting tired now, Michael. I'll say goodnight next time, okay?*

MICHAEL: *Of course. Sweet dreams. Goodnight.*

ELISE: *Goodnight. XX*

Rimski's "inside man" job lasted approximately five hours. The Garrand brothers, when they heard about it, didn't blame him or accuse him of incompetence; it was just a couple of accidents which put paid to his criminal misadventure.

He had shown up at 8am for his first day as a minimum-wage delivery driver for a car-hire firm, based out of a Warrington industrial estate. The boss had sent him out straight away as a passenger in a brand-new Audi A4. The driver was an obese, smelly individual called Eddie, who was following another driver, by the name of Lloyd, in another Audi. As soon as they were off the industrial estate it became clear to Rimski why the men did such a low-paid job; they drove like escaping bank robbers, doing 60mph down normal roads and turning corners with the help of the handbrake. On the way to collect a vehicle, Lloyd went down the wrong street. Without any warning, he performed a stunt driver's handbrake turn. Eddie let him come back past him before carrying out the same manoeuvre. Rimski held on for dear life, cursing the Garrands.

They collected a Volvo estate car from a telecommunications firm, and this became Rimski's ride, his mission being to stay behind the two Audis, until Lloyd delivered his vehicle and jogged over to become Rimski's passenger (he wasn't going to share a car with honking Eddie until he absolutely had to).

Eddie's Audi was delivered to a residential address: to a woman in a flimsy nightgown who seemed disappointed in the quality of the delivery men. After doing the necessary paperwork with the woman, Eddie lumbered over to the Volvo and eased his massive bulk into the back seat. He didn't seem to notice both front windows being opened. Apparently, it was now time for breakfast at a nearby greasy spoon, the speeding journey helping to give them plenty of time for lounging around, before heading back to base.

Rimski drove them back to the firm, where the office staff didn't question their time of absence. Eddie, quite bumptious, took it on himself to teach Rimski how to valet the Volvo, prior to it going out again. It was a sight watching the man contort himself in stages down to vacuuming the interior. Then the oil and water were "checked", before it was taken outside the bay to be washed. Rimski had so far been horrified at the mundane cleaning part of the job, imaging having to valet fifty cars before the Garrands decided to start stealing them. Then he saw the power jet-wash, which was like a rifle, and would be great fun. As Eddie was sweating like a pig by that stage, Rimski took over the washing of the Volvo, hitting it with short bursts of jet wash. Suddenly he realised that his groin was getting soaked. He was relieved to find that the hose had sprung a leak, and not himself. As it was near to the handle he decided to cover the hole with his left index finger while operating the trigger. He vaguely recalled later that Eddie had advised him not to do that, as he blew a hole in his finger.

Thankfully, the more hygienic Lloyd performed First Aid to stem the flow of blood, and then drove him to A&E, with his wrapped finger up above his head. After a surprisingly short wait to see a nurse, it turned out not to be too bad. The wound was cleaned, given two little stitches and bandaged.

Back at the firm, Rimski saw the boss approaching, but instead of being allowed to go home, he was handed the keys of a BMW to deliver. It was like that then, was it, thought Rimski.

It was just Lloyd leading him in another Audi. Rimski kept his damaged finger off the wheel and the gear stick as he stayed behind Lloyd. Rimski's confidence was growing, although he didn't have a clue where he was half the time. Lloyd headed onto the M62, Rimski imagining speeds of up to 100mph, but the leader stayed at seventy, perhaps taking into account the new man's injury. But off at the first junction, Lloyd stayed at seventy, up the off ramp, still doing seventy, then around to the left to join a dual-carriageway. Rimski followed at the same speed, and instantly realised that he didn't have the skill to make the turn. Two things happened together; he realised he was hurting the tyres badly, and he found himself going sideways. It was true, he found, that at times like that everything went into slow-motion; he had plenty of time to watch the direction bollard approach the side of the car, but after he'd wiped that out everything sped up, until eventually he came to a stop on the central reservation, in a groove of turf, and with an astonished HGV driver looking at him in passing.

Rimski gathered himself before getting out of the car. Lloyd had doubled back rather quickly and parked up, so they examined the damage together. The driver's side door was caved in and the driver's side wheels were destroyed.

Probably not a write-off, but pretty bad for a first day. Lloyd seemed fairly amused by the whole thing, and was already suggesting the story of a loose horse running into the carriageway as Rimski's excuse for the crash. Rimski looked at the man as if he were quite mad.

21

PRAWNING AGAIN

Michael had just left his building and was thinking about prawning, of all things, when he came across Joanne Garrand, sitting on the pavement, with her feet in the road. It was a suitably odd enough sight to take his mind off Elise McHugh.

'Joanne? Are you all right?'

Joanne took a moment to place the voice and then the face, before showing him her expensive right shoe, minus the expensive heel. She was bleeding from her right knee.

'Hello, Michael. You've caught me in one of the situations we women most dread.'

Michael went to her aid. She removed the other shoe and stood, leaning on him in her bare feet. She seemed less intimidating without her high heels.

'That's a nasty cut, Joanne. Shall I go and get Stephen?'

'God, no. He'd only laugh his head off. I'll just go home

and get cleaned up.'

'It looks very dusty around the wound. Come up to mine and get some water on it straight away. I insist, come on.'

They went a few yards before she was struggling to walk.

'Allow me to carry you,' said Michael.

Joanne laughed. 'How gallant! No, seriously, I'll... No, Michael, you're right, in fact. Would you mind, really?'

Michael took her up in his arms and headed to his front door. Two things came to mind: had he ever picked up a woman like that before, and could he bang her head on the door frame as if it were a comedy sketch? Instead, he carried her up to his flat carefully, pretended not to be strained as he used his key, with her arms around his neck and an amused expression on her attractive face. He put her down on a kitchen stool.

'Thank you for this, Michael.'

He found a brand new cloth, wet it from the tap and, without thinking, began to clean up the wound. 'Oh,' he suddenly realised, 'would you like to do it yourself?'

'No, no, you're fine, carry on. I'll take the pain.'

They exchanged smiles at that.

'It's not too bad,' he said. 'You're just a bit of a bleeder.'

Her smile broadened. Then she took the opportunity to look around his apartment, her brows knitting as she spotted the football goal. Michael took the chance to inspect her neck and the top of her chest on show above her sweater. He tried not to ogle the infamous boob job. Then he was happy with the knee, finding a plaster to put on it.

'You'll probably be bruised for a while,' he said, 'hitting the pavement like that.'

'Thank you for looking after me, Michael.'

'Would you like a drink?'

'I would, actually. The trauma has made me quite parched.'

He stepped two yards to open the fridge, revealing his beer stocks and Hope's soft drinks. 'Or an ice pop,' he suggested, 'it's a warm day.'

'I'd love an ice pop.'

He brought two from the freezer compartment. 'Refreshers ice pops. Delicious.'

They moved; she hobbling a bit, over to sit by a window, both enjoying their ice pops. She looked out over her husband's scrap yard.

'Lovely view you've got,' she couldn't resist saying, with a grin.

The only reason I took the place. Hey, not bad neighbours, ghostly quiet at night. Most of the time.

'Yes, most of the time. You've got a great space here, you know.'

'Oh, I've driven past your new eco-home. Very trendy, I must say.'

'We're having a garden party very soon. You'll have to come. You can bring your girlfriend.'

Michael smirked as he imagined flying Elise in from

Singapore for a Garrand garden party. 'You know about Keira and me?'

'It's a small town. Keira's lovely. I'm pleased for you, Michael.'

'I'm pleased for me.'

'I was sorry to hear about you and Samantha. I so wanted Hope to go to Byrchall's with my two.'

'We had her down for the Hope Academy.'

'Oh, equally as prestigious. I read your last book, by the way.'

'Did you? Can I call you a fan?'

'Sure, I'm a fan.'

She suddenly laughed.

'What?' he asked.

'I was imagining Stephen looking up and seeing us sitting here licking ice lollies.' Michael laughed too. She finished her lolly, so he took the stick from her. 'I'd better be going.'

Michael stood and made a back for her. 'Come on, giddy-up, I'll piggyback you to your car.'

She laughed, then stopped laughing and looked at him for a fraction of a second too long. 'I'll be all right. Thanks again.'

He walked down with her, thinking about that lingering look. They said good day and he shut the front door after her. 'Right,' he said to himself, 'what did I go out for?'

CINDY: *Michael, are you there? Can you talk?*

MICHAEL: *I'm free! That was an old English comedy catchphrase for you. I'm free! Have I confused you now?*

CINDY: *No, anything you say make me happy. I really hate being here. I want to be in England. I read wonderful book now by English writer, Jodi Ellen Malpas. Do you know of her? Tell me things of England, please. England wonderful place, no?*

MICHAEL: *England wonderful? No! Well, it has its good points, but at the moment it's pretty crap. Let me change the subject and give you another catchphrase: I come from Urmston. Haha. That's from a marvellous comedienne called Victoria Wood. I know, you've never heard of her.*
Are you in Sidoarjo much longer? When you get home you'll feel better.

CINDY: *Ohh, I wish I was in Urmston now.*

MICHAEL: *Hahahaha! No, you don't. Believe me, you don't.*

CINDY: *What's wrong with England? England is nice in my books. Tell me things.*

MICHAEL: *Where do I start? Ignore the fact that all the*

governments have ruined us financially. The smaller things, let me think, such as, we have to pay more for goods than other countries, the roads are a disgrace despite the billions of pounds of tax, TV talent shows have fake screaming piped on to them, there are three-dimensional adverts at the side of football goals, tennis players ask for a towel after every shot, people get knighted for winning a cycling race, my favourite chocolate has shrunk in size and gone up in price, I have to pay £20 to see my dentist while foreigners get in free, burglars can have fifty convictions and still not go to prison. Apart from that it's great here. But, hey, come for a holiday any time, baby.

CINDY: *Michael, you are my daebak friend. I know you only kid for coming holiday, kekke, but never mind, I get there one day. How is Hope, by the way?*

MICHAEL: *Hope's great, thank you. I'll tell her you asked after her. Oh, Cindy, it's so hard talking like this. Is there anything I can do for you?*

CINDY: *You can come and beat up my boss, he reall dickhead. No, only three more days here then get train home. I so happy able to speak with you. How long can you talk tonight?*

MICHAEL: *As long as you want.*

After Cindy had finally become tired, they had bid each other goodnight and Michael started preparing his evening meal. He had a nice piece of tuna to grill. As he threw together a salad, he got to thinking about prawning again. It seemed to sum up the differences between Elise and himself; a divorced, thirty-something, failed writer, starting to talk dirty with a nineteen-year-old, with a completely different culture and with her whole future set out in front of her. While he slept last night she was out on a Singaporean beach with a teenage boy, catching and cooking prawns. Where did he fit in with that kind of thing? A sudden melancholy came over him. He squashed his tuna down hard on his George Foreman grill chefs serving raw meat and fish was another thing that could have gone on Cindy's list. Should he nip it in the bud with Elise? He decided he would tell her his concerns in his next message.

22

CUSTOMS DECLARATION

Elise replied to Michael's message containing his concerns over the relationship.

ELISE: *Oh, I see. I won't force you to keep talking to me if you want to go. I'm having a lot of fun with you, and don't want to finish it. As for prawning, he is just an old school pal. Nothing romantic happened. He didn't even try to kiss me.*

MICHAEL: *Elise, he didn't even try to kiss you!? What's wrong with the man? I'll knock him out if I ever see him! :p Okay, sorry, I got a bit worried about our issues, you know, age differences, 9,000 miles apart, cultural matters, you being a bit of a bimbo, that sort of thing.*

ELISE: *Hey! Mr Himbo himself with his naughty*

words. :) Anyone could write a dirty story, you know. :p

MICHAEL: *Oh, yeah? Go on, then. I'm waiting.*

ELISE: *Not me! Hehe. I'm an image girl. Do you not have Skype?*

MICHAEL: *Ummm, I was waiting for that. My feelings on that is, if we see each other, I ask for things, you refuse, I ask again, you refuse again, then we've got nowhere else to go.*

ELISE: *I see what you mean. I'll leave that for now. I've got a new image for you.*

MICHAEL: *Send it! Send it!*

ELISE: *It's not nude, silly.*

MICHAEL: *Keep it! Keep it!*

ELISE: *Too late. Check your email. I'll be waiting.*

Michael checked his inbox, finding an unusual, black and white shot of Elise with her head turned away from the camera, her ponytail caught in mid-swing. It was really quite artistic.

MICHAEL: *I love that photo. Thank you.*

ELISE: *I've just sent another one.*

Back to his email. Elise, kneeling on her bed in just pink underwear, her folded arms under her breasts, forcing her bosom upwards.

MICHAEL: *OMG. What are you doing to me? Is that brand new? Have you just done that for me?*

ELISE: *Of course it's brand new. Do you think I've got a ready supply of them? Yes, it's just been taken. I'm still in just my panties and bra, I'll do another one. What can I be doing to prove it's right now?*

MICHAEL: *Are you kidding me? Just take off the underwear, then I'll believe you.*

ELISE: *Tut tut. Last chance, tell me what to do to prove it to you.*

MICHAEL: *Elise, you're getting me going here, girl. I don't know, suck your thumb.*

ELISE: *Getting you going? Are you hard? Hehe. Okay,*

give me a minute.

He waited, trying to ignore his erection in his pants. Finally the new email appeared. She had returned to the same position, but now was sucking her left thumb. Michael swore and laughed at the cheek of the girl.

MICHAEL: *I need to see your body.*

ELISE: *Come to Singapore and you can see my body.*

MICHAEL: *That's a bold statement from the other side of the world. Do you think if I see you in emails that I won't then travel?*

ELISE: *No, I trust you. I'm just not ready to do that. Sorry. Have I spoilt the mood?*

MICHAEL: *No, don't worry. Are you staying in those panties and bra?*

ELISE: *I'm now in shorts and a pyjama top. Are you still turned on? Can I imagine holding it?*

MICHAEL: *I'm imagining you doing more than holding it. Where exactly are you?*

ELISE: *In my room, about to watch a movie. James Bond. Should I eat chocolates or popcorn?*

MICHAEL: *I'm imagining being beside you on the bed, settling down to watch. Will you take off the shorts?*

ELISE: *Hehe. Okay, done. Not the top?*

MICHAEL: *No. I'm eating the popcorn. From my position I can just see the start of your pussy. You have opened the pyjama top and have six chocolates lined up from between your breasts to below your navel, eating them slowly. You offer me one, but I say I will stay with the popcorn. You look up at me in the darkness of your bedroom, and say, "Baby, after the film, I'm going to suck you off". I'm happy to hear that. I put the popcorn aside, and pick up the highest chocolate from your chest in my teeth, transferring it to your grinning mouth. I kiss your breasts while waiting for you to be ready for the next chocolate, taking it up to you the same way. I leave the last one in place while I spend a few minutes licking your pussy, then collect it in my teeth, deliver it, and linger for a long kiss.*

MICHAEL: *You beg me to go back between your legs. I love the paleness of your inner thighs, spread for me. I knit three fingers together and finger fuck you while using my mouth on your clit. Clearly you are finding this an intense experience. I'm happy to be of service.*

MICHAEL: *I kneel up between you and you take hold of my massive cock, guiding it into you. You are gorgeous like that. I love doing that to you.*

Michael paused, wondering if he should just plough on with descriptions of the intercourse. He at least noticed she was still online, but had she fallen asleep on him? He laughed. Then he noticed in her profile information that her birthday was only two weeks away. He would have to get something sorted for a present and quickly entrust it to the postal service.

ELISE: *OMG! I wasn't planning Me Time, but that was so good. Did you come?*

Eh? He didn't tell her he was too busy typing to actually do anything.

MICHAEL: *Honestly, not quite, but it was good fun. Did my words help to get you off?*

ELISE: *Definitely! Thank you. I wish you were here so much.*

MICHAEL: *I wish I was there. Have you not got a... tool?*

Sorry. You know, what most women have in their panty drawer.

ELISE: *No! Haha. There's a shop for those I pass every day, but I couldn't buy one. I'd be too embarrassed.*

MICHAEL: *Get one online. Hey, I notice it's your birthday soon. I'll get you one.*

ELISE: *I need to bath again.*

And she was offline. Fuck, thought Michael. He stood up, thinking what to do while she was away. He washed the pile of pots in his sink. Then he thought he might as well shop for a vibrator online.

The first site he found seemed as good as any other. With wide eyes, he perused their wares. Anal love eggs were probably inappropriate at this early stage in his friendship with Elise. He recognised certain vibrators. Then he remembered that she was a virgin ("nothing goes up there") so looked at a rabbit-ears clitoral stimulator, in pink rubber. That would do the trick nicely. Fifteen quid. He could send her some books as well. He found his card and made the purchase.

She was back online within twenty minutes.

ELISE: *Ah, all clean again. Back to my chocolates. Where*

were we?

MICHAEL: *Elise, how many children do you want?*

Elise: *With you? Hehe.*

MICHAEL: *Yes, with me. I want three little McHugh-Lincolns. You can still have your career. I don't mind being a house husband, as long as the maids are pretty. Hehe. Yes, Francesca McHugh-Lincoln, Maria McHugh-Lincoln, and you can choose the third name. I'll join one of those parent and child groups in the afternoon, meet nice women. Hehe. And take the kids to the park and use them to meet nice women. Hehe. I know, I know, I'm in the doghouse.*

ELISE: *You'd better get my present now, after that. :(Hehe, one of those would be a brilliant present, Michael. But you don't have to send me anything, really.*

MICHAEL: *No, no, I insist. But, haha, God knows what I'm going to write on the Customs declaration!*

23

QUIM

CINDY: Michael, we have finished inspection early. I go to the train station in the morning. God has answered my prayers. After finish Jodi Ellen Malpas book I'm going to read one about Anne Boleyn. You know Anne Boleyn?

MICHAEL: *Are you kidding me? I'm descended from the Boleyns.*

CINDY: *Are you!? Seriously?*

MICHAEL: *NO!*

CINDY: *You are such a bad man! :(Teasing your Cindy.*

MICHAEL: *I'm sorry. Please forgive me.*

CINDY: *Let's read Tudor together. Heya, Wolf Hall.*

MICHAEL: *Won't that be a bit heavy for you?*

CINDY: *Uh? Wolf Hall, yes?*

MICHAEL: *Wolf Hall, yes! I'll order it today.*

CINDY: *Good. What are you doing?*

MICHAEL: *I'm about to have lunch. I've just come back from the tyre garage. I've had three nail punctures this week! The tyre man asked me, "are you putting these in yourself?". Haha.*

CINDY: *How is my little gangsta gurl?*

MICHAEL: *Hope's fine. I'm seeing her tomorrow. I played her your songs, last time she was here. She liked them very much.*

CINDY: *Aww, :) Send her my love. I go now. Have a good day. I message when I can.*

MICHAEL: *You stay safe. I love you.*

CINDY: *You love me? Aww. Bye bye.*

Michael's inner doorbell disturbed his afternoon session on the novel; he really would have to disconnect the thing. Surprisingly, it was Keira, carrying a bulky item in an Argos store bag.

'Hi,' she said, 'your oddball neighbour let me in. You know, the one all in black.'

Michael took the package from her and they kissed. 'He wanted to kiss my hand.'

'He's like that. You've brought me a present?'

She laughed, stepping into the apartment. 'Not quite. It's one of my son's birthday presents.'

'Oh, what is it?'

'An indoor basketball set.'

'Wicked. I'm sure I'll enjoy it no end.'

'I wondered if you could come round and help me put it together.'

'I've heard some chat up lines in my time, but that takes the biscuit. Let's put it together here. Then we can carry it through the town like a pair of loonies.'

They embraced casually and kissed again, both amused at the suggestion. He glanced inside the bag, opened the box and spotted the toy's wrapping. 'Oh my, bubble wrap. I need to pop some of that. Please don't stop me.'

Keira smiled, waiting for him to bend back up so she could kiss him again.

'Have you ever made love on bubble wrap?' he asked her.

She screamed with laughter, broke away and sat down on his couch.

'What have you been up to?' she asked. He thought of his sexting with Elise. 'And how's the book coming along?'

'It's good. Not long now. Coffee?'

She nodded. 'Please.'

They talked across the apartment while he brewed the coffee.

'Your walls are a bit bare,' she commented. 'Why not get some artwork?'

Yes, you may be right. I tell you what; I was reading the paper yesterday and this bloke has made himself a mosaic in his bathroom of the Manchester City football club logo. I want something like that. Not City, of course.

'Liverpool FC?'

'Don't be ridiculous. Chicago Bears. No, only joking. What about one of Hope? On the wall between the windows there.'

'That would be amazing, Michael. Could you find someone to do it? That's the question.'

'I'm sure I could. I suppose they would blow up my favourite photo of her, and then copy it by building up the pieces in tile. Yes, I'll look into that.'

He came to sit beside her with their coffee, and she put her legs over his. They talked about various things, including their children, her job, whether they would team up in the next club golfing day. He finished his coffee first.

'Shall we?' he asked.

'Shall we what?'

'Oh, come on, don't be coy.'

'*What?*'

Let's put the basketball thing together. I'm sure it's only plastic tubes; it'll go back in the box for you to carry home.

'Michael! Come with me now. You can have a quick play before I have to go to school.'

'You've said that before.'

Nevertheless, he accompanied Keira to her home. It took him about fifteen minutes to assemble the basketball game. It stood about eight feet tall, so not really an indoor toy, but she had a conservatory, so it went nicely in there. He took free throws for another fifteen minutes, before she kicked him out to go and collect her son.

'Come for dinner tomorrow night,' she told him, as he walked down the drive. 'I'm doing an Indian.'

'It's a date.'

ELISE: *Michael, hello. I'm taking a break from the project we are working on. I'm sorry I might not be much fun tonight. Can you forgive me? We should be done in a couple of hours, then maybe you can help me get to sleep. Hehe.*

MICHAEL: *Okay, do what you have to do. I'll be here. I*

wonder what you need to help you sleep?

ELISE: *Oh, good, someone ordered food. The break will be longer. What's new there?*

MICHAEL: *One of my balls smells.*

ELISE: *Whaaaat!?*

MICHAEL: *I have a few balls I kick around between writing sessions. I found one under the settee. It really pongs for some reason. What do you need later to get you to sleep?*

ELISE: *We could talk through a sixty-nine.*

MICHAEL: *Yeah, right, such a shy girl.*

ELISE: *Or you could write me a new story and we can relive it when I'm in bed.*

MICHAEL: *I'm not a writing machine, you know. :) Jeez, I'll see what I can do.*

ELISE: *Okay. Boy, I eat too much. There's talk of us taking up boxing here as exercise. I'll get toned for you. Laters.*

MICHAEL: *I like your puppy fats, thank you very much. Laters.*

MICHAEL: *Elise, your warlord Englishman is riding up from the docks as we speak. Your three maids are terrified of me and you have to beat the eldest one to go and wait for me in the porch.*

Are you prepared for my arrival? I've been fighting Chinese pirates for six weeks, with only my cabin boy for sport.

MICHAEL: *My horse clattered to a stop in the portico of the Singapore mansion I had installed you in. I jumped down, threw the reins at a groom and strode inside, my boots ringing on the cobblestones. The door was opened by one of your maids, actually quivering in terror as she took my hat and cape. I couldn't remember if she was the one I made join us in that threesome recently. I retained the parcel I carried, and went in search of you.*

I barged into your bedchamber, finding you reclined on your bed, naked, not even attempting to cover your sex. No doubt fair warning had arrived of my ship sailing into the harbour. I threw the parcel to a chair and stood, legs akimbo, appraising you. I had mistresses in Hong Kong, Macau and Port Arthur, but you were my favourite whore.

You told me you had missed me. I told you to get your

arse off the bed and welcome me properly with a kiss. You obeyed me promptly, rushing into my arms, allowing my coarse tongue to probe into your sweet mouth, while my calloused hands groped your bottom. I then took a moment to reacquaint myself with your breasts; my cabin boy has a nice hole but no titties. Your breasts seemed fuller, that you were perhaps with child. I fondled your belly but found it as flat as ever, moving my fingers down to your bare quim.

Once I was naked I threw myself onto your bed, telling you I had a present for you. You were so giddy with joy, I had to laugh. I let you fetch the package and you knelt on the bed to open it. It was lingerie, flimsy and rudely filthy. You thanked me and I ordered you to put it on, which didn't take long. There was lace around your breasts, delicate cotton spreading open to your sides and the tiniest of white, cotton g-strings.

I was already aroused, but now I was massive. I made you kneel in front of me and suck your thumb coquettishly. I told you I had an itch that only your tongue could deal with. Your sweet, innocent face was puzzled. I spread my legs and beckoned you in. Still you didn't know where I wanted you. I pointed to the part of my underneath, between my ass and my balls, and said I wanted a long lick there. I watched your head go down, and then felt your tongue probing the exact spot. I held your head with one hand and made you stay there for some time, licking away.

24

BRITISH POSTMAN SUPPOSED GOOD

ELISE: *Michael! I just read your story. Nasty man you. That will keep me up all night, not help me sleep. And to think, I just sent you a photo of me at the beach. Shame on you! :p*

Michael checked his email. He found a headless shot of Elise, he presumed, wearing a skimpy blouse and shorts, paddling at the water's edge.

MICHAEL: *Mmmm, a leg photo of some random bird at the beach; you're going backwards, baby.*

ELISE: *I love the word bird. What kind of women do you like?*

MICHAEL: *I love all kinds of women; brunettes, blondes,*

redheads, the occasional Welsh bird.

ELISE: *Hahaha. Welsh bird? Is a Welsh bird a woman who struggles to get home from the pub at night?*

MICHAEL: *You're priceless! Haha. I don't know where that came from, but you're not far wrong. I'm descended from Welsh people, by the way.*

ELISE: *I've sent another photo. Then I'm going to sleep, okay? Tomorrow I'm seeing a movie later on, so please forgive me. Goodnight XX*

MICHAEL: *I'll survive without you, I suppose. Enjoy the film. Going to check new picture now. Goodnight.*

It was Elise, posing in a one-piece swimsuit, completely decent but still extraordinarily sexy. He realised he quite loved her.

On the way to the movies, Elise, Tricia and their friend, Silvia, stopped off at the Vanda boxing club, which was quite near to Raffles hotel. After the recent talk of how good it was as a way to get fit, they wanted to see what it was all about. They found the place extremely busy, with men, women and children all training. Tricia and Silvia couldn't wait to sign up for it, while

Elise needed a little bit more persuading.

At the cinema complex, Tricia parked (in a fashion) and they headed inside, Silvia throwing a few uppercuts that made them all laugh. They were giddy all the way through the foyer, buying the tickets and their refreshments. Elise, being the film buff, had chosen what they were to watch, as usual. At least they settled down by the time they got to their seats. Mostly they chatted in hushed tones about Tricia's boyfriend, or about Silvia's potential boyfriend. Elise thought she had mentioned Michael once, but only as a book friend. She ate her popcorn, watching three noisy lads choose to sit right in front of them; uh, so obvious. Then she almost choked as she realised one of them, directly in front of her, was *him* again, the boy she seemed destined to forever bump into, and he turned with a smile for her.

'Hello,' he said, 'you're here too.'

'Yes,' was all Elise could think to answer.

'We've almost met a few times. I'm Dylan.'

Elise saw his hand come over the seats, so shook it, blushing because she knew her friends were watching and would tease her throughout the film. 'I'm Elise.'

'I love these kind of movies.'

'So do I.'

He pretended to have a crick in his neck. 'Would you like to sit with me, a little over there? We could chat before the film starts.'

'I think it would be rude to leave my friends.'

'Oh, I'm always trying to get rid of these guys. But I understand.'

Elise found herself being lifted out of her seat by the stronger Tricia.

'She'd be glad to join you,' Tricia said to Dylan.

Without a choice any more, staring daggers at her giggling girlfriends, Elise took her popcorn and moved a few rows to the side, where Dylan waited politely to sit down once she was seated.

They didn't speak for nearly a minute, then they talked non-stop, about their lives, school, movies, his music, his ambitions to be a doctor, until suddenly realising that the film had started. She let him eat some of her popcorn – normally she was very territorial when it came to food snacks. In a lull in the early action of the film, she leant in and returned to the subject of his career, asking which he really wanted to be: a doctor or a musician. He joked that he had little chance of being a professional at either one.

Near the end of the film, perhaps aware that she would soon be gone, he broached the subject of taking her out. Responding honestly, she said she was sort of dating a writer. It was at a delicate stage. He said he understood. He was being very chivalrous about it, though he was clearly disappointed.

As the credits rolled, and people began to move all around them, he spoke up, 'Perhaps I could give you my number, in case things don't work out with this guy. I hope they do for you. But...'

'I suppose that would be okay,' she replied, glad that he could not see her relief in the darkened cinema.

They exchanged numbers on their phones.

'Not the best film ever,' she said.

'No, quite bad. But thank you for watching it with me.'

'You're welcome. Well, Dylan, I should rejoin my friends.'

'Yes, goodnight, Elise.'

They smiled at each other; then she left him standing there in the aisle. Her friends at least waited until they were in the foyer before starting to take the mickey. At Tricia's car, Elise spotted Dylan and his friends just exiting the complex; they exchanged waves, then she was in the Audi and away.

CINDY: *Michael, heya. You got Wolf Hall yet? Thought British postman supposed good!*

MICHAEL: *Cindy, British postmen supposed good! hahahahahaha*

Michael looked at the mail on his desk. Apart from the bills, he had one package, which he opened carefully, as he intended to reuse it. Slowly, as if he were a bomb disposal expert, he withdrew Elise's vibrator. He examined it closely, feeling the latex rubber of the two rabbit ears, then placed it down on the desk in front of him and kept looking at it.

MICHAEL: *Cindy, heya. Postman has just been. He's a miserable bugger who needs a bath and a shave, but never mind. Opening a package right now. What have we got here? No, sorry, no Wolf Hall yet. Maybe tomorrow. Start without me, I'll catch up. What are you doing?*

CINDY: *No! I wait for you. Now I cook meal. You want I photo meal and send you, hey?*

MICHAEL: *If you must. :p*

Michael waited until the image came though on his email. There were several dishes on a table, with little, grasping hands in the shot, perhaps belonging to one of Cindy's younger relatives. He recognised fried chicken, which looked very appealing; there was rice, but also some weird stuff, white unidentified balls, something submerged in a brown liquid, and greenish things floating in water. He imagined himself taking a holiday in Cindy's home town and trying not to be a fussy eater.

CINDY: *Make you hungry, kekke? I send another image.*

MICHAEL: *Ravenous. What image? Dessert?*

The photo was of Cindy in a kitchen, smiling amidst the

chaos of food preparation. She looked extremely cute, the fringe there as always.

CINDY: *You must come here and I will cook for you. :))*

MICHAEL: *Yes, I must come and see you. I will think seriously about it, now that the first draft of the book is almost done. I promise.*

CINDY: *Ah!! That make me so happy, Michael. You are daebak!! I so so so want you to come.*

MICHAEL: *I suppose I will just have to renew my passport, look into the visa situation, money etc. Don't worry, I won't bring any heroin with me to Indonesia. Haha. Seriously, I'll sort it out. I have a cousin who backpacked for ten years. He knows everything there is to know.*

CINDY: *Fighting!*

Michael left Cindy to eat with her family. He returned his attention to Elise's present. For a moment he imagined Cindy receiving her own vibrator from him, using it in front of him, then put those thoughts aside. He put the present back in the envelope, wrote out Elise's address on a card and Sellotaped it over his address. Then he sealed the envelope and put it aside for the morning.

25

DOE EYES

Over breakfast, Michael checked his email. There was nothing of any interest, except the promise of another photo from Elise; hopefully, when he opened this one, she would be completely naked.

She wasn't obviously and explicitly naked, yet the image was astonishing in its cuteness. She was posed, sitting on her bed, possibly nude apart from maroon knee socks, with her legs tucked up to her body, hiding her face as well. Apart from the erotic socks, there was the gorgeous sight of bare left thigh, side and upper arm. Some of her jet-black hair cascaded onto her left shoulder. Perhaps the cuteness came from the crossed feet, and the general impression that she was awaiting instructions, sitting there like that.

He found a message from her on *GoodReads*, saying she had a late session at school, but would talk to him very late in Singapore. There was a notification that his Giveaway had finished overnight and his five winners had been chosen. The first glance showed no Indonesian winners, which was a relief; he had two America, two Canadians and, no way, Singapore. Elise McHugh! Elise won a copy of his book! He laughed his head off for a good minute. Then he finished his toast, and sent out some messages; first to his publisher, Henry.

MICHAEL: *The giveaway ended last night. One of the people I wished good luck to actually won. How about that? As for the new book, first draft will be done today. I'll send it very soon.*

MICHAEL: *Cindy, the giveaway just ended. You didn't win. Sorry. Speak to you later, hopefully.*

MICHAEL: *Elise, listen to this. You only went and won my giveaway. Well, you probably already know, being seven hours ahead. That's saved me some money. Hehe. You'd better write a review. Okay. I'll be here whenever you get home.*

With that done, he got on with finishing the novel. The hours flew by, he ignored lunch and found a thrilling conclusion by around 3 o'clock. He celebrated finishing the way he celebrated finishing all his novels, by doing nothing different in the slightest. He made a sandwich and a coffee, sitting by the window overlooking his old school. A game of rounders was in progress, with a lot of high-pitched squealing and laughter.

With no word from Elise, he shot some pool. Then he decided to get on with packaging and addressing the books to the four winners. They were for California, Arizona and two in eastern Canada. When they were done, he left them alongside Elise's birthday present, ready for the Post Office in the morning.

ELISE: *Michael, I'm home. Terrible in Singapore today. There are fires in Indonesia polluting the air here. Have you missed me?*

MICHAEL: *I've missed you terribly. I've had an erection here waiting for you just in case you fancy it.*

ELISE: *Hehe. I would really like to satisfy you. I would come to your room, climb above you and kiss you through your boxers. I would pull them down, your massive cock springing up to your belly. I would lick your length from top to bottom and back up again. Then I would start sucking hard. Oh, Michael, is the erection really there?*

MICHAEL: *Of course it is. I was looking at some naughty stuff while waiting for you. Will you take care of it? Use both hands as well as your mouth.*

ELISE: *I'm slowly licking and sucking you while giving you the doe eyes.*

MICHAEL: *Oh, I love the doe eyes bit. Keep going.*

ELISE: *What have you been watching, naughty boy?*

MICHAEL: *Horrible things being done to Japanese women. Is that really bad? But it got me big.*

ELISE: *I know it did. You sit up and fondle my breasts. You tell me I am beautiful. I move up you and lower myself down slowly onto your cock.*

He was indeed very aroused by then.

MICHAEL: *Wonderful. You are beautiful, you know.*

ELISE: *We are like sexaholics, aren't we? Hehe. Every little innocent stuff will turn out to be naughty between us don't you know? Anyway, I need to bath now, got early class tomorrow.*

MICHAEL: *What!? You've just lowered yourself onto my cock, and now you're going for a bath? What a passion killer!*

He sat there, but she had gone to have her bath. He continued to sit there, starting to steam a little. The last thing he wanted to do was upset Elise, but that was a bit uncalled for. Quite unthinking and selfish on her part, in fact. He felt really silly, still with an erection. He let it subside a little, before moving off from his desk.

He ate one of his favourite flapjack biscuits, looking out over the scrap yard. He would have to think of making some proper evening meal soon; finishing the book had messed with his routine. He kicked a ball about for a while, every few minutes checking if she was back. Fifty minutes later she returned, oblivious to what she had done.

ELISE: *I'm back. Did you miss me? I can talk until 1 am. What did you think of my socks photo?*

MICHAEL: *I liked it. What would you like to talk about until 1 am?*

ELISE: *Oh. Why so vague? There was a joke in class. Has anyone ever walked in on you when you were masturbating?*

MICHAEL: *Could you ask me that question another time, please? I have a funny answer but I'm not feeling naughty any more. Sorry.*

ELISE: *Why the sudden grumpiness, Michael? What did I do? I'm busy now because my deadlines are near. My project meetings go on late, so I can't bath earlier. I don't want to go to sleep thinking I have made you grumpy.*

MICHAEL: *What did you do? You put me in you, then went for a fifty minute bath. What am I supposed to do with that?*

ELISE: *I'm sorry. I got to bath right? Maybe next time I bath first, then message you, but I was keen to speak to you. Sorry. Are you really angry? Do you want to stop this?*

MICHAEL: *No, I don't want to stop this.*

ELISE: *I have to wait for you to wake up before we can message, yeah.*

MICHAEL: *I'm sorry. It's just in England, teenagers have stress and exams of course, but there's not this night school.*

ELISE: *You don't have it in England, but that doesn't mean it isn't happening in Singapore. Go online if you don't believe me. There are dozens of night schools. I'm not lying. Do you not have any trust in me? I enjoy this special thing with you. If I didn't would I talk to you every night and take pictures like I've never taken before? Goodnight.*

MICHAEL: *Elise, I didn't accuse you of lying about night school. Just that it's alien to my upbringing. I'm sorry we seem to have fallen out.*

There was just silence. She was alongside the red online sign, but after switching screens, she seemed to have gone off.

MICHAEL: *Okay, you're off to bed. I'm trying to figure out what happened there. I hope you realise I wasn't doubting you over the night school.*

Why did I get so grumpy? Imagine we are physically together somewhere. We've been talking dirty, you've had me in your mouth, you slide yourself onto my erection. Then, right at the start of intercourse, you go for a fifty minute bath. ANY man in the world would HIT THE ROOF if you did that to them, not just me, but it's okay to do it to me? Why, because I'm on the computer? Can't you see that? And you wonder why I'm suddenly unchatty.

You know I fancy you like crazy. But we have a few issues. I'm guilty, feeling that I am keeping you from guys your own age in Singapore. I only want what's best for you. I'll keep trying. I'll try to get to your emotions around your busy schedule. Or you can not talk to me and go back to before we met.

26

SEX TALK

ELISE: *Michael, I don't want to stop talking to you. I enjoy talking to you. I understand now why you got grumpy, I will not do it again okay? I will see you like normal guy and not someone from the computer. I will text you after I bath and show you my full attention then.*

You don't have to feel guilty. Cause I can get to see normal Singapore guy if I want to. But for now I don't need to so don't worry okay?

I've missed you.

MICHAEL: *Hiya. I was just going to ask you what you want and I would give it to you, but you have told me. Listen, I was silly. Sorry again. I hope you know where I was coming from with that. Of course you can bathe whenever you like. If I ever get to Singapore then I hope it won't happen like that, though. :p*

ELISE: *You'll come to Singapore!? Yay! When, tell me.*

MICHAEL: *I'll start making arrangements from tomorrow. It might be a few months. I don't know. When are you done with school? School, that sounds terrible. I wish we could call it college. That's pretty bad but not so worrying for me.*

As long as you promise I'm not hindering you with your real life.

ELISE: *You are not hindering me. I am meeting new guys. There are two guys who are very interested in me, however I don't see myself with a future with them so... you know. No, you've got all the right to be grumpy. I've learnt my lesson and I won't do it again. I've bathed and am all clean and fresh for you.*

MICHAEL: *Who are these two guys? I'll kill them! Haha. Oh, so you've bathed already?*

ELISE: *I'm yours the whole night, what do you want to do with me?*

MICHAEL: *I want to get you really turned on, crazy with desire, put my cock all the way in you... then go away for fifty minutes! Hahahahaha. Oh, come on, you must have* been expecting that? Turn that frown around, miss.

Actually, I would really like to have my mouth on your fresh, young cunt. But plenty of time for that. Have you got a particular fantasy in mind?

ELISE: *You're the one with the imagination. YUP, I'm clean and relaxed and you can do anything to me.*

MICHAEL: *Maybe I could give you and your friends a PE lesson? Lots of hands-on action, exercise and showers.*

There was a pause in the chatter for a few minutes. He took the chance to trim a rogue fingernail and look out the window.

ELISE: *Before you get mad, I'm at my parents', and I had to help my brother with mathematics.*

You cheeky man. My friends! I was thinking more like we haven't seen each other for two months and you miss me and my body terribly. What would you do?

MICHAEL: *I'm not mad. Stop assuming I've got a nasty streak. So, I can't be strict with you? Damn, I was imagining your doe eyes while I was forcing your legs up to your chest on the floor mat, with you wearing only a leotard. So I've got to be loving but passionate?*

Oh, I remembered the thing about someone walking in

when I was masturbating. Want to hear that first?

ELISE: *I'm seeing us kissing on the doorstep, banging and hitting each wall while tearing our clothes off kind of thing. Hehe.*
I want... some Me time. I feel like it.
Yes, please, tell me the story.

MICHAEL: *I know you want Me time. Build to it. Keep your fingers away from your sex. I was about fourteen. Masturbating on my bed one afternoon with music headphones on. When I'd finished, I realised my mum had put a cup of tea on the bedside table.*

ELISE: *What???!!! paint the walls with my brain. How? Did you feel embarrassed?*

MICHAEL: *That's an urban legend about the cup of tea! Please forgive me. It never happened to me.*

ELISE: *WHAT YOU ASS! I believed you. I thought it really happened. I should refuse to talk to you now. :(;)*

MICHAEL: *Imagine you are not wearing a bra and have a dress on you don't mind getting ripped from your body. Give me ten minutes for the next message, then they will come at you quickly.*

MICHAEL: *I've missed you so much. I'm sorry we fell out. We grasp at each other as if our lives depend on it, holding so tight, kissing, using tongues, then frantically I have to devour your slim neck. You've got me massive straight away, straining through my trousers against the thin white summer dress you are wearing. I can feel your nipples hard against my chest. No bra, good. I bring my hands up to cup you through the flimsy fabric, kissing you really hard on your open mouth. We are both gasping, in need. You feel me through my pants, my erection facing downwards and becoming uncomfortable. As you realise this you unzip me and take a firm hold on the throbbing member, getting it facing upwards. Your touch drives me insane, bruising your small breasts with my groping mitts. While my tongue is down your throat I scrabble at the buttons down the front of your dress, finally ripping the garment wide open. You gasp and laugh, but are pleased that your bare breasts are in my hands now. My mouth finds its way down there, kissing and licking between the two tight globes, settling on the left nipple for a firm, almost painful, suck.*

You haven't taken your hand away from my dick, working it up and down, you naughty girl. Now I slip my right hand down the front of your tight white cotton panties, moving through the pubes you promised to shave, immediately finding a slick slit, warm and moist to accept my middle finger. You whisper into my ear not to hurt you. I ignore you and try to finger you as deeply as possible.

I back you through to my bedroom. I really, really want to be in you. I want to fuck you. The dress is thrown away, I rip your knickers down with one hand, and you are naked apart from high-heeled shoes, which can stay on for now. I lose my shirt and trousers, my cock held tight to my belly by the waistband of my boxers. It's dark in there but you can just make out a drop of pre-cum.

We fall to the bed, still madly kissing and touching. I tell you to open your legs and you ask if I am going to leave you waiting again. I spread your thighs with my hands and dive onto your soaking cunt with my mouth. There's your answer! I thrash from side to side, trying to fuck you with my tongue. At the same time I am reaching up, unwilling to stop fondling your breasts. You seem to have lost all sense of where you are.

MICHAEL: *I see your vibrator has arrived. I grasp hold of it, bringing it into play as I continue to lick you out, pressing it just right on your swollen clit. It sends you into back-arching spasms. I take a break with my tongue, keeping the vibrator in place as I kiss your quivering belly.*

I'm ready to enter you with my cock. I give you the vibrator, lose my boxers and move up to where the noise is, entering you easily. Your eyes open and you smile, I tell you I love you and move really deep. There's so much juice I can hardly feel you, but never mind, I just have to get even deeper and penetrate you with force. Can you handle this, my balls slapping against your underneath, my thick stem shafting in and out with squelching noises competing with the constant buzz.

MICHAEL: *I've ordered you to change position so that you are riding my cock. I love looking at your naked body while you are doing that. I sense you want to use the toy again, but I forbid it, telling you to make do with my full hip-swinging upper thrusts.*

My cock pops out accidentally. You reach under and put it back in. The fucking then continues. I tell you I will use the vibrator on you when we finish with doggy-style soon.

"Oh, God, you'll put me in a mental home. Please let me have control of it."

I shake my head.

MICHAEL: *I need a little bondage. Lie on your back and lift your hands, while I tie them to the bedstead. Wow, you look so delicate and vulnerable. I kneel before you, showing off my erection. Then I put it back in you without the aid of a hand, and the fucking goes on, with your rib cage stretched and your armpits exposed, your face flushed bright red. In, out, in, out.*

MICHAEL: *I've missed spanking your lovely little bottom. I withdraw from you, lift you easily up off the bed, and spank you hard, half a dozen times. Being a good girl you accept it without saying anything.*

Are you ready for doggy-style? You know I prefer to cum in that position. I'll untie you. Maybe you could have a little suck and a firm fondle of my balls before we carry on?

MICHAEL: *Get on your hands and knees, and show me your sex. I see you really want more, don't you. I put the vibrator near to your asshole while I finger fuck you. Cum drips all the way down to the sheets. Okay, I'm edging forward.*

MICHAEL: *I take the vibrator underneath you and clamp it on your clitoral area, then enter you from behind. I start to fuck you with long slow strokes, feeling you really tight and pulling on me. Briefly I grab your hair as I am riding you, then as your howls intensify I build my speed, thrusting right to the top of your cunt and out again. Back in, fucking you, fucking you, fucking you. Still I don't cum, you are making too many squeals of pleasure. You must be having multiple orgasms. In again all the way!*

MICHAEL: *I can see your thigh wobbling with the strain of this long fucking. You've cum, haven't you. I am going to keep fucking you hard until you say something to make me cum. Say something dirty, Elise!*

ELISE: *Come for me Michael. Come so fucking hard. Imagine me with another girl alongside me.*

(I tried)

MICHAEL: *Oh, you mean a girl I'm fingering while I'm doing this to you? No, I only want to think about you. I'm still pumping really hard, I don't care if you can't take any more. Then I cum hard inside you.*

Slowly I withdraw. I kneel there, making you stay in position because I want to see my cum run out of you.

Oh, beautiful, there it is, all creamy and hot, dribbling out. Will you let me hold you now, baby?

ELISE: *Aww, why so sweet? :)) Of course you can hold me. I put my head to your chest and we cuddle up.*

MICHAEL: *I hold you close, face to face. I love the way your breasts don't even think about being anything other than upright. I can't say the same for Michael junior, he has fallen down to the left, knackered. We kiss and hold each other. Thank you for doing that with me.*

27

QUOTE ME A FIGURE

It had been five years since Michael last went abroad, to Majorca, with Hope and Samantha and Samantha's mother (may she rot in hell). He dug out his passport from his desk drawer; as suspected, it had only just expired.

He took a walk to the Post office for a renewal form, bumping into the Garrand brothers on the way back. They tried to persuade him to join them in the pub, but he talked his way out of it.

Back at his apartment, he intercepted the postman with his Amazon package; he was now the proud owner of a copy of Hilary Mantel's *Wolf Hall*. He examined the book over a cup of coffee, then perused the passport form, and also brought up Singapore visa information on the computer. When he had bored himself rigid, and was still not actually sure that he needed a visa between Britain and Singapore, he settled down to further editing of his novel.

The Garrands had mentioned the upcoming golf day, which was being themed as a mixed-doubles event that year. He wondered if Keira played golf at all. He rang her mobile, unconcerned that he might disturb her plastic bobby wanderings, and asked the question. She laughed and answered in the firm negative. But she was willing to give it a go. He politely rang off. "Give it a go" – what was he supposed to do with that?

Ah, he remembered he had a golf-putting game somewhere. With childish delight, he found the box on top of his wardrobe, and his putter near the front door (from the time when there were a lot of burglaries happening) and set it up on the carpeted area of the lounge. Great fun ensued, with the four golf balls occasionally running up into the hole in the box and being sprung back towards him. He was disturbed by a message bleep on *GoodReads*. He laughed, remembering the start to that sci-fi film, was it *Independence Day*, when the bored SETI technician was putting golf balls in the lab when a noise started to emanate from the moon?

The message might as well have been from the moon; it was from Irene Hannah in the Philippines, the friend who had gone silent after the mother-in-law joke.

IRENE HANNAH: *Michael, could I ask you something? I'm so embarrassed because we've never seen each other in real life. But would you help me financially? With my education? I'll pay you back when I get a job. I promise. Tell me what to do to prove I will pay you back and I will do it.*

Fucking hell, thought Michael.

Michael decided to start *Wolf Hall*, settling himself down in a window seat. A couple of chapters in, it was clearly superior writing, with a wonderful style, but he found it a bit heavy going.

Someone was contacting him on *GoodReads*.

ELISE: *Good evening, Mr Temperamental. Had a good driving lesson today. And a lovely meal with friends. On my way home right now. I hope you'll be free later.*

MICHAEL: *At your service, madam.*

Immediately another message came in, but proved to be from Cindy.

CINDY: *Michael, hello. I want say I enjoy become your friend, I enjoy everything we chat about. I feel comfort with you. When I'm tired or my job, and when I can't call anyone, you're always there. I m timid girl, like wallflower, but doesn't mean I don't enjoy convertation. I listen to Black Sabbath right now. I love all rock classic music, but I'm not a hater of other genre.*

I want to become a good mother and wife then I can leave my mark on this world, mark of better generation...

I watch Tudors television show last night, with Rys Meyers man, kekke. I so annoyed, it so good but I start with Katherine Howard episode. I have to find all show. Hey, reading buddy, you have Wolf Hall yet?

MICHAEL: *I've just started it. Are you sure about this? I can't even get my head around it.*

CINDY: *Eh?*

MICHAEL: *Oh, nothing. Loving it. Loving Wolf Hall. How about you?*

He waited patiently, but the enigmatic Cindy was gone. He sat there having a quiet think. Really, he should be helping Cindy with her education, or her overall circumstances. But maybe Irene Hannah was a really lovely person; that was the trouble with those kind of relationships, they were difficult to be completely sure about someone. He hadn't given to charity in many years, except for Hope making him get involved with her Red Nose day at school. Maybe it would be an uplifting, enjoyable thing, very philanthropic: helping Irene Hannah away from poverty while she studied to improve her situation.

MICHAEL: *Irene Hannah. Quote me a figure. Best*

wishes.

Michael spent the early evening "making" a chicken curry out of a jar. While it was in the oven, he returned to *Wolf Hall*, finding it enjoyable, if incomprehensible. Irene Hannah came back to him, up late in the Philippines now that there was money on the line.

IRENE HANNAH: *Michael, please tell me how I can prove myself before I say what is needed.*

MICHAEL: *Well, you could talk to me more regularly.*

He almost said the word intimate.

MICHAEL: *Perhaps become intimate.*

IRENE HANNAH: *I have to use my grandmother's computer. I have no internet of my own.*

MICHAEL: *Maybe I could help you out with that first. See how we go.*

Silence. He put his rice on for his curry. Opened a bottle of Budweiser. Opened some windows to let some of the cooking smells out.

IRENE HANNAH: *I don't want to mess you around. Maybe I just quote you the figure and wait.*

MICHAEL: *Go for it.*

IRENE HANNAH: 6,000 pounds.

'Fucking hell!'

Michael forgot her while he had his curry. Elise had not shown up yet, so he washed his pots. Then he remembered Irene Hannah. He wasn't about to give the woman £6,000. He had a little laugh to himself about it. Maybe they could work something out? There was always an answer. He looked at her profile images again and liked what he saw. He wandered around his apartment, puzzling over the terrible arrangement he was considering setting in motion. Asking the poor girl to prostitute herself. Fuck it, he thought. He wasn't very likely to ever see her in real life or even set foot in the Philippines. He loved what he had with Elise; that was special, but why should he deny himself other fun? Last time he looked, he was no longer married to anyone.

MICHAEL: *Irene Hannah, send me an intimate image of yourself, so I know one hundred per cent that I am dealing only with you. It doesn't have to be obscene. I'll transfer £500, and we'll see how we go over the next few months. I do want to help with your education.*

Irene Hannah appeared to be sleeping on it. Elise filled the void.

ELISE: *Michael, school really tired me and I had to go to a friend's birthday drinks, but I want to be here for you now. Oh, but I have to bath first, baby, really humid here. Please forgive me, I'll be quick. You can imagine me in the shower. I will have the jet really fast. Then I smell all girly, just for you.*

MICHAEL: *Haha, sounds like my teenage years, school followed by birthday cider in the park. I'll be here, sweet.*

Nothing much happened while he waited for Elise to get clean for him. It was nice to do absolutely nothing, just sit there, not even to delve into his book. The phone rang; Keira, inviting him to a late supper. He asked her if "late supper" was code for something else, and asked if they could discuss golf. She had laughed, set a time, and rung off.

ELISE: *There! Done. All yours.*

MICHAEL: *You're not in your shorts, are you?*

ELISE: *Er, no, I'm in my sexy nightie. Of course I'm in my shorts.*

MICHAEL: *Oh, all right, then. Is there anything on your mind?*

ELISE: *What have you been up to today?*

MICHAEL: Solidly waiting for you.

ELISE: *I'm sure. :p   What happened to that woman in your town?*

MICHAEL: *Could you be more specific? :p*

ELISE: *Oh, sorry. I walked into that one. The woman you liked. Is she still on the scene?*

MICHAEL: *Yeah, she's still around. I've had a big pause here, Elise, looking at the flashing cursor, because I don't want to keep anything from you. I'm seeing her tonight.*

ELISE: *Ah. Even longer pause this end. Will you be having sex with her?*

MICHAEL: *Most probably.*

28

KOREA

Irene Hannah sent Michael a photograph of herself, apparently self-taken at some kind of beach restaurant: lots of white sand and blurred red lights. She was smiling, very pretty, and with a bit of cleavage on show, but not what you would call intimate. Michael had shaken his head at the misunderstanding, maybe he should have been explicit in his instructions. But then he just enjoyed looking at the nice photo. Anyway, he had already decided not to follow through with his plan to exploit the young woman.

MICHAEL: *Irene Hannah, thank you for the lovely photo. I'm afraid it's not what I meant, and I don't think we can ever get onto the same wavelength. Maybe it's a cultural thing. Would you let me send you £ 500 towards your education. Then we'll say goodbye. I'll need bank details?*

ELISE: *Good morning, sunshine. How are you today? Mwah!*
Imagine me, waking up for school with you. You are on your back, one arm across your eyes. The sheets cover your

abdomen. Michael junior is standing proud. Feeling cheeky, I pull down the sheets slowly. I blow cool air on your cock. I see you shiver a little due to the cool air but you are still deeply in your sleep.

I start to lick you from the bottom to the top of your cock. And I straddle you to have a more comfortable position and start sucking you off. Woken up by the pleasure, your hips move up in rhythm of my sucking off. One of your hands was on my head, the other gripping the sheets.

I hollow my cheeks and move up and down your cock while looking at you with doe eyes. After some while, moving up and down. You start to move your head, according to your rhythm; before long you hold my head at place while you spurt cum into my mouth. I sit up with cum in my mouth, looking at you I swallow the cum down. Then I walk confidently away to the bathroom to wash up.

I hope this is good, my baby.

ELISE: *Sorry I left quickly last night. I came out of the shower and someone I care for very much told me he was going to have sex with another woman. It upset me. But now I realise you have your real life there. I understand. I can't expect you to wait until you can come out here. Love you.*

MICHAEL: *My first response to your story was... :))))))))))))))))))))))))))))))*

Stephen Garrand waggled his shoulders, dug his feet in a little more, and played a gentle 8-iron golf shot down his garden. Joanne Garrand came outside via the conservatory, appearing a little sour-faced at his activity on the lawn, until he glanced in her direction, whereupon she smiled cheerfully. 'Oh, you're out here, darling,' she said. 'I was going to look about before making plans for the garden party.'

'Garden party?'

'Barbecue get-together, then. Will you come round with me?'

'Only if you hit a dozen balls first. I don't want you letting me down in this competition.'

'Oh, Stephen, you know I can make it go nearer the green for you.'

Stephen tried to comprehend "make it go nearer the green for you".

'Give it here, then,' said Joanne.

Stephen grinned, handed over the club and stepped aside. Joanne got into position around one of the balls on the grass, addressed it, swung, and did exactly what she said she would do; moved it a little way forward. She expected and got his advice about looking at the ball, and tried again. When she was finished, she looked for his opinion.

'Not bad. Not bad at all. Now, go and collect them.'

'Get lost!'

They hugged. Then they went for a wander around their

landscaped garden, considering where the bouncy castle (bigger than the one Shirley hired) could go, and about seating, and maybe some novelty area for the adults.

'What do you mean by novelty area?' he asked. 'A jacuzzi?'

'I don't know. Something different to other parties. Mini-paint-balling, perhaps, archery...'

'Archery!? You can't have bloody archery at a garden party.'

'Well, we'll have to think of something. I want people to say, "remember what we did at Stephen and Joanne's party that time?"'

'We could have bear-baiting. Or badger...'

'Oh, Stephen.'

'I can only think of padded Sumo wrestling, or a ground water slide on the dip over there. You know, people will take a run up and launch themselves down it.'

'No, no, baby. Can't we have clay pigeon shooting?'

Michael was listening to music on Youtube; a mixture of the *Beatles*, *Kings of Leon*, *Adele*, the theme from *The Thorn Birds*, *Cavatina* from *The Deer Hunter*. Then he listened once more to Cindy singing. He was playing that again as a message came in.

CINDY: *Are you free? What are you doing?*

MICHAEL: *I'm listening to you singing.*

CINDY: *AH! Don't mock me again. What are you really doing?*

MICHAEL: *I swear on my daughter's health, I'm listening to the thing you sent me. You have a beautiful voice, Cindy. Where are you?*

CINDY: *I on my way to Korea.*

Michael laughed. Of course she is.

MICHAEL: *To see your relatives?*

CINDY: *Yes. Did I ask you to come? Maybe you say no. I say goodbye for a few week. What you forget me already? No forget me! :) You my special Michael, I speak soon, kekke. Bye.*

MICHAEL: *Give my regards to your family. Have a lovely time. I'll be here waiting.*

Michael decided to do some exercising – some serious exercising, with Singapore in mind. He changed into his sweats, and started with some stretching exercises learnt during a brief martial arts phase, during his teens. Then he began to run up and down the communal stairs. There was no chance of his making any noise, and it was very airy and cool out there. Before he got too exhausted, he came in for some water and to let his heart rate calm down. Next, he was playing football for a good twenty minutes, sometimes lying on the floor, volleying and saving shots.

Now completely shattered, he knew there was a new message, so slumped in his office chair.

ELISE: *That's all I get for a response, mister? Hmm? :p Late school again, sorry.*

MICHAEL: *Hey! :) You know I will expand on my thoughts. I was just giving you my initial speechless reaction.*

I grinned broadly when I realised what you had written. You naughty girl, waking me up with a blow job. And making such a deliberate show of swallowing my cum, as well! "you spurt cum into my mouth". Wherever did you learn such crude language? I'm here, waiting around your education.

29

BAYBEATS

Michael woke up ridiculously early. It was the day of the golf event, not that he was particularly excited about that. Well, he thought, yawning while excavating his eyes, at least he would get to see Elise's first message sooner than normal.

He showered and made coffee while waiting for the computer. Three messages awaited him on *GoodReads*; two from Elise and one from Irene Hannah. He wondered about those people with five thousand friends, most of whom they never spoke to, but perhaps they did get dozens of messages a day.

ELISE: *Good morning, sleepy head. Yay! Your present arrived in the post. OMG! I've looked at it, but not used! Hehe. Naughty man I can feel your thoughts. No school today. About to go on another driving lesson. Maybe we can have some Me time a little later.*

ELISE: *Michael, you know you are always telling me I'm not to ignore dating Singaporean boys? Could I have permission to go out with one tonight? I won't go if you mind. It's nothing serious, but he's asked a few times. It'll come to nothing, don't worry. You're my number one.*

He wished he'd stayed in bed now. Of course she must date over there, but it was a very strange feeling. He looked at the times of her messages: ninety minutes apart.

MICHAEL: *Elise, thank God! Dating at last. Please don't scare him off, it might be months until another fool comes along. :p You don't need permission, silly. I'm going playing golf, anyway. So you have a lovely time.*
We'll do some special Me time in the very near future.

He sent the message and sat back heavily into his chair with a sigh.

IRENE HANNAH: *I don't have a bank account. Could you send the money to my uncle's?*

Philanthropy was suddenly off the agenda. 'To an uncle?' he said out loud. 'You can fuck right off!'

Michael was ready when the buzz came on the intercom. Wendy owned a silver BMW X5, which was about ten years old, but still an impressive looking vehicle. He climbed into the back, kissing Keira beside him, patting Tony on a shoulder in the front passenger seat and thanking Wendy for doing the driving.

As they quickly left Newton-le-Willows, Michael appraised the attire of his golfing partner (partner for better or worse). She was wearing cream-coloured, cropped, Capri trousers and a pink fleece, with a pink baseball cap. He himself was in his best dark trousers and with a maroon sweater; he wasn't exactly Rory McIlroy, but he wouldn't stick out, either.

'Are you nervous?' he asked her.

'A little, I suppose.'

He took her hand into his lap and she stretched over as far as the seat belt allowed. 'You'll be fine after the first bacon roll of the day.'

'Yummy.'

Tony called, 'After the golf day, we're planning one of those track days, you know, driving fast cars.'

'Bagsy I'm not partnered with Wendy,' joked Michael.

'Hey!' objected Wendy, with a smile in the rear view mirror for him.

Michael had expected the golf day to be held at one of the local courses, as usual, such as Haydock Park or Leigh Golf Club, but for some reason they all had to make their way to one just south of Manchester airport. So close, in fact, to where Hope and her mother were living that he felt he should pay a visit. But he wouldn't.

Travelling along the M6 and M56 motorways, they played the game of trying to spot their neighbours, either overtaking them or being passed by them. Then Wendy settled into a mini-convoy behind Alfie and Shirley Garrand in the Porsche Cayenne, who were themselves following Stephen and Joanne in the Audi Q7; Michael finding it amusing that they had not shared a vehicle. He bet Christmases were a right hoot with those two headstrong sisters-in-law.

Michael's thoughts turned to Hope, as they came off the motorway at Manchester airport. He assumed her mother and the South African would be holidaying soon, so he should be having his daughter with him for a couple of weeks.

Immediately they became ensnared in the roadworks for the new Metro tram system. 'This is taking them seven years!' exclaimed Tony. 'Seven fucking years!' There was a lot of laughter in the X5. 'Get the bloody Japanese in to do it!'

Dylan picked up Elise for their date, with another woman in the back of his car. As she hesitated on the steps to her apartment building, all Elise could think about was describing the first impression of her date to Michael. "He brought another woman with him". How Michael would howl with laughter at that!

Dylan ran around to open the passenger door of his Honda, his face open with apologies, quick to explain, 'It's my sister; she's volunteering as well. As soon as we get there I'll banish her from our company.'

Elise smiled. 'Oh, no worries.' She smiled again and reached back to shake the girl's hand, as Dylan ran back to the driver's seat. He seemed delighted that the car was still running.

'Off we go,' he said, smiling at Elise.

They were going to be volunteers at the Baybeats musical event at the Esplanade. It was a showcase for young musicians and would be packed out with teenagers. Elise still wasn't sure exactly what she would be doing, but felt comfortable being out with Dylan and his sister.

They talked on the way. Elise tried to engage with Dylan's sister in the back, but she seemed very shy. Elise wondered how much the girl would be of use in a volunteering capacity. Dylan was very excited. Gallantly, he explained that part of that was down to finally being out on a date with her, but mostly because he was a supporter of the Baybeats events, and also that it would look good on his efforts to enter medical school.

'I thought you wanted to be a musician?' asked Elise.

'That's my passion. But a career as a doctor would be amazing.'

Elise watched his profile as he drove, liking him even more.

Keira drank the morning coffee, but avoided the bacon rolls.

She chatted with girlfriends, some of whom were less than pleased to be dragged along to the event. The men were nearby, devouring breakfast and looking forward to the matches.

Michael bit aggressively into his bacon roll for the benefit of a watching Keira, then leaned in to hear what Rimski was talking to him about. Rimski was in a minority there outside the clubhouse, being the stooge of his golf-playing wife.

It was a glorious morning in south Manchester, with a haze amidst the trees down the first fairway. There were quite a few police sirens in the distance, with a few jokes being made about it being Manchester, after all.

Stephen Garrand was taking charge, as usual, waving a piece of paper like Neville Chamberlain. Michael assumed it was the order of play. Suddenly he felt a hand on his lower back – had Keira breached the apartheid and stepped into the man domain before being asked? It was Joanne Garrand, apparently coming from the Ladies room. It flashed through Michael's mind that she was wiping her hands on him.

'Play well,' she offered.

'I always do.'

Shared smiles, disturbed by even louder sirens. Were they to suffer the noise during their day out? Then, from the shrubbery to the left, burst a scruffy man with a flowing mullet of a hairstyle, running across the first tee right in front of them all, quickly followed by two portly policemen and two useless PCSO's. Cheers rose from the Newton crowd. Michael looked at Keira, but before she could react, Alfie Garrand leapt forward. With six fast strides down the grass slope he flung himself into a magnificent rugby tackle on the fugitive. Hilarity and laughter followed him, as he pinned the man down and raised a fist to them all in triumph, smiling his head off. Finally the officers got there, puffing and blowing, and relieved Alfie of his prisoner.

Covered in mud and grass stains, Alfie returned to the group a hero. Only his wife seemed less than enamoured at him making a public spectacle of himself. Keira had come across to hug Michael, both of them equally amused.

'Got to be a good citizen,' Alfie was calling.

At first, the noise and excitement at the music event was overwhelming for Elise. But she tried to get into it, with Dylan close by. Apparently, she was there to just check that people were having a good time. If, for example, someone found they disliked one particular type of music, Elise could look at her clipboard and suggest something else at another location. The first time she helped someone she looked straight for Dylan afterwards, and found him beaming at her. Also, they had been given cameras to take snaps of the revellers, and white boards to let them write down their excited thoughts.

Elise ended up thoroughly enjoying it and, during a break, she and Dylan managed to find a private place for some kissing and cuddling.

30

MY TOY

MICHAEL: *The morning after you gave me the amazing blow-job, I sit in your bedroom and watch the sun move across your sleeping form. You are wearing that tiny, pink top I like to see you in, then there is bare stomach, before the sheet cuts off the view at your hips. I come over to the bed, slowly drag the sheet down and take a look at your nude bottom half. Your cunt is peaceful and just lovely, yet still inviting. I open your thighs a fraction more. You stir but don't wake.*

So I begin my leisurely fun down there, licking and rubbing with my mouth, getting inside a little bit, but generally focussing on where I think you enjoy it most. Now you wake and a smile creases your pretty face. 'Naughty baby,' you mumble, still half asleep.

Nothing distracts me as I devour my favourite place on earth. Suddenly it is all wet and hot, filling my senses as I lick and suck and probe. I don't finger you this morning, even though you are lifting off the bed in a frantic need to be fucked, this is all about returning the favour, using my mouth until you gush onto my tongue and I know you are cumming. Let it happen, baby! Enjoy it.

Awww, was that nice?

Nothing from Elise for two days. As far as Michael knew, her date with the Singaporean boy had turned into a love-in. He was still doing his exercises, trying to get into shape for his Far East adventure, and he had a dentist appointment booked for that afternoon. There was nothing obviously wrong with his teeth, he just wanted to ask about getting them cleaned.

Still nothing back from the Passport office in Liverpool – no doubt they had a massive backlog through their own gross incompetence. Later that day, he would bore himself again with information on getting a visa (assuming he even needed one in the first place). How long would he be going for? A week? Two? Should he mention it to Hope? Was it that set in stone?

He had just sent his latest novel to his publisher. There was nothing to do until the man came back to him with his thoughts. Maybe he should get the trip arranged. Get out there before she fell in love with this guy. But get out there, 9,000 miles, to take the virginity of a woman he had never even met? That was so alien to Michael. Maybe the teenagers of today, more used to the internet, would fly around the world to do that sort of thing. And besides, was Elise even ready?

He was in a bit of a mood by the time a message came through from Elise herself. He was relieved it seemed to be as happy as normal.

ELISE: *Have you missed me? Sorry, baby, so busy. Are you free to talk?*

MICHAEL: *Go on, then, put me out of my misery. How was the date with lover boy?*

ELISE: *Oh, Michael. It wasn't really a date. I'll tell you later. Thank you for the little story. You should check your mail.*

He did so. An image showing Elise's legs being shaved, up against a wall. Why was she shaving her legs lying on the bathroom floor? Then he realised it had come through upside down, turned it and admired the legs in a better context.

MICHAEL: *Have you just taken that? Please take more, but go higher up.*

ELISE: *Higher? How much higher?*

MICHAEL: *All the way.*

ELISE: *Nada, no nude shots for you, sunshine.*

MICHAEL: *Elise, please!!*

ELISE: *Sorry. I'm just not comfortable with that, you know. Forgive me?*

MICHAEL: *It's okay. I just get carried away on a wave of lust. I apologise for being male. So, I take it you've bathed already.*

ELISE: *Yes, I've learnt my lesson.*

MICHAEL: *What are you wearing right now?*

ELISE: *Just a towel, that's out of shot in the photo. Would you like to take it off me?*

MICHAEL: *Very much would I like to do that. Have you tried your present yet? How was MY toy?*

ELISE: *Hehe. I was coming to that. I thought it best to try it alone first, so did last night. That's one of the reasons I didn't manage to message you, sorry. It blew my mind. I kept it on my clit. Pretty intense! Thank you so much.*

MICHAEL: *Have you any idea how horny you just made me? Kept it on your clit?*

ELISE: *Really? Turned on, are you? Can I see it?*

MICHAEL: *I'll show you mine if you show me yours. Sorry, too easy to say. Would you really like to see? Silly question. Give me a minute.*

He freed himself from his jeans, and took several shots that made him look as big as possible; he was proud of the great strides he had made in photographing his cock these last few weeks. He transferred the images to the computer, then sent them across to her.

ELISE: *Oh, so big! Thank you. I'm sorry I can't do completely intimate for you. I am trying, please be patient with me. Will you talk dirty to me while I look at your photos?*

MICHAEL: *Why, is it Me time already? You're outrageous.*

ELISE: *It needs to be done. I'll still be here afterwards, baby.*

MICHAEL: *Can't whatshisname help you out?*

ELISE: *Now, don't be moody. I'm using my fingers, but your toy is at hand...*

MICHAEL: *Oh, for a GIF of that! I can see it. Are you really spread? Elise, look at my cock image and imagine it competing with your fingers for the right to rub your cunt. Will you let me rub you with it? I won't go inside, just move my length up and down you.*

MICHAEL: *Oh, I'm sorry, it went in you a little bit there. Keep rubbing with your fingers. Hold my balls with your other hand. Today the scrotum is firm, sometimes it's fairly loose; who knows, one of the mysteries of the universe? What, you want me in you again? Okay, I plunge myself into you!*

MICHAEL: *Are you using My toy? Put it all over yourself down there. Then you can focus on your clit. Right, we're going to need cameras! I know what I said about it leading to requests and refusals and requests and refusals, and eventual arguments, but I have to see what you're doing. At least take a photo, Elise. Hide your sex with My toy as you are using it. Come on.*

Michael sat there, quite agitated. He knew he shouldn't push her, but there must be millions of sexts flying over his head right that second and yet he was being censored.

ELISE: *Michael, I can't show myself yet. Give me more time. Do you want to stop talking to me if I don't do what you want?*

MICHAEL: *Of course not. I'm sorry. Please understand the state I'm in when we talk like this, though.*

ELISE: *I'm sorry too. Wow, that was a nice feeling, it went on and on. If you were here I couldn't be shy.*

MICHAEL: *I've sent off for a passport. What practical things need doing? If I transferred some money for my stay. Maybe you could organise my hotel. The flight will be easy. But when? Two months, four? Christmas? I don't want to come when it's 100% humidity and be like a wet lettuce with you.*

ELISE: *You'll stay with me! And you don't have to send any money, you'll be my guest. Just carry in the allowed amount (try not to get body searched hehe) Oh, come. Come. Michael, come!*

MICHAEL: *Only if you shout that out loud, not just typing.*

ELISE: *I've done it! What will the neighbours think of me? Come, Michael, come!!*

ELISE: *I'm very tired now. You've satisfied me. Can I say goodnight next time? Write me a story to wake up to.*

MICHAEL: *So demanding. Okay, will do. Sleep well. Love you.*

ELISE: *Love you too. Good night. X*

31

GARDEN PARTY

MICHAEL: *Elise, you need a holiday. Go away for two weeks of sun to Spain! Hehe. Or come on a cruise around Iceland with me. Temperature of minus 8, eating your lunch outside with your coat on, sightseeing volcanoes with snow around them, then back to our cabin for sex before dinner. Then we can go and see a brand-new movie, have some drinks, some supper, and fuck all night long.*

We can make love in the morning before we arrive in the Arctic Circle. More sight-seeing, eating in a local fish restaurant. Back on board we can shower together, you're too sore for sex so you suck me off. You dribble my cum out of your mouth and giggle at how offended I am.

At night we go on deck, arm in arm, to watch the Northern Lights in the sky, have another drink, then go to bed to find out how sore you are. It might have to be anal.

Elise saw this message, but didn't respond, being out with Dylan again. They were on a more normal date; he had picked her up from school, taken her home to get changed (waiting in the car despite her amused protests), then for a pizza in the Ice Edge Café one of her favourite places, and finally to watch a movie. This time they had managed to talk more, finding out about each other's families, and what was most important to them. She mentioned books and *GoodReads*, but withheld anything to do with Michael. She questioned Dylan on his medical ambitions again, comparing them to her own mangled plans. She told him about Tricia and her finally deciding to go to Seattle to continue her studies. Dylan told her she could change her route in life, and she had laughed at the thought of giving six or seven years up to train as a doctor.

'You don't have to be a doctor,' he had said. 'There are many branches to go along. Be a dentist, that's quicker. Oh, you hate dentists? A nurse, then? Something specialist, like pharmacologist or physiotherapist.'

'Dylan, the movie's started, don't bore me, yeah.'

He laughed, actually taking hold of her hand. 'Sorry.'

This is a first, thought Elise, watching a movie with one of her hands being held. Actually, it was incredibly sweet.

Not that she intended to mention it to Michael, after Dylan had dropped her home, with one kiss. She showered, got into her favourite pyjamas, made a cup of cocoa, and checked other messages, before contacting Michael.

ELISE: *Heya. I've been out with that boy again, only because he has his days off together. It's nothing serious, I just didn't want to keep it from you.*

So, how is your day?

Michael wasn't there to reply, being on the way to collect Hope at a minute's notice, as her mother had another one of her vital business meetings to attend. This time when he got to the Moss Nook house, he pulled Samantha up on her erratic behaviour. They had a few words, before Hope was there with a hug for her dad, quite happy to be staying over with him.

They collected fish and chips from the *Fishician* take-away on Newton-le-Willows High street. Children's programmes replaced the tennis he had been watching, and they settled down together to eat.

'I've brought *Wreck It Ralph*,' she told him.

'Oh, God, sweetheart, does that involve my knees on the hard floor?'

'No, silly, it's a DVD.'

'Oh, cool.'

So, after tidying up the meal, and getting cups of tea with Jaffa cakes (the only thing left in his cupboard) they settled down to watch the animated film. As usual when they watched a film, Michael thought it was very cleverly made and they thoroughly enjoyed it together.

Hope decided to go for a bath, so he took the opportunity

to check his mail. His publisher had sent the first draft back to him with observations and some clear mistakes that needed amending. He would start on that tomorrow. He replied to Elise:

MICHAEL: *I have my daughter with me. Her dysfunctional mother is gadding about somewhere on a business meeting. So I can't talk, baby. I hope you'll find something to occupy your time. :p*

In the end, it turned into a three day stay for Hope, which Michael was happy with, of course, but livid with Samantha for messing around with his daughter's schedule, and he let her have it over the phone. It meant Hope missed a Friday in school (spent partly food shopping with him in Warrington), but also took her into being able to attend Joanne Garrand's much-hyped garden party on the Saturday. Keira's son was with his father, as planned, but she was more than happy with the change that saw Hope going with them. Some of Hope's friends would be there also, and she knew the Garrand children.

Michael managed to speak to Elise during his daughter's visit, but there was no sexting. He told her about the party, which fascinated her and she expressed a wish that she could be there with him, even apologised, but mention of Keira didn't go down too well.

Their final communication before he ordered the taxi (planning to drink heavily, even if Hope was with him) had been quite cool, as she had informed him that her project was reaching its conclusion and she and her school pals needed to focus on it solidly for two weeks. Two weeks! He didn't want to be restricted in his messages with Elise for two weeks, not after getting to such an intimate stage, but in the end he promised to be patient, and she promised to make it up to him as soon as the project was handed in.

He said goodnight; it was two o'clock in the afternoon, and 9 o'clock in Singapore, but Hope was dressed and had done her hair, and he was still to order the taxi.

'Dad, come on,' implored Hope, finding her trainers.

Michael switched off. 'Parteeee!'

'Oh, mister.'

The taxi went for Keira first, then doubled back and headed out to the Garrand residence, dropping them amid a line of about thirty cars parked on the main road. Hope immediately saw friends, Jack and Ruby Peplow, with their parents, and asked if she could run off with them into the party. Michael waved her away.

'I'll see you in five hours,' he called after her, 'make sure you eat something.' Keira laughed. 'Jack Peplow,' he pointed out to her. 'Last year she said she was going to marry Jack Peplow. I'll have to vet his parents, of course.'

Keira laughed. 'Oh, of course.' She was linked with him, her hair blowing in the wind, wearing bright colours and sandals. They followed two people they didn't know around the side of the large, unusual property.

'Bit of a grand design,' Michael commented.

'They certainly like glass.'

The first thing they saw was the massive bouncy castle; so big it had two teenage attendants, already hard at work. Then, smelling barbecue, they were engulfed in friends from the town, chatting, catching up, doing a few air kisses (Michael), finding cocktails thrust at them. Finally, Joanne Garrand spotted their arrival and rushed over to welcome them.

'Sorry, hi, you two. Keira you look lovely (air kisses), Michael, hi (actual lips on cheeks kisses). You've got drinks, great. Stephen's around somewhere. We've got caterers, so I've not let him cook.'

'Don't want the salmonella thing again,' joked Michael, before feeling Keira nudge him in the side.

'Too true,' said Joanne.

She was in a white dress that reminded Michael of a Jane Austen novel, with a blue bow around the waist. Her exposed upper chest seemed very thin; not unhealthily so, just as if she were training too hard. Her hair looked great. He was no expert on women's hairstyles, but it swept across her forehead and seemed permanently wet.

Joanne was quickly gathered up by other people. Michael took Keira's hand and moved to a free part of the patio. He could see Hope telling Jack Peplow how he was going to pay attention to her today, and the boy nodding, or at least that was how it seemed from a distance. There was an awning over the caterer's gun-metal industrial cookers, and an outdoor bar where he would find something better soon. Then music started up, from above them. Everyone craned their necks to see a DJ set up on the Garrand's bedroom balcony. If he had to guess, Michael would say they were starting with something from *One Direction*.

A brief parting of bodies allowed them to see the place from where noisy adult voices were emanating; there was a Bucking Bronco machine, covered in black and white cowhide. Michael strained to recognise the youth currently being thrown about on it, before he was dumped into the blow-up rubber catchment area, much to the hilarious amusement of his friends.

'Don't even suggest we try that,' said Keira, smiling.

'I bought something like that one Christmas for my ex-wife. It was one of those horse-riding exercise machines, you know. She wasn't particularly impressed.'

'I'm not surprised.'

Party conversation flowed all around Michael. He found he was watching Keira as she laughed and joked with mutual friends. Although part of him permanently longed for Elise, there was a quality and loveliness to his date that was undeniable. Before Elise, he would have thrown himself into this relationship with Keira. She kept glancing at him. He asked her what proper drink she wanted, and set off to get it. On the way back, he clinked glasses with Stephen Garrand.

Stephen was preoccupied with watching a fight down near the bouncy castle. It was a relief to Michael to see that it was nothing to do with Hope, and was quickly broken up by the staff and reacting parents. 'Always something,' joked Stephen, grinning. Michael laughed.

'How's business, Stephen?'

'Business is very good. How's the book coming along?'

'Book's done. Would you like to read it? Give me your thoughts before I make it ready to publish?'

'Michael, mate, I think the last book I read was in Mr McLaren's English class when I was fifteen.'

Michael grinned. Then their attention was taken by yet another fight, one that lasted about seven seconds, but which was completely different to the catfight witnessed on the High street by Michael and Keira; this was stand-up, slug it out, flying fists, from Joanne Garrand and Shirley Garrand. Something had lit the spark, something had brought years of simmering animosity to the boil. It was fantastic stuff.

Of course, Stephen departed Michael's side rapidly, to join the scrum of people keeping the women apart. Michael, highly amused, counted six women with a shocked hand to their mouths as he headed back to Keira.

'They're unbelievable,' Keira said to him, shaking her head.

'They're certainly that. And I was starting to get peckish, as well. Shall we go for a McDonald's?'

'The party will be called off, won't it?'

He grinned. 'You reckon?' He gave her a peck on the cheek. 'I'll upset Hope with the news.'

32

'NEBRIATED

Elise's final push to finish her project on time got underway, with no messages to Michael until at least 10 pm, Singapore time, for two weeks.

Michael tried to deal with having his fix of Elise rationed. At first, he complained to her. Then he sulked. Then he acknowledged that he shouldn't interfere with her education and promised to be patient. He got on with the amendments to his novel, continued to exercise, with his Far East trip in mind, and spent time with Keira and Hope. He and Tony got drunk a couple of times, but he was always there, ready to speak to Elise.

ELISE: *Are you drunk, mister? Hehe*

MICHAEL: *You sound like my daughter when you call me mister. :)*

ELISE: *I'm young enough to be your daughter.*

MICHAEL: *That's true. Yes, I'm slightly 'nebriated. My pal Tony's here. He wants to talk dirty to you. He won't be as good at it as me though.*

ELISE: *Hahaha! No, I don't want your friend to talk dirty to me. Tell Tony to get lost.*

MICHAEL: *I can't. He's asleep on the sofa. Boy can't take his liquor. Don't worry, I don't share you with anybody.*

ELISE: *That's good to hear, mister.*

On about the fourth day, he took a shot of himself in the bath; not his most explicit image, but Elise said, when she saw it, that she liked the novelty of being able to see him when on a quick break. So he went click-happy, all around the apartment, sending her six a day. She laughed when they spoke late at night and promised that she would make things up to him on the very night her project was handed in.

ELISE: *Has my package arrived there yet? I posted it ten days ago.*

MICHAEL: *Package? No. Wait a minute, I'll ask the*

maid. Hehe. No, no package yet. What's in it?

ELISE: *Hilarious aren't you? Just a pair of my panties.*

MICHAEL: *I'll watch for the postman! I'll stake out the entranceway. Are they soiled?*

ELISE: *Don't be gross! I was having lunch today and my friend almost saw your latest image.*

MICHAEL: *I don't mind that.*

ELISE: *I'm sure you don't. How do you get hard every day?*

MICHAEL: *How do I get hard every day? I can see over into a nurses home from here.*

ELISE: *You pervert. Are you big now?*

MICHAEL: *I have a semi, after thinking about your panties. Do you want me to get big for you?*

ELISE: *I want you to cum for me.*

MICHAEL: *That's not an instantaneous thing to do, you know. If you give me a few minutes, baby.*

ELISE: *I tell you what. On my last project day we'll both try to cum together. I promise I'll do whatever you tell me to do.*

MICHAEL: *Sounds good to me.*

ELISE: *Can I say goodnight next time? Very tired.*

Michael went through with the goodnight formalities, then made some coffee. He was quite relieved not to have to cum on cue.

Cindy was back from Korea.

CINDY: *Michael, I'm here. Did you miss me, kekke? I not distrub your job? Today is full with rain sound, I love when I hear rain sound outside my window. How is Hope? I still wait for Hope arrive airport. I watch X-Factor soon, heya. Michael, may I ask you something What and when that make woman beautiful in your eyes?*

MICHAEL: *Welcome home, babe. I'm sorry I missed Korea. It's somewhere I've always wanted to go. :p*
What's this question about beautiful women? That's tough to answer. I'll try. To me, it doesn't matter her ethnicity, or her hair colour. I suppose she has to be in

238

proportion to her height, and her breasts not huge. As long as she is pretty and has character on show, you know, personality, then I will consider her beautiful.

CINDY: *I had my photo taken in Korea. I email it you, check. Man say I beautyful.*

MICHAEL: *Before I even look, I know you are beautiful.*

Michael checked his mail. Yes, beautiful Cindy was there, flanked by some seriously ugly Korean relatives. He actually made the frame with his hands, like a professional photographer, to only be able to see Cindy; who was smiling, adding to her impressive cheekbones. She wore a light-coloured dress with a small denim jacket.

MICHAEL: *Cindy, without doubt you have beauty and personality.*

CINDY: *:))) You make me happy. And my Belgian friend arrives today for visit. So good.*

Who is this Belgian fucker? thought Michael.

MICHAEL: *Who is this Belgian man? Remind me. Why is he coming to see you?*

CINDY: *Is my Michael jealous? He loves my country. He lovely man. 24-year-old from Rotterdam. We just friends. He never touch Cindy. Never. When do you come for visit, Michael?*

MICHAEL: *Cindy, you can be friends with whoever you like, of course. Just not him! No, no, joking. :) Just joking. He sounds a really nice guy. At last something good has come out of Belgium.*

CINDY: *Ehhh? You not answer question. When Michael come to my country?*

MICHAEL: *Oh, sorry. I'm organising a Far East tour as we speak. I can definitely stop off in Indonesia.*

Nothing more came through from Cindy. Perhaps she had fallen asleep, or was preparing herself for the arrival of Belgian Boy. Michael had a smile to himself. What did he do with his time before these *GoodReads* women?

That made him think about Irene Hannah again. Asking him to send funds to her uncle! But what if she genuinely didn't have a bank account? What if he had blanked her, and she did face a bleak struggle to pay her way through school? His stomach rumbled, time to think about his evening meal.

MICHAEL: *Irene Hannah, I've not forgotten you. I was a*

bit shocked that you asked me to send money to a man. Listen, let me send some money in your name via Western Union, towards your education. Then we'll say goodbye on good terms.

Dylan accepted Elise's busy period without argument, so much so that she was a little disappointed, to tell the truth; at least Michael had expressed his disappointment with a manly sulk. She intended to still see Dylan occasionally in the next fortnight, perhaps for lunch or a drink, but really did want to throw herself into perfecting the project.

He was collecting her from school in his Honda. She turned off her phone, with the image of Michael's latest erection, and jumped in, leaning over for a hug (it was still too early in the relationship to kiss, just as a welcome). They said hello and asked about each other's day. As it was so humid, he took her to have fruit-flavoured shaved ice at the NEX shopping centre – Elise seemed to have favourite places for all the food stuffs. Here they chatted about his latest set of measures to get him ready for medical school. He would have liked to give up the hotel porter position, but it looked like he would have to work solidly up until enrolment day.

ELISE: *Michael, sorry I'm so late. This project is a pain in the ass, man.*

MICHAEL: *Hehe, I thought I was the pain in the ass man? What are you wearing? No shorts, I hope. I want you exposed.*

ELISE: *Well now, look who's horny. What have you in mind for me? I've showered, now wearing just a big tee.*

MICHAEL: *Take off the tee-shirt. Don't be embarrassed. Lie on your back on the bed and lift your legs so your feet touch the mattress either side of your head. I'm going to ignore your holes for now and focus on the intimate area inside your thighs. Can you stay in that position for fifteen minutes? Oh, stop complaining, other men would do weirder things to you, believe me. Don't you want to obey me? Hehe.*

ELISE: *Okay, you can consider me doing what you asked. :p I'm not saying I'm actually doing it. I would like to be kissed there. I'm imagining it, baby.*

MICHAEL: *Good girl. I give you all my attention there.*
Then I let you up so you can walk about the bedroom in front of me. I watch your little bottom moving, and your small boobs bounce slightly. You look over your shoulder and see what I'm doing to myself. I so want to use you.

MICHAEL: *Seriously, have you given any thought to how*

horrible it will be the first time I press my cock up your asshole? Think about it. Will you go through that pain for me? Hahaha.

ELISE: *I don't know! :) The amount of pain I have to go through, first my hymen then my anus? Woah, it's so overwhelming you know.*
I fancy a kissing session. Please.

MICHAEL: *Oh, I kiss you until you can't kiss any more. Pause... imagine more loving kissing. Then we can relax and cuddle on your bed.*

ELISE: *Aww, baby, I can see the image. Hold me from behind.*

MICHAEL: *I start to play with that part of your ass/legs again, but you slap me and bring my arm back around you. I'm stirring again, against your warm, nubile body. Just a sec... reach down, bring it up between our bodies. That's better. Maybe I'll get to go in one of your holes if you're in a good mood.*

MICHAEL: *The cuddling didn't last long. I got my way and started to shaft your moist cunt from behind. You reach underneath yourself and feel my cock move against the palm of your hand on its way inside yourself. You love that feeling on your hand, of such a thick, angry member. I'm holding you by your breasts as my hips go back and forth, giving you such pleasure. I take it out, much to your annoyance, and slide it into your willing ass. You huff! Always the ass! I let your reaching hand feel my shaft again as I fuck you differently, your pleasure more emotional than physical, giving yourself in an unnatural way to the man you love.*

I spurt my cum into your ass, still rutting furiously. We collapse in a sweaty heap. Oh, all right, more cuddling, if you insist.

33

ST IVES

Irene Hannah came back to Michael overnight, expressing her thanks and saying how wonderful that would be. So, not wanting to send money online, he looked up his nearest Western Union office. He had a choice between Wigan and St Helens; neither one being an overwhelmingly appealing option. He thought again of the John Bishop joke, "I've never met a woman with hairy ears, and I've been to St Helens" and headed over there in the car.

It cost him £2 to park. *Two pounds.* Then he found the office very quickly in the Hardshaw shopping centre. He did the deal with a very helpful assistant, then decided to make the parking cost worthwhile, so browsed a few shops. He bought some toiletries for himself and, in a sports shop, he found a nice Fila top that he thought would fit Hope, as well as buying some thick socks for her (with next winter in mind).

Getting home, he accosted the scruffy postman outside his

building. There was nothing for him. Go and have a wash and brush-up, mate, thought Michael. As he was about to close the door, a delivery van pulled up. Here at least was his passport. He signed for it, thanking the man. He ripped open the envelope and quickly scanned the document as he jogged upstairs. 'Jesus, Michael, you'll have to hide that photo.'

MICHAEL: *Elise, I can't wait for this project to be done with. I hope you haven't forgotten your promise to me. The postman just came. Biff! Bash! Bosh! Wallop! That's what he gets for not bringing your package.*

I'm looking at your adorable profile image. I can't tell you what I would like to do to it. Well, I can, I suppose. I want to cum on it. You don't have to swallow any stuff, just let it run down your pretty nose and drip off your chin. When I've stopped pumping right in front of your doe eyes, I'll wipe you off with tissues, then take you into the shower.

I'm going to shower for real now. Imagine the soapy water running off my balls.

Elise got home earlier that evening. The bus had been insanely crowded and hot. She was so tired, and grateful for the apartment's air-con, and that Tricia was already cooking. She joined her friend in the kitchen, where she was poured a glass of wine. After a moment's small talk, Elise noticed that Tricia seemed giddier than normal.

'My acceptance letter came,' Tricia announced, beaming from ear to ear.

'Is it London?'

'No, Seattle!'

Good enough! They squealed and did a kind of jig around the kitchen, then composed themselves and clinked glasses.

'I might go a few months early,' said Tricia. 'Stay with my relatives, while I get used to the country.'

'Arrgh, you're leaving me, honey.'

'I know, but you can come for a holiday.' She became serious all of a sudden. 'What will you eventually choose to do?'

'I don't know. I might become a doctor.'

'*What*? A doctor?'

Elise laughed, then shrugged. They embraced.

Elise wandered into the cooler living room and checked her messages. When she saw the one from Michael she laughed, but decided to hit the shower before replying.

ELISE: *I've just bathed. I imagined the water running off your balls. My friend Tricia is moving to America to study. She's such a lucky girl. You, bad man, attacking the postman! Tut tut. It should come soon.*

Elise was delighted that he was there, waiting to reply.

MICHAEL: *I think I've broken my hand.*

ELISE: *What!? How!?*

MICHAEL: *Punching the postman. Actually, it turned out to be an ugly post lady with short hair. She took the blows well, bless her, before falling on her fat arse. How was I supposed to know it was a woman?*

ELISE: *You're terrible, you are.*

MICHAEL: *Are you not going to America with your friend?*

ELISE: *I wish! I don't know what I'm going to do. I'll have to make a decision soon. Can't you look after me? Can't we live in a big house overlooking the sea?*

MICHAEL: *Of course we can, darling. Just so long as it's not the South China Sea. I can't take humid 24/7. We'll build a house in St Ives, Cornwall. Look it up. You can do the interior decorating. Just leave space for my indoor football goal.*

ELISE: *I'm eating now. I'll look up that place before I come back to you. Will you be there.*

MICHAEL: *I'm feeling horny, what do you think?*

Since the garden party, Rimski had changed his opinion about Joanne Garrand's enhanced breasts. He had been one of the people to spring forward to separate the fighting sisters-in-law and, as a result of pulling Joanne away, had inadvertently copped a feel. Admittedly, it had only been across his forearms, but there was enough pressure for him to decide that they were, in fact, wonderful things, and that she hadn't completely ruined herself with the surgery after all. He still didn't like the woman, though.

His support remained strongly with the younger Shirley. If only his starting position had been different and had allowed him to get to her before the other people, he mused, one afternoon in the yard. The Garrand brothers were no different with each other, he observed. Shirley had visited since the incident; wearing a little cut on her nose and a black eye. As usual, she had warmly said hello to Rimski, asking about his post-cataract operation eyesight, and Stephen had behaved completely normally towards her. Rimski remembered how bad the fight had been, though. The two women really despised each other. Surely Joanne wouldn't leave it at just keeping her distance from Shirley. Would she pressure Stephen into some big changes?

Not that Rimski was particularly bothered. He would get on with whatever was asked of him, as usual. He was doing just that, near the entrance to the yard, so was in the prime location to see Joanne Garrand's Mini Cooper pull up. As soon as she got out of the vehicle, he was entertained by the enormous sunglasses she was sporting; clearly Shirley had done some facial damage. Joanne looked at him, at least her head inclined in his direction, before she found her husband. His wide, aggressive stance was more of a "what?" than a "hello, darling, what brings you here?"

She was clearly in a terrible mood. 'Why aren't you answering your phone?' was her opening gambit. 'I'm taking your mother to the airport, remember?' Rimski looked to see old Mrs Garrand in the passenger seat of the Mini. 'The school's been on. Your daughter's been fighting. You'll have to go and deal with it.'

'Fighting? What are you talking about?'

'She's been fighting. What more can I say?'

'Well, is it any fucking surprise? I wonder where she got that from? Why don't I take my mother to the airport, and you go to the school?'

'I'm not going there to be shamed.'

'Christ, Joanne. You're some piece of work.'

'Listen, Stephen, your mother and her suitcase are in my car. You know her legs are bad, what's the point of making her move? Just go to the fucking school.'

Stephen raised his hands in defeat. 'All right, all right. I'll go and get our daughter.'

With that, Joanne spun on her heels and marched to her car. Stephen looked at Rimski, but didn't say anything. They watched her speed away with the elderly Mrs Garrand.

34

PRIVATE IMAGES

ELISE: *Have my panties arrived there yet?*

MICHAEL: *Oh, and good evening to you. It's half past five here. Finally talking to me, then? :) I just knew you were sending panties. No, nothing has arrived yet. You know, there's a man in Toxteth, Liverpool, who works at the main Post Office sorting depot, who sits wearing your panties every night while he watches TV. Haha.*

IRENE HANNAH: *Michael, I got the money. Thank you so much. Please stay and be my friend on here. I know I've not deserved your friendship. Tell me how I can make it up to you.*

CINDY: *Michael, somehow I think how to taste your lips, how to taste your skin, how you sound... LOL #I'm going insane. I read too much erotic romantic novel, hehe. Seriously, my Belgian friend ask to be more than friend. I say I want to him May I back off? He go away upset. I so confused. My family conservative, I can't talk them.*

There was also a new friend notification. Michael smiled. 'I'm popular all of a sudden.' It was another friend request from Gary in Canada, the man Michael had ignored a few months earlier. Michael grinned. 'Hey! Gary, my man, you're here again.' He accepted Gary as a friend.

He had absolutely no idea of what to say to Irene Hannah. And he didn't want to say "I told you so" to Cindy.

MICHAEL: *Cindy, I'm sorry to hear about your friend. I'm here. You can talk to me.*

MICHAEL: *Elise, I'm so good, aren't I? I'm still giggling about the Post Office man. He's sitting there in just your panties. Hahahaha. And his wife is there doing the crossword as if nothing is out of the ordinary! Hahahaha. No, seriously, they'll probably show up tomorrow. Unless you put the wrong address on. I've got a weird neighbour we call The Prince of Darkness. Maybe he got them. You didn't put your address in the package, did you? I dread to think what he'll send you back. Hahahaha!*

ELISE: *You're a very bad man, you know. Haha, ohm*

gosh, imagine if I sent to the wrong address. Worst nightmare ever. I'm tired, baby. I just wanted to check in with you. Will say goodnight next time. But project almost over, so then I'm all yours. Friday night, yeah.

MICHAEL: *You promise? Goodnight, sleep well.*

ELISE: *Goodnight. X*

Michael opened a can of beer and put something resembling a pizza into the oven. He seemed too busy to eat properly at that moment, with another *GoodReads* message waiting and an email in too. The email was just from his publisher, saying his first draft was currently being read by some reliable friends of the man.

JOHNNY PISSMEOFF: *Hey, man. Loved your books. I'm a new fan. Just wanted to say. Sweet.*

IRENE HANNAH: *Michael, oh, I opened an account straight away with the money you sent me. I thought you would like to know.*

CINDY: *Michael, please when do you come visit? I know you be gentle man. I hope I not distrub your work? I hungry, cooking late. If you here I cook for you. I send you new photo of me cooking.*

MICHAEL: *Mr Pissmeoff, good to have a new fan. Glad you like the books. Michael.*

He shook his head, hoping that was appropriate for Mr Pissmeoff. Cindy's new image duly appeared; wearing a yellow bandana and a striped apron over white tee-shirt. She had her shy smile on; so sweet.

MICHAEL: *Cindy, I love the photo as always. Next time I cook I will take one of me. Summer's here soon, so I'll probably be cooking topless. Show off my muscles to you. No! I'm joking. I always cook in one of those aprons with a naked woman on the front. Seriously, it's an English thing.*

He ignored Irene Hannah and sat there drinking his beer, leaning back in the chair.

MICHAEL: *Cindy, I hope you are still reading Wolf Hall. I am. There was a part where Mary Boleyn said something to Cromwell about her sister Anne Boleyn and the King, "At night she lets him undo her bodice and play with her breasts".*
Cromwell replies, "I'm surprised he can find them". That made me think of you for some reason. Haha. No, no, I'm sure (well, I assume), that you have wonderful boobs. Hahahahahaha. Oh, I'm so in the doghouse now.

He was still giggling, as Irene Hannah came back to him.

IRENE HANNAH: *Michael, I appreciate the money you sent. I hope I can rely on your continued support. For your friendship perhaps you will let me offer what I have to give. Which is me.*

MICHAEL: *Irene Hannah, sorry? What do you mean?*

IRENE HANNAH: *I can perhaps offer images. Private images. Do you see?*

Oh, I see, he thought. Not that he hadn't considered it himself, but it felt different hearing it from her, unprompted like that. More beer, more straining the chair back.

MICHAEL: *Irene Hannah, let me think about it.*

He switched off and went to check his pizza.

All the next day Michael thought about Irene Hannah's offer. He admitted to himself it was what had first crossed his mind. But he didn't go on *GoodReads* to speak to her, nor did she contact him. A gentleman, now thoroughly ashamed, would back her education without conditions, and he wanted to do that, but still there was the niggling concern about being scammed, especially with that first attempt to have him send money to the uncle.

In fact, the night before, he had struggled to sleep, thinking about all the women in his life. He had realised, in his semi-conscious mind, that Keira had not featured in his thoughts; it had all been about the Far East, and one of the three had caused him to develop an erection with his dirty thoughts.

It was warm when he got up, deciding to go for a walk before breakfast. Still, by 10 o'clock, there was nothing from Elise. Throughout the day she stayed quiet. He did his household chores, and took a shower before going for dinner with Keira and her son. Then in the evening he watched a big football match (the Confederations Cup, whatever that was) with one corner of his eye looking for the *GoodReads* message box.

Elise came through as late as the previous day, claiming exhaustion and hatred for anything to do with buses or schooling.

MICHAEL: *Elise, I miss you so much, you know. I hate that you are so busy. Why on the bus so late? Singapore education is crazy.*

ELISE: *I had dinner with a friend after school.*

That annoyed Michael, even though it was the most normal thing in the world. The girl had to eat. Perhaps it was because he felt he was waiting around for her. He let it pass.

MICHAEL: *I'm no proof reader, but can I read some of your work, try to help some way?*

ELISE: *I've just emailed you one of my reports about tourism at the Asian Civilisations Museum. You could read through and tell me what you think.*

MICHAEL: *I think I'm bored rigid at the thought of it. Joking! I'll look at it in the morning.*

ELISE: *I like seeing you rigid. I'll delay my shower until we say goodnight, as I'm so late these days. How was your day, baby?*

MICHAEL: *I so want to be in the shower with you. Take an image. Please.*

ELISE: *No. No shower images tonight. Give me time, remember?*

MICHAEL: *(sulking here) I bet you'll have the water jet in the right spot.*

ELISE: *Eh? Oh, I get it. No, I don't do that.*

MICHAEL: *I just fell off my chair. Are you seriously telling me you have never aimed the water jet at that area?*

ELISE: *No, I've never done that. Do you?*

MICHAEL: *Are you kidding? I can't go a day without firing water at my balls.*

ELISE: *You're so naughty. Well. I might try it tonight. Just for you.*

MICHAEL: *I insist, and I want to hear about it tomorrow. When you shower, have the water jet as strong as possible between your legs, cold if possible. It's warm here today, yes, I know, not by Singapore standards. I think I will shower again later. I'll get the jet on my balls. I'll get big, thinking about you, pumping away like there's no tomorrow. I will try to cum as hard as possible for you. Can you see it? Can you visualise it, baby? I'm cumming just for you.*

35

HOUSE GUEST

It turned into a very interesting morning for Michael. First, he came to a decision over Irene Hannah; he intended to sponsor her, in stages, while trying to be a good friend, but she would have to prove herself with a couple of images. He justified this by telling himself that she had been the one to suggest it and, besides, there was no such thing as a free lunch in this world. No doubt she would send some coy shot of her boobs, then he could tell her they were cool and that she wouldn't have to do anything like that again.

He fired the instruction off to her, early on. Then, while having crumpets and coffee for breakfast, he read Elise's piece on the Asian museum in Singapore. He found it quite interesting, focussing on the different sections, the type of people the museum appealed to, and its practical side, such as fire safety and commercial enterprises on site. Then he went through it again, making notes of spelling mistakes, inappropriate use of slang and picking her up on one occasion where she seemed to be un-pc about the museum's attitude towards the disabled.

Then his mother phoned him. He assured her he was fine. He listened to her news. Basically, she was calling to tell him their holiday plans, because they always had Hope for a couple of weeks during the school holidays. There would be two weeks on a coach around Historic York and then a cruise around the Canaries come autumn – all right for some, he thought. The call was as good as complete when the door intercom buzzed. He told his mother he loved her and promised to visit soon.

The female voice from outside his building asked if he had any ice pops in: Joanne Garrand. He listened to her coming up the stairs, unable to think what could be the reason for the visit. At the last second he remembered the smudges of curry sauce on his tee-shirt, but it was too late for that kind of thing.

'Joanne! This is a pleasant surprise.'

She was in a dress that looked like nightwear. He wanted to ask if she was one of those women who dropped their children at the school gates without bothering to get dressed, but he controlled himself – it didn't seem the right moment. Joanne appeared to be fairly distressed, red in the face from the sun, but also from crying.

'You're probably wondering why I'm here?' He politely remained quiet, letting her go on. 'I've had a massive row with Stephen. *And...?* you're thinking. Well, I have a certain friend who I go to when these things blow up, just for a day or two, but she's in the Canary Islands.' Michael inclined his head as if to say that was a nice place to holiday. 'I don't share this kind of thing with other friends, obviously. I can't have Stephen shouting on my parents' doorstep again. So, I wondered if I could hide here for thirty-six hours or so. Maybe it's lame, but you helped me so nicely when my shoe broke.'

An extraordinary thought came to Michael as he stood looking at Joanne; if there ever came an apocalypse, could he be the leader of Elise, Cindy, Irene Hannah, Keira and Joanne? Not forgetting Shirley, and maybe his ex-wife, Samantha, in a domestic servant capacity. He immediately discarded the idea.

'That will be okay, Joanne. Have you got any bags with you?'

'No, just what I'm stood up in.'

'You're cooking tea, you know.'

'That's fair enough.'

'Or, you're going to the door when the pizza comes. It's usually Tommy Mansell who delivers, and he's a discreet bloke.'

'Whatever.'

He shut the door, finally. 'Well, are you peckish? Would you like a crumpet? You can't beat a good crumpet.'

Joanne smiled, swept hair off her forehead. He asked

whether she wanted tea or coffee, to which she answered the latter. He didn't ask her where the kids were during these occasional tiffs. She went to look out of the window, before remembering where she was, backing away and settling herself down on the sofa.

In the kitchen, Michael grinned, thinking how Elise would find this situation amusing, while Keira would most certainly not. He thought about the practical side of things. She'd better not expect him to watch soap operas, like *Emmerdale* and *Coronation Street*. Did he have any clean towels? She would be sleeping in his bed; he would have Hope's room. He slid the crumpets under the grill. He realised he was happy to have Joanne there, looking all vulnerable and feminine – not that she was ever not feminine, just that she had come in without her usual aggressive self-confidence. All he needed now was to chat with Elise, find out that Cindy understood *Wolf Hall*, and see Irene Hannah's breasts.

Whenever Michael had a guest, at some stage they went on the pool table. It was the focal point of the room, impossible to ignore, even if you didn't like pool. Joanne went for it earlier than most, straight after breakfast. Michael found it a little disconcerting that she was licking butter from the crumpets off her fingers between shots. Maybe he should get another pool table: "that one's yours, this one's mine".

He noticed her peeking out of the windows from time to time, which was understandable – she, more so than anyone, was allowed to enjoy the vista of the scrap yard.

They moved into the afternoon, without him questioning her about the unusual decision to seek refuge with him. She did ask him if she was stopping him doing something in particular, but he just joked that he'd only had to postpone his 10k training run. While watching an old Cary Grant film, they chatted away on a variety of subjects, from their children to her interesting fascination with all things Cornish.

'We were thinking of buying a second home down there,' she said, 'maybe in St Ives. So, so beautiful.'

'I went to Cornwall once, when I was younger, to see a girl. The car journey seemed to go on for days getting down there.'

'But worth it. Cornwall or Egypt, will do for me.'

'Wow, where did Egypt come from?'

'Don't the pyramids fascinate you? I'd love to go there. Stephen was talking about a world cruise. Do you think I could go on a world cruise with him? I'd be pushing him overboard. Anyway, Gibraltar, Malta, Venice, Egypt, India, Singapore, Thailand etc.'

'You should take me, instead. Would it be an overnight stop in Singapore?'

'Most probably. Okay, if I find myself in need of a travel companion.'

'Would you like all the weird food? The Far East is all octopus and squid, isn't it?'

'Fine by me. I love sushi. What food do you like?'

'Cooked.'

They had coffee and some of his *HobNob* flapjacks in the

middle of the afternoon. She phoned her children, telling them she was away visiting a relative, and took a few calls from friends, on one occasion wandering about subconsciously dribbling one of his footballs. Then at four o'clock she introduced him to the delights of ITV's game show, *Tipping Point*, which was a quiz based around the old penny arcade game of dropping coins into a two-tiered machine to push off the ones already in there. It was great.

At five o'clock he had his own quiz, asking her about her favourite pizza toppings, then phoned in the order.

'I'll go to the door,' he assured her.

He sat back down. She was watching the news, biting her nails. 'What was the fight about, then?' he asked.

'With Stephen?'

'No, don't be silly, I want to hear about the girl fight with Shirley.'

She guffawed, and ran her fingers through her hair. 'Hasn't town gossip reached you yet? No, it was nothing in particular, actually. Me and Shirley, we just don't mix, I'm afraid.'

Before the pizza was due, Joanne went for a shower; Michael telling her where towels were and saying she could wear any of his clothes she found. 'If you're feeling kinky look in the bottom drawer of the dresser.'

He took the opportunity to check his messages.

GARY: *Hi. Thank you for accepting me. I liked one of*

your books. I look forward to the others. Best wishes.

Oh, Gary from Canada, very good.

CINDY: *Michael, I've been eating so much lately. I not skinny any more and I love it. I have bosom :p finally YAY! Oops sorry talk about bosom. Did you know celibate is healthy for your body?*

She had stumped him once again.

MICHAEL: *Cindy, feel free to talk about your bosom any time. Sorry I've been neglecting you recently. I promise to give you my full attention very soon.*

ELISE: *Sorry, sorry, I fell asleep right after I bath. Forgive me, baby. Can we talk tomorrow? And Friday is only a few days away when I will be FREE!*
Goodnight,
XX

MICHAEL: *Elise, I miss our long chats. You get some sleep. You'll need it from Friday onwards! Hehehehe.*
XX

Michael could hear Joanne singing in the shower. How bizarre to have Joanne Garrand singing in his shower. A brief fantasy flashed through his mind about joining her in there, but he quickly squashed it. He would have to get rid of her before Friday night.

36

IRENE HANNAH

MICHAEL: *Elise, two days until you say you are free for me. All mine! Clear the decks for some non-stop naughtiness. Warn your friends that you are going into a very dark place for a while. Hehe.*

Seriously, I hope your college work is where you need it to be, and we'll have some fun talk to help you wind down from it all.

I must get on my lover. Sorry, I mean, I must get on, my lover.

Joanne Garrand, making herself pretty in the bathroom, was coming food shopping with him, probably just to avoid the onset of cabin fever. 'Come on!' he called, as if to a tardy wife. She came through and presented herself to him for his appraisal (which was a cute thing to do, if a little strange). She wore her own jeans and one of his, white, *Abercrombie & Fitch* tee-shirts, and his *Fila* cap, pulled down low over her forehead, like an off-duty movie star.

'Ready, sir.'

'Right, what's the plan? Give me three minutes. Slam the

front door and run downstairs, the car will be waiting. You can jump in and slump down in the seat.'

'You're a natural at this, Mr Lincoln.'

They played the game, giggling, and drove away from Newton-le-Willows, fairly sure no-one of any importance had spotted them. Only then did they realise they hadn't decided on where to shop.

'St Helens?' he offered, trying to sound cheeky.

'What!? Certainly not. We'll just go to Warrington, use two trolleys. If anyone we know spots us we can just say we bumped into each other there.'

'Okay. You're the one who seems to be the natural one at this. Have you had a lot of practice?'

'I might have had a little bit of practice at this sort of thing.' She grinned. 'I'm sure you've heard rumours about me.'

'Oh, yeah.'

They laughed. They were out in the countryside between the two towns, speeding along. She brought her feet up and hugged her knees, enjoying the freedom. He looked across; at least she hadn't put her feet on the dashboard.

At Tesco in Warrington, he had the forethought to let her out of the car at a different place to where he parked. 'Difficult to bump into each other if we arrive together.'

They synchronised meeting up at the entrance, with extravagant gestures of surprise and friendly smiles. They acquired two of the smaller trolleys and set about doing his shopping.

'Ready meals and then the beer department,' he pointed out with mock gravity.

'Not on my watch. Head left, fresh fruit.'

On the way, he grabbed newspapers and *Krispy Kreme* doughnuts, which he placed in her trolley. 'Well, something has to go in there, for effect.'

'I'm going to cook tea tonight, as a thank you for letting me stay.'

'Is this where I say you don't have to? What's your speciality?'

'Well, anything complicated when I don't have to do it myself.'

They reached the fruit and veg aisles, where he idly did some people-watching while she chose some items. Then at the fish counter she asked if he liked fish.

'I've always wanted to try monkfish.'

'Seriously? I can do that.'

He nodded, so she ordered some over the counter.

'I'll be off in the morning,' she said, as they moved on.

He was riding the trolley like a child. 'If you must. I like having you to stay. You can come again.'

She smiled. They moved towards the bread aisle. After checking they were alone, she gave him a nice hug.

They spent a good hour and a half shopping for him, making sure to even out the produce into both trolleys. He let her pick some wine to go with the monkfish. Near the tills, he stopped her, 'Now, I always pick the most miserable bitch imaginable.'

Joanne laughed, and forged ahead. But she did put them in a little queue towards a woman who was clearly unhappy in her work.

'Sullen Susie,' Michael whispered in Joanne's ear, making her giggle. 'Suicidal Sharon. Pissed-off Pamela.'

'Stop it.'

They were still happy, chatting together, as they headed out with the throngs of fellow shoppers. Suddenly there was a log-jam in front of them, six or seven people stopped with their trolleys, then came loud shouts and a scream. It wasn't exactly the parting of the Red Sea, but some people moved right, towards those queuing to come through the tills, and two women pushed themselves up against the wall, revealing the cause of the disturbance. There was a scruffy man in a long brown coat, apparently taking offence to being accosted by two security men and a female store manager. At his feet were a number of items which Michael assumed to be shoplifted. But he was more interested in the knife which was protruding from the right sleeve (no hand, just the blade). They couldn't retreat, as there was a build-up behind them, so Michael at least put Joanne at his back. Then everything went mental; the man lunged at the nearest guard, slicing his arm, blood spraying about, prompting more screams. The other guard had no choice but to act, or the maniac would no doubt injure many more people in his panic to escape. The guard came in with a kick, but slipped, perhaps on his colleague's blood – a colleague who was squatting down, in obvious distress. The knifeman threw a hunted look about him, at Michael, who was the nearest male. The guard was trying again to tackle the man, while his manager called frantically into her mobile phone.

Michael had no choice; he had to get involved, it was getting wild. He feinted to grab the man and felt a whoosh of the blade come by his face. This gave the guard the chance to pounce, bringing the knifeman down to the floor, yelling and thrashing as he went. Michael sprang forward to kneel on the knife arm, causing a scream from the maniac. He grabbed the man's wrist and pinned the blade to the ground. Michael gave pressure to the man's shoulders with his right knee, as the guard took an arm lock on the other wrist and exerted enough force to subdue the man and get his face against the floor. The man was strong, so it took an effort to keep him contained. Michael looked at Joanne.

'The police are on their way,' called the store manager. 'Stay calm everyone, please.'

As the knife slipped from the man's weakening grip, Joanne knelt beside Michael and pushed it away to the wall. Michael tried to smile at her through his exertions, then looked about at the general public. As always, in those kinds of circumstances, there were about twenty-five per cent taking pictures and filming on their phones.

'Such a hero!' called Joanne.

'I know.'

'Remember, at the golf, when Alfie tackled that bloke running from the police? That was just a laugh. What you did was very serious.'

'It was, wasn't it?'

She was cooking the monkfish, filling the apartment with the most wonderful, never smelt before, aromas, while he was looking at *GoodReads*. He had a possible new friend: Lulu from New Jersey. How could he refuse someone called Lulu? He just checked Lulu was, in fact, a woman before he clicked the accept button.

ELISE: *Michael, just bathing now, okay.*

That was timed fifteen minutes earlier, so maybe she would return before he had to go eat.

MICHAEL: *Elise, you make my heart go boom titty boom titty boom!*

Joanne called for him to do the plates and cutlery, which he attended to immediately. As he collected everything from the cupboards, he noticed she was looking about his small kitchen.

'Where shall we eat?' she asked.

'The sofa works for me.'

'If we must.' She glanced at her watch. 'Oh, I've missed

Tipping Point, cooking this meal.'

'And you think me uncouth for having no dining table.'

He placed the cutlery on the table in the lounge. He flicked through the TV options for something to watch during the meal – oh, cool, women's international football on Eurosport, but probably not for Joanne. *Top Gear* on Dave, maybe not, *Last Of The Summer Wine* on Gold, definitely not. *Man vs. Food* on... 'Not that!' she called. He continued to search.

'How about *On the Buses*?' No reply.

'Put local news on, see if they mention the supermarket incident. 'Oh, we might be pictured together.'

'We'll see about that later. How about *The Good Life*? That's quality comedy for our last meal together. It's the episode with the windbreak.'

'That's a good one.'

He wandered over to the computer, and *GoodReads*.

Elise: *Always the titty, with you, mister. Hehe. I'm too tired to talk to you today i'm so sorry. I fell asleep bathing. Please forgive me. Finish everything to do with project tomorrow. Our Friday, yay! Goodnight, baby.*

Disappointing, Michael felt, to be fobbed off again. Still, he replied with a friendly goodnight. While there, he checked his email. He realised that Irene Hannah had sent him a new image. He opened it, and found himself leaning towards the screen in delighted shock. It was quite astonishing: naked, from behind, on her knees. Her cunt in a long, bare, beautiful line. Her overall shape was sexy, half her face hidden behind the camera which was aimed back towards a bedroom wall mirror, shoes and clothes scattered about. Her hair jet black. Her left breast slightly visible, the back of her thighs long and fresh, her bottom sharp, her asshole just a shadow.

'Michael.' He clicked the image off, turned to find Joanne offering him the wine and a corkscrew. 'Would you do the honours?'

'Of course.'

'We're ready now.'

'Super.'

37

FRIDAY (EARLY)

There was a strong hug, and then Joanne was gone, skipping down his stairwell. Only after he had closed the door, brewed coffee and realised that he was wandering around his apartment, did he give thought to whether or not he was disappointed that nothing had happened between them. He really wasn't sure. According to local gossip, didn't she have an affair with the landscape gardener? It had been a novelty having her stay, anyway. He was looking out over the scrap yard. His eyes settled on Rimski, where the old man's face was turned upwards, perhaps catching the sun. Rimski gave him a little wave – the first time ever that had happened – being acknowledged. He lifted a hand in reply, then moved away from the window.

Michael settled himself down at his desk, determined to get some things done now that his house guest had departed. His publisher would soon be calling for movement on the finished novel, so he opened that up on his computer. At the same time he was thinking about Elise's upcoming 20th birthday. Of course, she had the vibrator (which might come into the conversation that evening) but he looked through her "to read" wish list on her *GoodReads* page for books to buy her.

There was a new notification telling him he had won a book giveaway. Seeing as he only ever won anything when there were over fifty copies on offer, and the competition was only open to Great Britain, he didn't look into it, instead would just wait for it arriving in the post. Thinking about the post, he jogged downstairs. Oh, yes, a small package from Singapore in his post box! Grinning like a teenager, he had it ripped open as soon as he was back upstairs, allowing a tiny pair of Elise's panties to flop into his hands. He sat at his desk, pleased beyond measure, wanting to tell her the good news, and also to say how excited he was that her project should be handed in by then. With Rimski in mind, he bent down a bit to do the obligatory sniffing of the underwear – very fresh, indeed.

MICHAEL: *Elise, your panties finally came. The parcel was open and damaged, and had been left in a neighbour's letterbox. She's a lovely lady, Gloria, just brought it to me now. Hehe. Only kidding, they arrived normally. I love them, thank you. They fit me perfectly.*

I can't wait for later. XX

A phone call came in: Keira. She told him she was going playing tennis and wondered if he played, or just wanted to come along. He asked if he had to run to her with a towel after every shot. She laughed, he said he was busy, and they agreed to get together on Saturday night.

Then, aware that he had just that second spoken to Keira, and communicated with Elise, he looked at Irene Hannah's nude shot again. It wasn't something she would post on her *Tumblr*. It was something just for him – or at least he thought it was just for him – she might have a number of overseas sponsors. Anyway, he loved it; he wanted more of the same, but also he was wracked with guilt. Even still, it was giving him a semi. Not the best time for the door intercom to buzz. He took his time going across there. Discovering it was Shirley Garrand downstairs didn't help his own downstairs to calm. How bizarre, he thought. Was the other Garrand woman now seeking asylum? He asked for a minute; he would go down there.

'Hello,' he said, opening up to Shirley.

Her arms were folded from leaning on the wall. She had on a light-coloured dress and pink flip flops which showed off pretty feet. He did realise it was odd to be liking her feet just then.

'Is Joanne here?'

It was a neutral question, neither accusing or interested.

'What makes you think she would be here?'

'My friend said she saw her car parked over there.'

'I'm surprised you're looking for her.'

'What's that supposed to mean? Stephen's cut his finger off in the yard. Everyone's looking for the silly cow.'

'Cut his finger off!?'

She changed her moody stance from one hip to the other. 'Well, sliced it so it was hanging off. He's been taken to A&E.'

'Well, I'm sorry to hear that. But she's not here.'

'Fine.'

With that, she departed.

'That's all right,' Michael said to himself. Before he could shut the door, he found himself looking down at a little girl. She was vaguely familiar as one of Hope's friends. 'Hello, sweetheart, you're Abbie, aren't you?'

'Yes. Is Hope here?'

'Not this week I'm afraid. Next week.'

'Oh. I've brought an invitation to my birthday party.'

Then Abbie's mother reached his door, and they exchanged cheerful hello's. Michael took the card.

'It's next Wednesday,' said Abbie's mother.

'Right, I'll phone Hope, tell her. I'm sure I can get her over for it. Thanks, Abbie.'

Smiles all round, and mother and daughter walked away happy. Michael checked the street for anyone else; all clear. He went back to Irene Hannah, ready to set the ground rules for how he wanted her to behave, what was expected of her sexually, how she must prostitute herself fully in order to keep his friendship.

MICHAEL: *Irene Hannah, thank you for the photo. It blew me away. Listen, you don't ever have to do that kind of thing again (not that you could beat it). I promise. You can rely on my friendship throughout your education. No strings attached. Okay? Speak to me when you get the chance.*

Friday afternoon in Singapore, Dylan's Honda drove out of Changi International Airport. He had a crying Elise in the passenger seat beside him and he didn't know what to do, apart from keep glancing at her. Should he put a hand on her bare thigh, should he pull over as soon as he was on a normal road and hold her in his arms, or should he start talking madly? He went for the hand on the leg. This brought half a smile from her, and she cupped his hand with her own. They had just seen Tricia off on her Seattle adventure. Dylan had stood there like a spare part as the two girls laughed, and hugged, and cried, and promised to Skype constantly. Then Tricia did the same kind of things with her mother and sisters, and then was away airside.

Elise's tears had not started properly until they had got into his car. If she had blubbed in the concourse, he was sure he would have reacted correctly on instinct.

'Well, she's gone,' said Elise, sitting up and trying to compose herself.

Dylan was relieved that she seemed to be pulling herself together. 'She'll be in touch as soon as she gets there.'

'Yes.'

'Would you like to stop somewhere? Get a cold drink or something?'

'Oh, no, Dylan. You've got to get to work. Thank you so much for bringing me.'

'It was my pleasure. I like Tricia. I'm sure she'll be fine. I love airports.'

'I know, you said.'

'I'm supposed to be going to Hong Kong, with my cousins, for a holiday soon. Maybe, perhaps, you'd like to go.'

'Dylan, I'd love to go. Thank you.'

'What are you doing tonight? Can I text you on my break?'

'I'd love you to text me.'

He drove her to her apartment. Once parked, he got out of the car, not to rush around to open her door, but just to be polite. 'I suppose you'll need a new room-mate?' he said.

Elise walked over and kissed him on the cheek. 'Maybe you could move in.'

Dylan blushed madly. 'I wasn't hinting at that, Elise. Please forgive me.'

She laughed, gave him a hug. 'Text me. Don't forget.'

'I won't forget.'

They smiled at each other as she entered her building.

She took a little melancholic look around the apartment it would be strange without Tricia. But it had been in the pipeline for a while, so she decided not to dwell on it. She would make a cup of tea before bathing. She clicked on the kettle. From the back pocket of her jeans she brought out her phone, to check her messages – five in total, all – suggestions from the girls. Even without Tricia, she had all those friends about her.

She brought up the old one from Michael, the Boom Titty Boom Titty one, and it made her smile.

ELISE: *Michael, good morning. I wanted to tell you how sorry I am for being busy recently. Tonight, I'm all yours. You can do what you like with me.*

38

FRIDAY (LATE)

In Newton-le-Willows, in the middle of the afternoon, Michael found himself chatting on *GoodReads* with both Cindy, and new friend, Lulu, in New Jersey. Lulu, as far as he knew, was a married, fifty-year-old, kindergarten teacher with a passion for reading crime and historical romance. Their chat was not particularly fascinating, and Cindy, though he loved her to bits, was having one of her waffling days, talking about the rain and about Belgian Boy still hanging around. Being that he was waiting expectantly to resume serious sexting with Elise, and indeed had already eaten an early evening meal, it did cross his mind to get Cindy to talk directly to Lulu.

It seemed Elise was teasing him, building up the sexual tension, making him wait. So, in the end, he made an excuse to Lulu about having to talk intensely with his publisher on some technical matter, and remained on to Cindy, only – but she had gone quiet by then, anyway.

Rather than twiddle his thumbs, he took a look at his favourite porn site. Mostly, he found boring rubbish, but the occasional good piece of action presented itself, followed by something he considered "fucking great". It was purely coincidental that it involved three Asian women. Massively aroused, he thought he might as well record the development for Elise. He snapped about a dozen shots from various angles, and transferred them to the computer, where he checked them over, editing one to increase his girth, and deleting another for having a bit of underwear fluff on show. Then he sent them to Elise, as an appetiser, perhaps. He had an idea for a new sex story for her, if that was what she wanted. No doubt she would want some Me time. He looked at his watch, estimating it was nearly ten o'clock over there in Singapore. He remembered it was her twentieth birthday soon, and decided he must check exactly when it was, so he could leave a birthday message overnight for her to wake up to.

CINDY: *Michael, need to change profile picture. Okay, just want let know, kekke.*

He noticed it had, indeed, changed.

MICHAEL: *Oh, that's much better. :p*

CINDY: *Nah, no lik. I change again.*

He waited patiently. This one had her when she was younger, and with wilder hair.

MICHAEL: *That one fits the bill.*

Suddenly it changed to another, of her all serious in work clothes, apparently. 'Oh, Christ, we're going through the whole album.'

CINDY: *This one? I look professional, yes?*

MICHAEL: *A modern, doing it for herself girl, yes.*

It soon changed once more.

MICHAEL: *Cindy, baby, I'll leave you to your decision making, if you don't mind. Good night. XX*

Still nothing from Elise. He began to stew. It was quite warm in there. He had a case of numb-bum, so decided to go for a wander across his football area, dribbling a ball while thinking about the last few weeks with Elise – feelings of being a bit abandoned still, having to defer to her education. Despite that niggling problem at the back of his mind, the one vaguely covering the age and distance gaps, he was keen to get back on track with the girl, have more fun, be very naughty.

ELISE: *Sorry, I'm going out for a late night movie. I hope you forgive me. Sorry.*

Reading that made him livid. He felt a total idiot, waiting around all that time, thinking he knew this girl. Wow, now he was hot in there. Boy, oh boy, fuck me! The ball was smashed right-footed, crashing somewhere in the kitchen, breaking something. A used coffee mug failed to survive being near him on the desk, cracking on the wooden floor. He found he was pacing up and down. He tried to make himself think; had he misjudged the moment? No, he had left her almost alone to finish her important project, accepted virtually being abandoned and today was when they were to resume their intimacies. She had said so, on a number of occasions, promised, even.

'Shallow, selfish bitch.'

MICHAEL: *Elise, Well fuck you then! I'm done with this. Goodbye.*

After he had clicked a few buttons to remove Elise as a *GoodReads* friend, and blocked her from communicating with him again in the future, he needed to get out of the apartment. He made himself ready and carried his bike down to street level. Gloria, his American neighbour, was just coming into the building and, although he was seething inside, Michael behaved as politely as usual with the nice lady. Then he was off cycling – heading along beside the scrap yard and down the street where the younger Garrands lived. Shirley happened to be outside her house, gossiping with a friend. Michael called to her, 'Found Joanne yet?' without waiting for an answer; all he got was an open-mouthed stare, anyway.

He sped down past the church, through the lights with the *Legh Arms* pub (realising he hadn't noticed whether they were green or red), under the railway viaduct, then out along Winwick road towards Warrington. The terrain rose, hurting his legs and lungs and making him sweat (with him only being used to poodling around alongside Hope's bike). The countryside opened up either side of him, with the straight road being Newton-le-Willow's bridge to the rest of the world.

By the time he reached *The Swan* public house he was shattered, but he pushed on, around the roundabout, the exclusive Winwick Park Avenue estate on his right. Traffic was crazy here, so he mounted the pavement, until he reached *Burger King*, where he bought a coke and drank it outside in a big heap on the floor. He took deep breaths between quenching his thirst, watching in a great melancholic mood the happy families heading into the restaurant, and even envying the people passing in their cars, going about their busy, normal lives.

Michael quite wanted to stretch out there and then on the pavement outside the restaurant, but knew he would only attract the attention of the staff. Thoughts of Elise kept trying to invade his mind, and they were interspersed with the knowledge that he would have to struggle on the return journey soon. It was then that a deep gloom came over him, in the form of the Prince of Darkness's shadow, moving to sit beside him and offer a smile when Michael looked up.

'Hello, neighbour,' said Prince. 'You look a bit distressed, my friend.'

Michael managed to find a grin, patted Prince on a leg. On their way to a car were three forms, similarly dressed in all black. For the first time, Michael realised that the Prince of Darkness actually had friends; up until then he had thought him a jovial, oddball, loner.

'I've just overdone the exercise,' Michael said. 'Thank you, I'll be fine. It may take me two hours to get home, though.'

'We could hang a rope out the back of the car and drag you along? On the bike, of course.'

They both laughed.

'I appreciate the thought,' said Michael.

Prince of Darkness slapped Michael on the back, and set off after his friends. Michael watched them go, in a pink, Fiat Punto, with large eyelashes sticking out of the headlamps.

39

IGNORE GOODREADS

The next day, oblivious to Michael's words and actions, Elise went for another driving lesson (with her test coming up soon), followed by lunch with Dylan, who had come out of work to meet her. He presented her with a present of a trio of New Adult books. Delighted, she kissed him hard on the mouth, causing Dylan to blush, as there were dozens of fellow diners nearby. She squeezed his hands on the table, before excitedly examining the novels.

During the meal, they talked of his plans again; Dylan intending to take every available shift at the hotel before quitting to take up his place at medical school. Elise had once more expressed her admiration for his chosen path, and again laughed off his suggestion to do something in that field herself.

'Seriously, Elise. There are a million and one things to do in medicine.'

'Baby, if you saw how restless I was in a classroom, you'd know I could never work in a lab, for example.'

Dylan was thunderstruck that she had called him baby. She was puzzled for a moment, slurping her drink through the straw, staring at him, then giggled and put it down to his unique personality, before moving the conversation on to something different.

She made her own way home after lunch, back to the quiet apartment. Could she share it with Dylan? What would her parents think? She bathed, put on shorts and a tee. It wasn't until about 3 o'clock that she went on *GoodReads*, and what she found made her gasp – she could not believe it – she had actually won a giveaway (and not one of Michael's where she wouldn't actually be receiving a copy). She laughed out loud, did a little celebratory jog – little old Elise in Singapore chosen over all those greedy Americans. On the subject of Americans, there was a message from her friend, Janelea, in San Francisco, talking about her new job in a book store. Elise fired off a reply, congratulating her, expressing her jealousy to be able to work with books, and about Tricia being in Seattle. Maybe they could meet if she went to visit Tricia, she suggested.

Then, leaving the best 'til last, she read Michael's message: *Well fuck you then! I'm done with this. Goodbye*. Aghast, her hand went to her mouth. What had she done!? She attempted to fire off a reply to urgently get an answer, at which stage she realised that Michael had actually de-friended her. Horrified didn't cover it. Tears filled her eyes. She was mystified. Then she remembered putting him off the previous evening, to go to the cinema with Eilynn, only because her friend had split from her boyfriend. How could she have said no to her? Perhaps, with hindsight, she should have explained that to Michael. But, even so, to de-friend her so brutally was a shock. Then annoyance set in – how dare he? How *dare* he!?

She forced herself to get up. She made a drink of tea. She tried to ignore thinking about him.

At least Dylan loved her – she picked up one of the books he had given her and tried to read. That was impossible. Men! Or at least, man! That Englishman.

Michael picked up some rolls and milk from the convenience store on the High street. Suddenly, the hot weather had arrived, and the people of Newton-le-Willows had on their shorts and flip-flops. Flimsy vestlets exposed tattoos, some aggressive, some full-shoulder ones of martial arts curved knives, etc (and that was just the women).

The post was there on his return, but no more panties. There was a package which was obviously a book, and clearly sent from his publisher, as the man always put a little address label on the back.

Michael examined the book in his kitchen, waiting on his coffee. He was considering eggs for breakfast. The novel was titled *The Red Thread*, set in 1830s Singapore. He searched his brain for what he had told his publisher about Singapore, apart from the initial good luck message for the giveaway. Never mind, he thought, he must have mentioned the place in conversation, or it was just a coincidence.

Tai-Pan by James Clavell was one of Michael's favourite novels, set in 1840s Hong Kong, so he was quite interested in the new book. It didn't spark thoughts of Elise, as she was with him constantly since he woke up; he was just trying to keep busy and not dwell on how it had ended. He decided to start the book right after *Wolf Hall*. That reminded him to check on Cindy's progress with the Tudor novel.

It was his day for Hope, which would assist with trying to get over Elise, but Hope was off school with a cold, so he was going to be with her at Samantha's house in Manchester, there being no chance of his ex-wife and the South African changing their plans for the day. He didn't mind, he planned to eat Samantha out of house and home, drop a few pans into her precious bespoke sink, and maybe loosen something on the South African's exercise bike in the conservatory. He would set off immediately after breakfast, ignore *GoodReads*. Cindy sprang to his mind, but, no, ignore it for that day entirely.

It was an insanely humid evening in Singapore. Elise, heading to her parents' house for a meal, sat on the crowded bus, too uncomfortable to even blink, just aware of all the people about her. She cradled her phone on her lap, unhappy that there would be no message, or an image, coming through from Michael. She felt enormous relief to get off the bus at the family home and be able to have a drink of iced lemon tea in the cool kitchen, while her excitable brothers filled her in about their day. She greeted two of the maids, Lily and Lina, as they came in, both girls happy to see her. Elise checked what they were having for the meal, while also looking at her designated place on the counter for any mail; empty. Very disappointing; nothing from overseas.

Her mother entered the kitchen, embracing Elise. They chatted about school, and how she felt about Tricia going to America (without any mention of Dylan possibly replacing her. In fact, there had never been any mention of Dylan in that house).

'Oh, baby, you can go and visit her soon. It's a shame she didn't choose London, though, you would feel more at home in England.'

Elise could only smile her agreement, while inside she was squirming. Her brothers were pulling at her arms, wanting to discuss what films to watch after the meal. She laughed and hugged them until they begged to be set free, then went off with them to the lounge. She discounted all their film options, until settling on two possibles, which she left them arguing over, as she went to shower.

Before, during and after her shower, she cried. Then she stood in front of the mirror trying to compose herself. It was so silly; she missed someone she had never met – missed them so very much. She tried to giggle, to stop being silly. Her phone was sitting on top of the bamboo laundry basket. She picked it up hurriedly, deciding to take some shots. First she went in close and photographed her black eyes. Then she focussed on the drops of water on her upper chest. Then she aimed at her naked torso, making sure to cut it off at her mouth, and took several images.

Michael got home at 9pm, exhausted by Hope, after playing water-gun fighting, football and a form of badminton where she changed the rules constantly in her favour, and that was even before they walked to a local park and had an hour on the swings and zip line. All on the hottest day of the year, so far.

Samantha and the South African came in at a quarter to eight with curry, insisting he stay to eat. He wished he hadn't, as it was chicken dhansak, his least favourite Indian, and they gave him the smallest portion of rice he had ever seen in his life – it really was like the rations given to plane crash survivors in the Kalahari desert.

Hope, still flushed and in a mood, because her mother said she must have a shower, hugged him all the way to his car. He kissed her, promised to see her as soon as possible. She brightened, smiled, and went back to her mother at the door. Michael waved and drove away.

Once home, Michael rushed to check *GoodReads* for a message from Elise. Cindy was there, and his publisher,

Henry, was there, but no Elise – then he remembered blocking the girl, so she wouldn't be there anyway. His huge fatigue added to his misery.

HENRY: *Michael, I've emailed you the thoughts of my beta-readers about the new novel. Let me know what you think and how long you feel you need to work on them.*

CINDY: *Heya, Michael. I'm going to the beach tomorrow. New hispanic friend (girl) is teaching me to surf. Have reading Wolf Hall, good. Are you enjoying?*

MICHAEL: *Hello, Cindy. Boy I so want to be beside the sea right this second. It's hot in England right now (don't mock) it's hot enough to send English people loopy. I don't understand much of Wolf Hall. Can you help me out, kekke? ;).*

40

DUAL BLOWJOBS

The next day, Michael spent a couple of hours during the late afternoon fixing the jammed back door at Keira's house, but only because he was on a promise of a free supper and one of her famous blow-jobs. Despite the loud expletives and general banging around, which came as part of the package when asking someone with minimal DIY skills to attempt such a job, she sensed his mood was pretty low. She was beside him, in the utility room. He hugged her, kissed her right temple, put his mood down to problems with the revision on the novel, and promised to cheer up. She accepted that and went to put the kettle on for a cup of tea.

Actually, since he began tackling the annoying door problem, Elise had stayed out of Michael's mind. He had inexplicably slept in until noon, waking from a wild dream in a total sweat. For once, he could remember the dream; of being in a bare underground labyrinth, cycling around, trying to control criminals on skateboards, and finally when one of them came at him with a knife, he drew his gun and shot him dead. As he tried to get over that and gather his thoughts, he found they were then filled with Elise. Throughout the early afternoon, he had so wanted to message her, but stubbornness had intervened, and he filled his time with showering and shaving and fussing about with domestic chores around the apartment.

'Have you any plans to go away on holiday?' called Keira.

That stumped Michael. 'Err, nothing solid. You?'

'We might go to North Wales again. Why don't we all go? Hope as well.'

'I'm liking that plan. When you have a date in mind, I'll force myself to speak to Hope's mother about it.'

He slammed the door again and it seemed to close properly. Keira came back with his mug of tea. *There*, he gestured, *man has prevailed*!

'You're so my hero,' she said. 'I feel obligated to you now.'

'I know you do.'

'Let's go into the garden.'

'But your garden's overlooked by neighbours.'

'I don't mean go into the garden for *that*. To have the tea. The night's young, big boy.'

She had a lovely patio with two sun loungers and some purple flowers in big Roman pots. It was a shame the rest of the garden looked like a building site, with a dilapidated shed and muddy flagstones from the previous tenants' four by four.

The grass was destroyed, but that was more from her son and his friends playing on it. Keira's son was staying with a mate overnight. Michael almost commented on the garden, before remembering that his gardening skills were worse than his DIY. At least they were in the shade, as they chatted away together. It was so refreshing out there, and the air was yet to be filled with the smoke of a thousand barbecues.

'Would you like a shower before we eat?'

'Do you mean a shared shower?'

'I'll come in, if you want. No, you go up when you're ready, I'll prepare something in the kitchen, then follow you up ten minutes later.'

'I'll be all nervous anticipation.'

'Well, I hope there'll be something to show for it.'

'I hope so too.'

He left her with a kiss and headed upstairs. He had a quick, thorough shower, and had only started to use his imagination and have Keira slipping out of a flimsy dress (she was actually in scruffy jeans) and only attained a semi-erection, when she entered the bathroom. He watched her through the steamed-up glass door, stripping off, taking far longer than in his dress fantasy. Then she opened the shower door, her hair down, her breasts pale against her tanned upper chest. First, she cupped his soaked balls. Then she took ownership of his mildly angry cock. She held on to it as she knelt. It became more impressive the second it entered Keira's mouth. She sucked him while still half in and half out of the shower. She had to let him free, so she could join him fully and close the door behind her. He was huge by the time she sank to her knees and resumed her attentions. Michael braced himself against the side walls, with his overview of her. He wasn't a head grabber during oral sex, preferring to trust the lady's abilities, and Keira needed no guidance; she was doing him marvellously, with both hands as well, and not ignoring his underneath. She had to look up at him, yes, there it was – he loved that.

It seemed to go on for a long time, but he didn't care about her knees, or her aching jaw. She showed no signs of flagging, so he enjoyed it to the full, finally coming into the roof of her mouth. That slowed her, but she finished him off, giving him more naughty eyes while she swallowed.

Elise had Dylan round at her apartment, to finish the evening. Coming straight from work, he had showered, but unfortunately not had the fun of receiving a visitor in the bathroom. Takeaway food cartons littered the lounge area, as they cuddled up watching the Timothy Olyphant film, *Hitman*.

Elise had done well not to think about Michael all day. Of course, she was a softer person than him, but perhaps her lack of experience with the break-up of relationships and overall heartache had protected her somewhat. Now she just wanted to be close to Dylan, to kiss him, as he smelled so nice and his hair was all messy. As soon as he next turned to her she planted an open-mouthed kiss on him. At first he was taken aback, but then he responded, leading to heavy kissing on the sofa. His right hand cupped her left breast, making Elise wonder if that was the first time he had touched her. There was a frantic discarding of tops – though, why, neither of them could say; there would be no full sex taking place. Nevertheless, Dylan was delighted, between breathless kisses, he marvelled at Elise's toned upper body. She reclined, enjoying his excitement, glad that one man at least wanted her. He surprised himself by kissing her stomach. Then he was trying to undo her belt.

'No, baby,' she said, stopping him.

'Just my mouth, Elise. Please let me.'

'No, but let me do it to you.'

Suddenly the old, shy Dylan was back, unable to comprehend the offer, even as she had his trousers open. Not that Elise was exactly confident of what she was doing either. She had touched a man intimately before, but now she was moving over a new threshold, into territory she had seen on *Tumblr* and been excited by in Michael's words. She reached in and held Dylan's balls. Awww, she thought, he looked so sweet, fighting a moral battle in his head, and then she was playing with his erection and he was still embarrassed, but more than delighted, then not caring, any more, loving the fact that Elise was playing with his cock. He watched with wide-eyes as she went down on him.

Elise kept turning her hand on him, as she closed her lips firmly around his member, remembering all she had seen and determined to put it into practice. She was so happy to be pleasing the lovely Dylan. She exerted more pressure and increased her speed. She could feel him straining on the sofa, then his hands were gently holding her head, as if he had a bomb in his lap. At one stage she felt that he tried to make her stop, but she was beyond that. Her jaw started to ache like mad, which made her think of one of Michael's messages. Damn him for interrupting what she was doing to Dylan. Damn him. Because her mind was briefly elsewhere, it shocked her when Dylan came. She stayed still, letting him finish. She didn't look at Dylan, guessing he was pleased yet ashamed. Instead, she got rid of it into a tissue, and went to the bathroom.

41

SALE

Two days went by in a daze for Elise; Dylan was either working at the hotel or continuing his plans for the start of medical school. There was no Tricia, of course, except for a giddy Skype message; Eilynn had found herself a new boyfriend and Silvia was studying hard. Elise went shopping, but bought nothing. She did enjoy seeing her family, but didn't stay long once they questioned her depressed mood.

It was in that down state of mind that she decided on some intense Me time, straight from the bath, on her bed, using Michael's vibrator present. It added a different dimension to the daze, three times, in fact. Afterwards, thoughts of Michael flooded back in. She realised that she had not even responded to his cruel dismissal. She didn't want to shout back at him; she just wanted to still know him. She thought of contacting him via one of his other friends on *GoodReads*, but discounted that immediately as a desperate and silly measure.

But how? Email, of course! She could email him. Still naked, she opened up her laptop and started to contact him, but what to say? She was lost in a jumble of emotions, unsure whether to express how offended she was before negotiating a continuation of their friendship, or just to blurt out that she missed him terribly. In the end, she said a bit of everything, then attached the topless photo she had taken recently in the family home. It was only after she had hit send that she realised how massive a step that had been for her, sending something like that.

At the time that Michael received the naughty email from Elise, he was laughing his head off. Of course, he still felt bereaved inside to be without her, but at that very moment he was actually kneeling on his office chair, so as to get a complete view of the police raid on the Garrand compound (seven van loads of coppers, no less). He especially liked the obvious indignant rage of the two brothers, and the headless-chicken runaround of the staff, including old Rimski. Actually, Michael had been aware of the police presence in a back street since early morning, when he went for a newspaper. Apparently, they had been waiting for just the right time to pounce, presumably to gather evidence as it arrived and make as many arrests as possible. He laughed heartily again before sitting back down to open the new email. What he found, delighted him, but also made him feel extraordinarily guilty. *Oh, baby*, he thought, with a wry smile and his head dropping to the right. Elise McHugh was an absolute darling, and he was a grumpy son of a bitch.

MICHAEL: *Elise, I'm so sorry. Please forgive me. I've missed you so much. And thank you for the beautiful image. I don't deserve it, and you didn't have to do that.*

ELISE: *I'm sorry I let you down. But there was a genuine reason. Can we be friends again? I'm glad you like the photo. I hope I will receive many in return.*

MICHAEL: *I'm doing that already for you! No, I'm not. I'm watching a firm I can see through my window get raided by the police. It's great fun, but it's terrible here, crime-ridden, please take me away from it all.*

ELISE: *Geez, I tell you to come here, don't I? Stop watching that and say naughty things to me. Hehe. Call it make up sex. I've sent you a new friends request on GoodReads.*

Michael immediately accepted Elise again, and they continued their chat on the book site.

ELISE: *What phone have you got? Does it make movies?*

MICHAEL: *What!? You want me to film myself!? I'll*

investigate the phone, but I'm not promising. How are you, anyway? What have you been up to?

They talked for nearly an hour. At one stage he told her he was looking at the topless image, and asked for something more, which she declined. He pushed for it, she declined more firmly, and they left it at that. He played with his phone, discovering the movie function. They both laughed at her keenness to receive a naughty moving image, but when she tried to explain how he would have to use the *Dropbox* file sharing system to get it to her he glazed over at the technical element, so they agreed to try that another day.

The day's heat had built up while he sat chatting. He had a little fan on his desk but it wasn't much use. A fresh email came in, from the company he had bought the vibrator from.

MICHAEL: *Elise, could you ask the monks to do a little ceremony, something to cool the weather here? And, there's a sale on at the sex toy company! What shall I get you next?*

ELISE: *Stop it now! And you're a wimp with the weather. Wait until you get here, then you'll know heat.*

So, they made plans again for his trip to Singapore; buy some new clothes, pay a visit to the dentist and, more importantly, telling Hope all about it. It was his birthday in exactly two months, and he asked if that would be the best time. She replied that it would be the perfect time.

ELISE: *But I'm nervous, you know. About losing my virginity. I so want to, with you, but you understand.*

MICHAEL: *Wow, talk about pressure. It's like travelling 9,000 miles to do an assassination hit on someone. I hope that didn't sound terrible. Listen, we've still time. If you want, we can agree that I'll visit, we'll have a great time, show me Singapore, we can play around a little, but leave the big thing until you come to Europe, in the new year.*

Michael had every intention of taking Elise's virginity in Singapore, but it seemed like the gentlemanly thing to say at the time.

ELISE: *Oh, that's so sweet. We'll see, okay.*

MICHAEL: *You promise not to wear pyjamas for my visit? What are you wearing right now?*

ELISE: *I've been naked since we started talking.*

MICHAEL: *Naked? Really?*

ELISE: *But don't get any ideas. I'm tired, and I have a big day tomorrow. Write me a story. It's been a while since my last one. Let me wake up to it tomorrow.*

MICHAEL: *You're leaving me? Sigh. That makes me want to be less than romantic in a story. I feel a spanking coming on for Elise.*

ELISE: *I might like that. Hey, no romantic, nice stories, right. Goodnight, baby.*

MICHAEL: *Right! Understood. Sleep well.*

MICHAEL: *Elise, when we live together in Singapore, we sometimes bathe together nicely, washing and talking and lounging together in the warm water. I know, I know, you don't want nice. Well, this time, you were in a giddy mood, constantly playing with me, soaping my length and my balls. I knelt up in front of you, waving my cock near your face. You couldn't stop laughing, refusing to suck it. I looked down at your wet body. As always I loved your lovely breasts and your petite shape, down to your shaved pussy below the water line. Still you giggled. At least you were using your hands on me. I playfully told you to stop being immature, and asked if I could come on your face. You screamed in the hilarious negative. I begged you, especially as you were being really rough with my erection. I doused your head with a soaking sponge to try to stop your giggling, but it forced more laughs from your adorable mouth.*

This went on for a couple of minutes, me kneeling there as a plaything to your giddy fun. Then I came on your face. You had it in your mouth, on your tongue, up your nose, in your hair. You pretended to be annoyed, but you loved it really. Anyway, your giggles stopped as you tried to deal with it all. I went back to my end of the bath and relaxed. I'd come on your face. Job done.

42

WHO DO YOU THINK YOU ARE?

MICHAEL: *Elise, I've just had a message from a lady called Nancy in Massachussetts, who has ordered one of my books and can't wait to read it. See, I have the capacity to cause people great joy :p*

Please wait, I'm about to write you another nasty story as requested.

Before he did that, he looked again at Elise's topless shot, received the other day. Her boobs were fairly regulation shape, i.e. small and curvy, but what made them lovely was the way they blended into her body so smoothly, they didn't take your attention in their own right, they were a continuation of how adorable she was.

MICHAEL: *The guard enters the prison cell and simultaneously pulls the sheets from the two beds. Both women are naked, looking up at him with fear in their eyes. Their names are Helen and Elise...*

Arrgh, Elise, I don't want to write something nasty.

Can you imagine me sitting, holding you from behind, both of us naked? I cup your breasts and you sigh back into me. We feel high and turned on just to be that close, whispering sweet nothings. Then the fingers of my right hand slip gently between your legs, running down your slit, not seeking to enter you, just running along the sides. Then you turn and straddle me, taking my cock and directing it to your hole, before slipping down onto me.

While you are riding me, I grab hold of your butt and squeeze firmly. I can see your thighs doing all the work, but by holding your bum it seems that I am causing you to rise and fall. Your delightful breasts are bouncing ever so slightly. There's not an ounce of fat on your nubile body I've fucked all your puppy fat off you (sorry, not so nice). You are so beautiful and sexy.

You decide to get off me. So you've done enough work, have you? Lazy girl. Actually, I don't want you to do any work. I want to give it to you, long and slow. I place you beneath me, spread your legs so that your tendons are strained and enter you deep, watching your eyes roll upwards and your nails claw the sheets. It's very long and slow, then long and fucking fast. Thrusting and fucking, fucking and thrusting, faster and faster, so thick in width as well that you can't take it any more and you cum throughout your vagina in great gushes.

I don't want to cum in you. I ask where I can cum and you open your mouth. No, I've cum in your mouth, in your cunt, your ass, on your face on your tits, on your back (loved that one, you didn't), on your bed sheet, up your shower wall. You realise what I'm thinking as I pull out of you, my throbbing, sticky member in my hand. I grab your favourite pair of panties off the bed, but you quickly fight me for them, before guiding me helpfully back inside you.

MICHAEL: *Elise, I've just re-read that. Ooops, maybe I should have stayed with the prison story. :p*

Michael played with his camera again, practising how to make movies by filming his bare feet up on the desk. The story had turned him on, and his computer screen was again filled with a semi-nude Elise. It was as good a time as any to give her what she wanted, so he freed himself, allowed himself to rise as big as humanly possible, began to play a little. He watched the action through the camera, but held back from filming, just getting the feel of juggling the two disciplines. Elise looked extremely hot on screen, but he felt something a little stronger was needed once that was found and playing, he got down to serious business.

Nobody was bothering with Michael, apparently, either on *GoodReads* or in real life. After a shower, he got on nicely with the revision to his novel. Lunch and doing a spot of laundry took him into the afternoon; Elise no doubt working hard at her studies. He ordered a couple of pairs of new jeans off the internet. He had his dental appointment the following morning. Then the day after that, he would tell Hope of his upcoming holiday to the Far East. He would use the term "friend"with her at this stage to describe Elise.

He returned to his desk as a new idea formed for a little story for Elise.

MICHAEL: *You hold an envelope in your hand and you teasingly say it contains four erotic bum shots, but I can't see them today because I was late talking to you. I apologise again, blaming my car breaking down and ask to see them. You say "naw, naw, bad boy" and go to put them away in a drawer. I laugh and grab hold of you. You scream with laughter and hold the envelope out away from us. I try soft talking you, kissing your ear, but you are in a giddy mood so I have to beg.*

Still you hold out. I can take the envelope from you easily, but I play along, enjoying your body against mine as we wrestle for it. You throw the envelope across the room and as we scramble for it we both tumble laughing into a heap. You make a move for it on your hands and knees but I grab an ankle and haul you back. You are almost wetting yourself with hilarity as I move over you to get at the envelope. Your arms clamp around my neck and your legs go around my waist, but I keep going, carrying your tiny frame with me across the carpet.

Eventually you know you must submit to my manly strength, and we collapse on the floor, with the envelope in my possession. We kiss, I stroke your hair from your flushed face. Then I look at the photos. I tell you I love you, that I will treasure them for ever and we kiss again, our bodies completely compatible against one another.

Michael could transfer the movie from his camera onto his computer, but could he find a way to put the file in drop box and make it available for Elise? Could he fuck. He was effing and blinding, his blood pressure almost through the roof. His phone rang; Keira asking him what he was doing. He almost told her, or was that his frustration playing games with his mind. She invited him to dinner, and he politely accepted.

Finally, he seemed to master the technology, just as Elise greeted him on *GoodReads*.

MICHAEL: *Hello, baby. How's your day been? I think I've put a movie there for you to view. Hope you're not too disappointed.*

ELISE: *Michael, oooooh! Listen, I've got a visitor. So I can't speak right now. Sorry. I'm desperate to see it, really, but I'll have to watch it like mad later. Sorry, sorry. XX*

Michael walked to Keira's house. It was a Thursday, a day on which her son usually liked to have a pasta bake type dish: something that also worked for Michael's taste buds. On arrival, there was a quick kiss for Keira, before joining her son and his friends for a game of football in the back garden.

He stopped that before he got too sweaty, sitting down with a beer while watching Keira finish preparing the meal.

'I've something to tell you,' she said. He looked at her; he was all ears. She laughed. 'Oh, nothing heavy.' She pointed at her son, who was waving his friends off home, through the side gate. 'His dad's picking him up later. I just thought I would mention it, as you'll be meeting him for the first time.'

'Well, you've not said he's a nutcase, so I'm sure it will be fine.'

'Oh, he's okay. I just thought...'

And the man was indeed okay, cheerfully civil with Michael, in fact, when he arrived an hour after the meal. There were handshakes and queries as to what Michael did for a living. The man seemed perfectly normal, pleasant in his interaction with Keira; so much so that Michael tried to remember why they had split up in the first place.

Later, just the two of them, they had a proper drink and snuggled up, trying to decide on a film to watch. Because they were deep in conversation, nothing was settled on, and they ended up viewing her favourite soap operas, and then an episode of *Who Do You Think You Are?*

Twenty minutes into the programme, Michael realised that the "celebrity" only seemed to be tracing the life of her father. Keira glanced at his bored expression, amused by the angst of it.

'I might go upstairs,' he said, 'and throw myself out of the window.'

43

MONOPOLY

Elise's visitor had been, and still was, Dylan Wang. A fire in his building had made him temporarily homeless. Then an argument with his father had seen him made unwelcome in the family home (at least his sister had been taken in again); he had other options, but Elise had made him stay, once her fright at the fire had calmed down and she was sure he was uninjured.

She had managed to see Michael's movie after they had turned in for the night (Dylan in Tricia's room); it had thrilled her, caused her to immediately indulge in a long session of Me time. She had put it on repeat. She had fallen asleep thinking about it, and about wanting Michael, wanting him to come to Singapore.

By the morning, having breakfast with Dylan before he went to work, she was confused. Her feelings were the same for her Englishman, but she cared deeply for Dylan. Michael was intense and exciting, Dylan was lovely and more suitable to be a reserved, Singaporean boyfriend, who wouldn't pressurise her for anything. But part of her wanted to be pressurised by Michael; maybe it was her English side exerting itself.

She walked Dylan out. She had a class later, but her day was very clear, really. They kissed (as there was nobody about in the foyer) and she waved him off. Back upstairs, she showered, then, wrapped in a towel and drying her hair, she watched Michael's movie again. Wow!

ELISE: *Michael, I've seen your movie. I think it's HOT. Thank you so much. I only wish I had the nerve to reciprocate with something similar. Please give me time.*

She cried out in exasperation and forced her hair back up on top of her head. Then, suddenly emboldened, she quickly found her camera, and returned to the bathroom. She set the shower running, placed the camera on a shelf, aimed at the water jet (careful to make sure it was well below the shower head), threw off her towel and stepped into shot. Actually, she shuffled into shot, really, quite nervous and self-conscious. She knew her left boob had started the show, before she offered her bottom to the camera, while she soaped up again for another shower. She made sure to run her hands around her butt, and go underneath her breasts. She was surprisingly turned on by the whole thing, her nipples so erect that she turned slightly to the side.

Later, in her bedroom, she was shocked with the results. The shuffle into the shower had exposed her pubic hair, and her turn to the side had almost been a full frontal. There was no intention to fire it off straight to Michael she would keep it in reserve for the time being. She edited her exit from the shower, then hit save, switched off and got back to doing her hair.

Michael had just received a message from Irene Hannah, giving him an update on where her studies were taking her, as well as some general chit-chat. And straight on the heels of that, Cindy had spoken to him, talking in riddles, but giving him the impression that Belgian Boy had tried it on with her again. His reply had been to advise her to speak to a relative about the man, perhaps to her father, or at the very least say that there was an angry Englishman about to head to a Channel port, but her last message had said that the man's time was up and he had flown home. Michael was glad that the matter now seemed closed. Cindy had left him with a new piece of her singing, for him to sit listening to, munching away as he was on macaroni cheese. Her voice was definitely hauntingly beautiful.

The ready meal had come from the microwave. Once again, bizarrely, he had been annoyed that the instructions on ready meals never seemed to match the wattage of the microwave.

Suddenly remembering this, as he sat there, he Googled that very question. He came across a man called Kevin, as equally apoplectic about the situation, wanting to know why the food companies didn't address the situation. Kevin had hundreds and hundreds of comments. Michael sat there, highly amused, reading some of them.

"Burnt your tea again, Kev?" "I'm so annoyed for you I've gone downstairs to check my machine". "Everything gets three minutes". "This is great stuff!"

It was silly, but Michael laughed his head off. Then he got Elise's message: ah, always nice to be appreciated.

MICHAEL: *I so wish you could send something similar. I'm not pushing you. I'd just really love that.*

But, apparently, she wasn't around any more. He waited. Singapore filled his thoughts, of seeing Hope the following day and telling her about his holiday plans. Soon, although it was another very hot day, he intended to ride to Burger King and back, but in a happier frame of mind than last time. Still he waited. He played some ball.

ELISE: *When you come to Singapore I'm going to show you the best places. I can't wait to be with you. I want to jump your bones, and we can do other things like play Monopoly.*

Eh!? thought Michael. Monopoly? She had genuinely, completely stumped him.

MICHAEL: *Monopoly?*

ELISE: *Yeah.*

MICHAEL: *Monopoly?*

ELISE: *Have you got a problem with Monopoly?*

MICHAEL: *No, I love Monopoly, I just didn't expect you to say that, baby.*

ELISE: *Hey, since we can't have sex 24/7 I thought we could do something silly and fun. It's in the Singapore edition, and we can be having drinks and snacks, maybe play naked, you know...*

MICHAEL: *Aww, that's so cute. Of course we can play Monopoly. I can't wait to see all the best (air-conditioned) parts of Singapore. Hehe. But I suppose I'll suffer between places. I want to see the ocean.*

ELISE: *You're so naughty. As for the ocean, we don't really have great sea views. Come tomorrow.*

MICHAEL: *Have a little patience. :) And no more Me time between now and then.*

ELISE: *WHAAAT!? Don't be cruel. What if I'm horny? Do you want me to bring out YOUR toy when you're here?*

MICHAEL: *Definitely. Wow, I'm imagining you lying naked on your bed, with your legs spread. I sit watching from the other side of your head, so you have to turn your doe eyes over a shoulder to see that I like watching you use MY toy. I can see a little tuft of your pubes, and your breasts are pert. Oh, you're really going at it! I so want to play a part in this. I approach you, pull you slightly off the bed, so your head is overhanging, and I put my cock in your eager mouth. I start fucking you and your eyes go wide, you lose the rhythm of the vibrator, briefly, as you try to accommodate my massive cock, starting to dribble saliva as I bang into your head...*

ELISE: *It's so thick and huge making my mouth full.*

MICHAEL: *That starts to become uncomfortable for you, so I help you up, all flushed and sweaty. I lie on my back and order you above me, facing away from me. My cock finds your asshole and you slide down onto me. I allow you to keep using MY toy on your clit while I pump up and down in your backside. You clearly love this. It's so dirty and pleasurable*

321

at the same time. You feel so completely full up there, and your pussy is ready to explode as well...

MICHAEL: *I want to cum soon. I get you off me and consider going into your mouth again. Then I put you into the doggy style position and use the vibrator on you. You are making the most unusual squealing sounds! I press harder and watch your body quiver.*

I press at your ass again and get all the way in. Then I fuck you solidly for ten minutes...

ELISE: *This attack from two sides is making me so full and incredible. I love it. And I'm so near to climax. I move on you.*

MICHAEL: *I can sense your thighs giving way. You look back at me with a pitiful, other-worldly expression, lost as you are in your pleasure, but I keep thrusting in and out, until finally I cum.*

44

HAPPY BIRTHDAY

Michael spent another day in Manchester, because, after collecting Hope from school, she was off to a birthday party for a new friend. So, while he waited to pick her up again, he sat around in Samantha's house, watching television and eating her snacks; apparently, she and the South African liked to shop at Waitrose, so the different food was a pleasant novelty to Michael. At one point he got bored with the Test Match cricket and the re-runs of *Top Gear*, so decided to wash the dirty downstairs windows for the lazy pair. The grass in the small back garden needed cutting, too, so he did that as well, more so for Hope's benefit.

When he went for her a few hours later, she came out of the restaurant hugging all her new friends, causing Michael to smile as it was so cute. He got her into the car with her three balloons and goodie bag (yes, I'll have one of those, thank you), and brought up the subject of his trip. As expected, she was only mildly interested.

'So, I might not see you for a week,' he said, 'but I'll bring you something back.'

'We'll get the atlas out when we get home.'

'That's a good idea. It's on the far side of the world. A long way away. Twelve hours on a plane, probably.'

'You're talking to yourself, mister. What's for supper?'

'What's for supper? You've just been to a restaurant.'

'But, dad, those kids' burgers are such a rip-off.'

So, they watched some *Wizards of Waverley Place,* or whatever it was called, on the *Disney* channel, he then watched as she ran around in *Assassin's Creed* on the *Xbox* (without stabbing anybody), they played a form of badminton on the new lawn, then had a snack of sandwiches and coke before Samantha was due home.

'Dad's going to see his new girlfriend in Singapore,' was the first thing Hope said, as her mother walked in the room.

'Is that so,' replied Samantha, removing crumbs from the corner of Hope's mouth. 'How nice.'

Michael remained quiet. Samantha looked stressed, all flushed. He liked her close-fitting, white blouse. The strange desire to cook her dinner came over him, but he quickly killed that, gathered his things, and had Hope jump into his arms. He carried her to his car and sat her on his bonnet while he tied his shoelaces. Samantha watched him, with crossed-arms, from the doorstep.

'Thank you for staying today,' she said to him. 'Hope, you'll leave a dent in that.'

'No worries,' said Michael. He lifted Hope off the car, kissed her and watched her walk up the drive. 'I'll see you soon, sweetheart.' He got into his car, shared a wave, and drove away.

Before he left home that morning, there had been a brief dialogue with Elise. When he got back in, he showered, took a beer from the fridge, and checked for new messages. Cindy and Irene Hannah just said hello – the latter asking if he could get her a certain book, which was proving hard to find in the Philippines. That could wait until tomorrow. He had a new friends request from an American male in Michigan, which he accepted immediately.

ELISE: *Check your mail.*

Intriguing. He opened his email. She was sharing something through *Dropbox*. For a moment he had forgotten what that meant, then it clicked in his head: a movie!

The shot was frozen on the running water of a shower, with a big Play symbol overlaid. *Wow...* That's Elise's shower. *Wow*. He was more nervous than if he had actually been there. Before he watched it, he went back to Elise's profile page on *GoodReads*, wanting to see her sweet face, before she changed everything forever. Something jumped out at him; in her details was her date of birth, and despite his terrible mathematics he realised that it was her 20th birthday tomorrow. He cursed, panicked about a present, one that wasn't a vibrator which she already had.

Putting the problem aside for a moment, he went back and clicked play on the shower movie.

MICHAEL: *Elise, baby. My God, I've seen what you've done for me. You're amazing. You are so sexy, and I'm proud of you for being so daring. Wait there... just watching it a few more times... back now. Thank you. You're something else, girl!*

He had already decided the best thing to do for Elise's birthday was to create a better new movie. Watching her in the shower had sent him bulging down his inner thigh, but he had to improve on his last effort at his desk.

He hit the shower (anything she can do) where he set the camera up on the window ledge, making it film the empty space of the cubicle. After checking the result, and making adjustments to the positioning so it was filming from below where his neck would be, he set it going again. Out of shot, he quickly stripped. Michael junior was definitely in the mood, if starting off completely facing downwards. He intended a long movie, and began with a proper shower. He soaped up everywhere and, while he did so, he fantasised about being in there with Elise. He quickly became aroused, and his soapy hands aided himself to a massive erection. Maybe it was the camera working, but he shocked himself with how engorged he had become, working it by then, and washing underneath.

He imagined Elise kneeling in front of him, her jet black hair wetted down her neck, her toned body glistening beneath him, going down on him as best she could. He was firmly playing, then thinking of entering Elise, in various positions. Now faster and firmer playing. Maybe it was because she was so far away and he was yet to have her, but he knew he lusted after her more than any of the women in Newton-le-Willows, or of any of his previous girlfriends. Extremely excited by them, seeing himself as deep as possible in Elise's body, giving her what she wanted, faster and faster, then he climaxed impressively (he wasn't a teenager any more, who could hit the ceiling, but that had been dynamic), and he hoped it looked okay on the camera, because he wouldn't be doing that again in a hurry.

Clean and fresh, Michael made supper of *Kelloggs Corn Flakes* and coffee, and settled down to watch *War of the Worlds* with Tom Cruise, for the fifth time. His efforts in the shower had been a real leg-trembling affair, but once he had recovered, he managed to put the shower movie in their shared *Dropbox* file, ready for Elise in the morning, over there in Singapore.

He checked the time; she would be fast asleep right then, he hoped. He paused the film, before Tom and his neighbours went to investigate the crazy lightning storm, and went to the computer.

MICHAEL: *Elise, Happy Birthday, darling. XX*
You're getting too old for me. :p Listen, I know you didn't want a card and a proper present, so I want you to find the new movie I just made for you. Enjoy. I love you, and I'm going to book the flight tomorrow. Speak to you later.

45

GOOD TO GO

After seeing Michael's shower movie, Elise felt quite distressed – delighted beyond words with what she had seen, and super pleased with the most unusual birthday present ever; it was just that she was going out with her friends to celebrate, and that would mean putting off Michael again, just when she wanted to please him most. Also, the following night had been ear-marked for time with Dylan – so it would be two evenings without connecting with Michael.

She watched it again, fast-forwarding through the normal stuff, which was still sweet, onto the hardcore show. Her laptop was at an angle on her desk, as Dylan was in the other room, studying, and he might just walk in. He would knock first, of course, but she was still in that quandary of having two men on the go. She knew Michael had that woman in Newton-le-Willows, but it didn't stop her terrible feelings of guilt.

She was delighted that he was booking his flight. The only issue was having Dylan staying with her. She had been intimate with Dylan, up to a point. She loved him to bits. But her Englishman was coming.

Dylan actually did knock on her bedroom door, shocking the life out of her. She banged shut the laptop and tried to compose her face, but he was waiting respectfully. 'Yes, Dylan, honey?'

'I'm going to the library,' he called. 'I'll be back in plenty of time to take you to meet your friends.'

She laughed. 'You can come in, you know.'

He popped his head inside, slowly. 'Are you decent?'

'Dylan, I said I'll get the bus.'

'I can't let you do that. Not when I could take you. Okay, see you soon.'

She blew him a kiss. She waited to hear him leave the apartment before reopening the laptop. She sat there watching it again, finding that she was rubbing her thighs together, getting quite hot and bothered. Inspiration came to her; a great way to tell Michael she was unavailable for two nights.

She lost her shorts and panties, before bouncing onto her bed on her knees, reaching into her side drawer for the toy and her camera. The movie was on a loop, the laptop slightly too far away, but she was already touching herself with one hand and preparing the camera with the other. She placed the camera on the bedside table, set it recording, and scooted around on her bottom until she was almost side on to it. She spread her legs, still going with her fingers. With no intention of going for an epic length of movie, like Michael, she incorporated the vibrator immediately. Checking the position of the camera, she decided to hitch up her blouse a bit more, let him see her flat belly. Her left hand was discreetly shielding the toy in action, but, nevertheless, it was extremely explicit what she was doing. And it was so good, as well, quickly getting her off. She even forgot the camera was working, as she pushed on for more pleasure.

Michael saw that Elise had sent him a message at lunchtime, after he returned from seeing Tony. What better man to be taking him to the airport when the big day came around? The reason for the trip, which would go to Keira through both of them now, revolved around him visiting relatives he had not seen in years – a bit of a clan gathering, in fact. Not that he feared Keira would be interested in accompanying him half way around the world.

The new movie had been titled "My birthday present back to you". It was quite possibly the most amazing thing he had ever seen. He had watched similar things in real life, of course, but to be sent that...

There was a storm brewing over Merseyside, electrical and big. It gave Michael a high feeling, the hairs on the back of his neck tingling, and he was too mesmerised to move away from the repeating movie. Lightning flashed across the apartment, followed quickly by a massive boom.

Finally, he dragged himself away. He rechecked his to-do list for Singapore. He just needed to get some Singapore dollars. Maybe he would venture back to St Helens and use that Western Union shop again, perhaps send some funds ahead of him to Elise. But apart from that, apparently, he was good to go!

Michael spoke on the phone with his mother, who told him she and his father had decided to go on a Rhine river cruise. It would coincide with his own trip, but he decided not to mention Singapore, just wished them a pleasant holiday.

Then Michael rang his ex-wife. He hadn't wanted to discuss anything to do with Elise while he was at Sam's house in Manchester, but he had to confirm that he would be missing his next day of looking after Hope. Samantha answered on the first ring, instantly impatient with him. He silently cursed her new lifestyle with the South African. She quickly quizzed him about the trip; he said it was to see a book friend. Long way to go for a book friend, she had said. But, anyway, the chore was done; there were no more hurdles.

Michael accepted Elise's apology for being absent for a couple of nights. He reiterated that he didn't want to interfere with her friendships there, however hard it was to not miss her. Then she was silent, and there was nothing from Cindy, or anyone else. He went to visit the barber, then jogged home as the rain came on again. He felt only slightly fitter with all his cycling and exercising. He hoped Elise would appreciate the efforts.

Late in the afternoon, the sky cleared, so he decided upon

another cycle ride. He liked the long straight road out towards Warrington, as he felt the pain half way down it, so stuck to that route. Once again, he was shattered as he rested at Burger King. He bought a smoothie and sat on his bike with it. It was after a couple of minutes of being there, that he finally noticed the family watching him from tables by the window; it was the two Garrand couples. Behind them, a wild children's party was in full swing, so obviously Shirley and Joanne had come together for the sake of the kids. It was bizarre for Michael to have to acknowledge them and receive waves and smiles (although Shirley just stared) and then mount his bike and take his dishevelled form away from their festivities.

After a shower, he checked *GoodReads*, out of habit. He looked at Elise's cute profile photo while having bad thoughts about her body. There was a new friend request: a man from Chicago called Jack. Michael pondered over Chicago, then remembered wishing good luck in his giveaway to Ivan in Chicago. Fair enough. He looked at Jack's image, found him to be a handsome thirty-something, but with nothing obviously crazy about him, so he clicked the accept button. Then he went on Amazon to order that book for Irene Hannah. Maybe he could take it with him, post it from Singapore. He laughed as he moved to the kitchen to prepare his evening meal.

46

SAMANTHA

It was two days before Michael was due to fly. Elise's mind was ablaze with where to take him, how to entertain him, how to make sure he enjoyed the best of Singapore, while subconsciously being a bag of nerves over the real reason for his visit; she hoped she didn't embarrass herself through her naivety, her shyness, and that he would be satisfied with her. There was also the mad problem of Dylan still staying in her apartment. She knew she had to make a decision. If it came to it, she would have to go to her friends and borrow one of their homes; no way could she put Michael up in a hotel. She would just say she had a poorly aunt staying at her place.

There had been no more movies exchanged. Michael had even joked that she should abstain from Me time until he got there. "What!!?? But what if I get horny?" she had replied. They messaged frantically, expressing their urgency to be together, while talking over the minutiae of what he would be wearing to travel in and what kind of suitcase he owned. They talked dirty, too. He mentioned what he would like to do to her in the Arrivals concourse at Changi airport, and she reminded him how strict Singapore was and that he would probably spend the holiday in prison. The back of a taxi was also a no-no, apparently, much to his amusement.

MICHAEL: *Elise, I just want to hold your body against mine. Feel your bare breasts against my bare chest.*

ELISE: *Aww, that's so sweet. You don't know how bad I want that too. Come here soon. I can't stop looking at the clock.*

MICHAEL: *What time is it there? Back here in the real world it's 2.30pm.*

ELISE: *Hey, cheeky! Are you prepared for the heat? I've got you some flip-flops.*

MICHAEL: *Flip-flops, really? No, I'm not happy with the weather forecast. Remind me, why aren't you coming here first? I could meet you at Heathrow, get you wet in my car in Heathrow's short-stay car-park. Hehe. Don't you want to see London?*

ELISE: *Oh, Michael, you could so make me soak my*

panties in Heathrow's car-park. Not the most romantic image, but okay. I do want to see London one day, but I want to see your home first, yeah.

MICHAEL: *Okay. We'll do London one day. I'll take you on the London Eye, and to the Tower, see where Anne Boleyn was executed – I believe she was a bit of a tease, too.*

ELISE: *Hey! Just you wait until you get here. You'll see I'm not a tease. I have an important question for you.*

MICHAEL: *Oh? Go ahead.*

ELISE: *When I collect you, would you prefer me shaved or...*

All day, Elise found that she was smiling at everyone, even on the bus, as she went from hair salon to nail appointment, to buying Michael his flip-flops for the beach. She had lunch alone at Marche restaurant, at Vivo city, eating lightly, with Michael in mind. Her friend, Silvia, was away on her job experience, so she had the use of her apartment. She went there first thing to change the sheets and generally clean up, as well as leave some food in the fridge.

Dylan, who was extra busy with his medical plans and hotel shifts, would be told that Silvia was poorly, and that

Elise would be there looking after her for most of the next week. Quite a simple plan, really. She was about to go out to meet Dylan for supper, and then, without any guilt, would throw herself into Michael's holiday. Never had she been more excited, with constant butterflies in her belly. She touched her stomach through her blouse, imagining Michael coming on her there.

Michael went for his last cycle ride before his trip, but only to the High street. Not being able to face up to visiting St Helens again, he went to pick up some Singapore dollars from the Post Office. Then he stopped by Tony's house again. It was not that he thought the man too unreliable to be there to take him to the airport, but that he did have a reputation for liking his sleep. Tony heartily assured him that he had an alarm clock and his girlfriend's heel to get him out of bed, and Wendy had seconded that. Michael declined a cup of tea, insisting he must go pack.

Carrying his bike upstairs, he passed his American neighbour, Gloria, bidding her good day. Getting himself a glass of milk, he examined the food in his fridge, deciding on unusual combinations for his dinner, to use up the stuff. He switched on the computer, then left it while he showered. In his bedroom, his case was on the floor, open and part filled. He realised he was excited and nervous in equal measures.

MICHAEL: *Cindy, hiya. Just wanted to let you know I'll*

be away for a week. Only going to Spain with the lads. A drinking holiday. Very bad. I'll miss you, and speak when I get back.

MICHAEL: Elise, not long now, baby. Are you free to talk? Tomorrow night I'll send a message just before I leave here, with all the details. I'm so looking forward to seeing you in the flesh.

CINDY: *No drinking. Tut tut Michael. Have loveley time, speak soon, kekke. NO DRINKING.*

That made him laugh. His door intercom sounded. Could Elise have possibly travelled to surprise him since they last spoke? Still giggling, he walked downstairs (burn a few more calories for Elise) and flung open the main door.

Hope cheerily hugged him, as she barged inside, and ran upstairs. 'I need the loo! Hi, dad!'

'Hi, sweetheart. What... what are you doing here?'

Hope's suitcase appeared in the doorway, attached to Sam's hand. She straightened, an expression of contrition on her face, but only found herself staring at Michael's aggressively pointed index finger.

'No, Sam!' he hissed. 'What do you think you're playing at?'

'We've got an emergency...'

'You can fuck right off, you selfish bitch.'

'If we don't go to South Africa we lose the contract. I'm

sorry, I know you had something on, but it's a critical situation.'

Michael, for maybe the first time ever, really wanted to strike this woman in the face. Or at least have her against the wall by the throat.

'It's not "something on", it's a 9,000 mile booked flight, with someone relying on me.'

'Michael, she's your daughter.'

'You cunt!'

The wind took Sam's hair, causing her to look away.

Michael looked up the street, wanting a fight. 'Is knob head here with you?'

'I'm here on my own, Michael. Can we not go up and talk about it?'

'What's to talk about?'

'Well, can't your parents have her for a week?'

'You disgust me. They're away on holiday.'

'Well, your girlfriend, then? Keira, or whatever her name is.'

Michael's mind was whirling, on how to save his trip to see Elise, while feeling the love and protectiveness towards his beautiful daughter. Frankly, there wasn't anything to consider.

'Can't you think of anyone?' asked Samantha.

'Just get out of my fucking sight!'

She didn't need to be told twice, vacating the doorway. Michael slammed the door and turned for the stairs. By the time he got up to his apartment, all things to do with Singapore were postponed. Hope was playing football.

'Well!' called Michael, 'my number one girl's here now.'

'Dad, get in goal. Come on, mister.'

'Right you are!'

47

ROAD TRIP

It wasn't a normal stay; Hope knew that. She knew her dad was supposed to be going away on holiday, but her mum's problem had made him stay. Her mum was so annoying at times. So she asked permission to watch her programmes instead of just grabbing the remote control, offered to make him breakfast and, after ringing her friends to catch up, and being invited out, offered to stay with him.

'No, no, you should go round. We've got all week, honey, don't ignore your friends. Maybe we could go to Southport one day, or to a fun fair.'

'A fun fair, dad?'

'Well, an adventure park, whatever they're called. What's the nearest one?'

'Alton Towers is the best.'

'Is that the nearest? That's in Staffordshire, isn't it?'

'But straight down the motorway.'

'Okay, I'll look into that.'

So he dropped her at her friend's house. He drove away, then stopped around the corner, and sat there in the car. Suddenly he was fatigued; emotionally, he supposed. It was twelve hours from the time he was supposed to be at Manchester airport. He must tell Tony. He must tell Elise.

Elise found herself at Pizza Hut, at Causeway Point, with her mum and brothers. Once more, thinking about Michael seeing her naked soon, she didn't want to eat pizza, but she so loved pizza, and it would be rude not to.

She did listen to family matters, as she munched away, but really she was almost delirious with the thought of jumping into Michael's arms at Changi airport. Before that, Dylan wanted to see her, urgently; the lie was in place about her caring for a poorly Silvia, but he said he just wanted a few minutes. She would meet him between his shifts at the hotel, see what was so important. She just needed to get through this meal. After seeing Dylan she would head home to bathe, and then try to sleep before looking in the morning for Michael's message to say he was on his way.

Elise's mother, still unaware of the existence of Dylan, dropped her daughter at the hotel, under the impression Elise was meeting a girlfriend. Elise kissed her brothers during a brief respite in their fighting in the back of the car, kissed her mother, and hurried into the hotel foyer.

She spotted Dylan straight away, on the far side of the atrium. He smiled, gave her a five minutes gesture, so she went through to one of the bars, ordered an orange juice and went to sit in a secluded part of the patio. She puzzled over what could possibly be so important. Surely he wasn't quitting his job early, expecting her to be available for him. If that was the case, then she would put her foot down and insist on caring for her poorly friend.

While she waited, Elise checked *GoodReads* on her phone; nothing from Michael yet. So she read through some of their old messages. Some amused her, some made her blush. In her emails she reacquainted herself with images of Michael's manhood. Soon it would be touching her. It gave her a thrill just to think about it. Before she felt the urge to squeeze her thighs together, she put the phone down and sipped her drink, watching through the potted shrubbery as other customers settled themselves at a table. It was quite a cool day; she so hoped it wouldn't become too humid for Michael. She just sat there and waited, smiling a little bit to herself.

'You're a bit early, mate,' said Tony, letting Michael in to his house. Wendy looked out from the kitchen. She smiled and waved. 'I was planning on having *some* sleep,' continued Tony.

'Can we talk?' asked Michael.

'Go into the games room.'

By games room, Tony meant the back room which Wendy had commandeered as a home office. It had French windows which were open to the garden, and they sat down there in springy chairs.

'Do you want a drink?' asked Tony.

Michael shook his head. 'Sam's only gone and left Hope with me.'

'Shit. What a scheming bitch. What are you going to do? Can your parents have her?'

'They're in Germany.'

We'd have her, you know that, but straight after the airport we'll be off to Harrogate with Wendy's parents' anniversary thing.

'I'm not leaving Hope with anyone. I just wanted to say it's off for now.'

'It's bad news, man. Remind me, where were you going again?'

'Singapore.'

'Did you not want to take my sister?'

'It's not cheap, you know.'

Tony grinned. 'Fair enough. What do the Singapore relatives say about it?'

Michael made to leave. 'I'm yet to find out.'

'Don't rush off,' said Tony. 'Stay for something to eat. Let the distant cousins wake up to the bad news. You would have been on the plane for, what, ten hours?'

'Tony, what would I do without you? More to the point,

what would I do without Wendy's cooking skills?'

'I'll go and tell the woman. I'll bring back some beer. Take your shoes off, relax.'

Michael did just that, he took off his shoes, but he struggled to relax. He sat there, looking out at the small Newton-le-Willows garden, worried sick as to what to say to Elise.

Whatever Dylan had to say to Elise, it would have to wait until morning, as his bosses were in a lather over some double-booking – he just had chance to hurry over to her, explain the situation, and sneak a little kiss. She laughed and assured him she wasn't put out. She warned him not to make a lot of noise when he got in. He kissed her again and took his leave.

Elise got the bus home. She bathed. She made tea. Then she went on *GoodReads* to leave Michael a message.

ELISE: *Michael, I know you're busy. I just wanted to thank you so much for travelling all the way out here. I'll look for your message in the morning. When you've done Singapore and I've done England I so want to do a road trip. Across America? I'll leave from LA and you leave from New York, and we'll meet in Oklahoma. Hehe.*

Check your mail, I've sent you something to help you on your way.

Love

She went to her email and sent Michael the shot she had kept in reserve for such an occasion.

Michael got home from Tony's feeling very low. He made coffee. He kicked a ball around. But there was no longer any chance to put off the inevitable. On *GoodReads* he saw the funny road trip message. Before he managed to reply, he went in search of whatever she had sent him via email. What he found almost made him cry; it was almost identical to the Irene Hannah photo, taken while on all fours, using a mirror. Almost consumed with guilt he had to force himself to look at her wonderful sex, focussing instead on the lovely curves of her ass. She had done that for him and he wasn't going yet. He was no longer just very low, he was completely depressed.

Elise woke, and was already reaching for her laptop before she remembered who she was. She took a moment, pushed her hair off her face. Before she got through to *GoodReads*, there came a knock on the door: interesting.

'Dylan, is that you?'

'I hope so,' replied Dylan. 'Can I come in?'

'You can.'

He was dressed for work. 'I left it as long as I could.'

'Come here.'

He obeyed and got pulled down into a hug, and made to sit on the bed beside her.

'I'm sorry you were messed around yesterday,' he said. 'No, it was unforgivable of me. I have something for you and I can't stand to wait until tonight.'

She laughed. 'What is it? Oh, you're not writing lyrics for me, are you?'

'What? No. It's this.'

He was offering her an oblong jewellery box. Her heart skipped a beat, both with delighted surprise and relief that it wasn't in a ring box shape.

'Oh, Dylan.'

'Open it.'

She kissed him first. Michael flashed into her mind and she felt so awful, but she kissed the lovely Dylan again, then opened the box. Her eyes were not yet awake, and now they filled with tears as she saw the gold bracelet.

'Dylan, it's beautiful,' she blubbed.

He was so relieved, it was almost comical. They embraced for quite a while. But then he just had to go to work.

'You'll soon just be a med student,' she cheered him with.

'I can't wait. I can't wait to improve my situation to make you happy. I love you, Elise.'

That made her cry even more. 'Go! Go before I dissolve, you lovely boy.'

He blew her a kiss and backed out of the room, looking at her until the very last second that he had to close the door.

Elise put on the bracelet. She loved it. She sniffled. She tried to compose herself. Now she had to put the wonderful Dylan away in his compartment in her mind, because she so wanted to hear that Michael was on his way to stay with her, to squeeze her at the airport, to laugh with her about all they had said to each other, to be intimate together and to finally take her virginity from her.

She went excitedly onto *GoodReads*.

TWO YEARS LATER

48

AIR CRASH INVESTIGATORS

Mr Sean O'Garra, the depot manager, pressed a little blue key fob against the connection post and the roll-top door creaked upwards. 'I'll get you one of these tags,' he said to Rimski, beside him, as they headed down a long tunnel. They passed small lock-up units of the storage facility, until they got down to where a couple of cars were stationary, their hatchback doors open. Two middle-aged men were, separately, taking parcels from mesh cages and placing them in order on the floor, prior to loading their vehicles.

'They look like air crash investigators,' laughed O'Garra, 'piecing the plane back together on the floor. You can drive in here, or stay where you are today, it's your choice. You've only got a small round, so you'll probably throw the parcels straight in after scanning.'

Rimski nodded, watching the ludicrous, time-consuming, actions of the two men; they must spend half an hour sorting parcels before they actually go out delivering them.

O'Garra pulled out a cage on wheels from amongst twenty others, full to about half way with parcels from well-known fashion brands, as well as lesser firms and packages being sent privately. With Rimski at the other side, they trundled it back up the corridor and out to the car-park, where Rimski had left "his" white van.

'I believe the Area Manager taught you about the handset,' continued O'Garra.

'She did, yes.'

'Good. I'll watch you scan the parcels this time. Any of the other couriers will help you with the little things that go wrong with the crappy machine. So, you know your area?'

'I'm familiar with it, yes. And I've got an A to Z.'

'Very good. You'll soon get the hang of it.'

Rimski began beeping the barcodes on the parcels with his hand-held terminal, pretending to take an interest in their addresses. O'Garra greeted the arrival of other couriers, sharing banter with them. Once Rimski was all loaded, O'Garra offered to take his cage back.

'Thank you,' said Rimski.

'I'll see you in the morning, then,' said O'Garra.

'What's the earliest I can get here? I like to get on with things, you see.'

'Well, the wagon gets here between six-thirty and seven, then we've got to sort the parcels. So, seven thirty, I'd say.'

'Do you not sort on your own, then?'

'No, too many. I've got a couple of lady couriers who help, before they go and do their rounds. Anyway, have a good one. Don't get too stressed, once you know the customers, it'll fly by.'

'Okay, then,' said Rimski, getting into the van.

He watched Sean O'Garra enter the depot, before driving away.

Stephen and Alfie Garrand were sitting in a McDonald's restaurant on the outskirts of Warrington, both enjoying Big Macs and shakes. There was other food on trays on the table, going cold, but their womenfolk had gone to the Ladies, immediately on arrival, much to Stephen's annoyance. Alfie nodded for him to look through the window, off into the near distance. Rimski's van had come to a stop. The man got out, looked around him, before going into the back of the vehicle.

Stephen slurped his banana milkshake and turned his attention to the big-haired blonde who was taking her seat beside him. Her eyebrows were tweezered to within an inch of their lives and her nails were like something out of Footballers' Wives magazine spread. She leant in for a peck on the cheek from Stephen, as if he would have pined for her going to the toilet; their relationship was in that early stage. Another blonde, of similar early-twenties age, sat herself beside Alfie. She was very pretty, but less of a doll. They continued their inane conversation from the Ladies and played with their phones while eating.

'He doesn't realise we can see him,' Alfie said to Stephen. 'What's he doing, helping himself?'

'It doesn't matter if he does,' replied Stephen.

'Who's that you're talking about?' asked the big-haired blonde, between stuffing her face with fries.

'Nobody, babe,' said Stephen. 'A business colleague is stopping by in a bit, we're gonna pop out for a quick word, okay?'

Stephen was divorced from Joanne, who still had the house on the outskirts of Newton-le-Willows, while Alfie was estranged from Shirley, who he believed was dating a local man, although he wasn't yet sure. Alfie looked at his date, as she devoured her chicken sandwich, with a look that suggested he was not that keen on her.

Rimski's van moved slowly into the car-park. Stephen and Alfie jogged out to meet it, both carrying their shakes. Rimski got out, his face expressing disappointment; he'd been hoping they would be waiting inside and would buy him a meal.

'How did it go?' asked Stephen, getting straight to the point.

'No problem at all,' replied Rimski, 'I'm in, accepted by the depot manager, got my day's deliveries in there.'

'Did you find out the time the wagon gets in?' asked Alfie. 'And get given an entrance key-fob?'

'I did. Both of those things.'

Stephen said, 'Make sure you get there early tomorrow, see that there's only one delivery driver, and count the parcel sorter people.'

Rimski nodded. 'No worries. What should I do with today's parcels? Deliver them?' He laughed at the very thought.

'Do what you want with them,' answered Stephen. 'Just make sure you do what you're supposed to do on the handset, so this manager doesn't get a phone call saying there's a problem with you.'

Stephen wanted to get back to his meal. 'Come straight to the yard after going there in the morning.'

Rimski nodded. 'Will do, boss.' He watched Stephen walk away, but gestured for Alfie to linger. 'I saw Shirley yesterday, with her new fella. Thought you'd like to know.'

Alfie pretended to be apathetic about the news, moving off after his brother. 'Anyone I know?'

Michael parked his car a few hundred yards up the road from the Hope Academy in Newton-le-Willows. It never ceased to amaze him that school could sometimes finish at 2.30 in the afternoon these days. As a child, he remembered staring at a clock on a classroom wall, praying for it to move to 4pm, but here were kids in the grey uniform, wandering along the street.

Michael got out and leant on the car, watching a fuller stream of children exiting the main gate. Finally, he saw Hope, and they exchanged waves. While he waited for her to finish a chat with friends, who were heading in the other direction, he looked at his daughter, now twelve, almost as tall as him, happy and settled, living with her dad for the last year and a bit. Her mother had decamped to South Africa, not quite emigrated, but as good as. There was still the fear that she would return, but at least Michael's legal hand had been strengthened by her behaviour.

Life was extremely good for Michael. He was an established thriller writer, selling well enough to make a living, now onto his sixth novel. He was still living in the same apartment, but having Hope there made him the happiest man in the world.

Oh God, he thought, seeing Hope take her leave of her friends, but have the famous Jack Peplow, classmate and all-round top boy, put a casual arm over her shoulder. There would soon be the problem of boyfriends to contend with. Michael tried not to watch as Hope and Jack approached. At least, as they got near and Hope pointed out her father to the boy, Jack had the politeness to disentangle himself from her. Hope waved Jack good day, then ran to hug her dad. Michael missed the spinning around bit, but accepted that she was growing up. Still, he had her juice drink waiting for her in the glove compartment, and they chatted away as he drove her home.

There was music coming from their apartment. While he parked the car, she let herself in and ran upstairs. Michael followed the guitar tune, coming in to see Hope still embracing Cindy, while she told her about her school day. Michael shut the door, smiling at the lovely sight.

Cindy disentangled herself. Apparently, she had baked rock cakes, and they were expected to enjoy them.

'Yay!' said Hope, who would eat anything.

'Yay,' said Michael, less enthusiastic over Cindy's cooking.

Cindy turned back to him, her fringe almost in her eyes, smiling happily. 'They not weird, Michael. I follow recipe.' She kissed him on the mouth. 'Meeting go well?'

He let her go, with Hope pulling her. 'Meeting go well.'

'They are lovely,' said Hope, 'but what happened to the icing?'

Cindy laughed. 'Eh?'

Michael held Cindy from behind, as his family laughed together in the kitchen.

49

999

Rimski pressed the blue fob against the pillar and the roll-top door slowly started to retract noisily upwards. At about three feet, both Garrand brothers, masked and tooled-up, scooted underneath and began running down the corridor of the storage facility, fluorescent lighting automatically coming on, as they went. Rimski, in a balaclava, waited for the door to go above six feet before following, at a steady pace.

A large van filled the tunnel, with full canvas sacks on the floor below its open back door. The delivery driver could be seen moving about inside, fetching more stuff. Alfie climbed up and confronted the man with a machete. The terrified delivery driver complied instantly, and allowed himself to be dragged out by his collar. Meanwhile, Stephen was in the process of terrifying Sean O'Garra and two middle-aged women, who were inside the bay, sorting parcels into cages. Stephen's baseball bat was up on his right shoulder, as he shouted and ranted, not with any clear instruction, just with the intention of bamboozling the three people. O'Garra had his hands up in surrender, getting himself between Stephen and the two women.

'Get the fuck over there!' Stephen screamed at him. Then the metal cages proved an inspiration to him. 'You and you!' he shouted at the women. 'Both of you get into a cage, squat down.' They did what they were told. 'Boss man,' he said to O'Garra, 'close the doors on them.'

The driver was standing alongside O'Garra by the time Rimski arrived. First thing first, four mobile phones were collected from the four raid victims, and all were thrown up the corridor by Stephen. With the two women out of action, the raid could progress as planned.

Michael brought Cindy breakfast in bed. With the curtains being quite flimsy, he could see that she was awake and watching him with a cute smirk on her face. She sat up, her hair tousled, yawning. She wore a large tee-shirt to bed; being in England with Michael still went against everything she had ever known in her life and she still tried to retain some modesty. Even so, she looked for a kiss and received a long, loving one from him.

'Why deserve this?' she asked, smiling, assessing what was on her tray.

Michael sat beside her. 'Because you are so beautiful.'

She smiled wider, bit into a piece of toast.

'Hope's on the computer. She wants to speak to your family after you've said hello.'

'Aww, we take her to them, soon, yeah?'

'Definitely.'

She pointed at her tray, as if realising the reason for his gesture. 'Oh, wait. Today you stand Godfather to friend Tony's child.'

'And?'

'Godmother is your ex-girlfriend, that Keira. You butter me to be close to her in church.'

'Aww, no, baby. Keira's cool. You know that. Everyone knows you're the one.'

Cindy grinned. 'I know that too.'

'Right, I'll let you eat in peace.'

'Tell Hope I get up soon.'

Michael left her alone. He heard Hope laugh hysterically at something online as he got to the living area.

'Is that Jack Peplow?' he teased.

'No, mister, it's not Jack.'

'Cindy's getting up soon. Don't you rush on there, you know she'll probably get emotional talking to her family.'

'I won't, dad.'

Michael started on his own breakfast.

'There's no milk,' called Hope.

'I'm a man, I don't need milk.'

Pulling a face at his black coffee, he sat down in front of the television to watch *Location, Location, Location*, just because it happened to be on. Phil Spencer was house hunting in Brighton.

'Hope, do you want to go to Brighton, for a holiday?'

'Not particularly.'

'You will be ready for the church?'

'Of course, silly.'

Sean O'Garra and the delivery driver had been made to put every sack of parcels back on the wagon, as well as three racks of expensive dresses from a major High Street brand, then they were forced into their own cages, and all four cages had been tied together. Alfie pulled down and locked the back shutter of the truck. Stephen considered locking the four people in their own room, but as soon as the first courier arrived the alarm would be raised anyway.

The truck was going to go the forward way out, so Alfie took Rimski's blue fob and ran up to the connector point. This door rose up. Alfie, keeping the fob for the original entry point, ran past Rimski, who was getting into the driver's cab.

Stephen checked that they were all done, that nothing silly had been left behind, waved Rimski away, slapped Alfie on the back, and then followed his brother at a run back the way they had come.

Rimski, who had driven buses as a younger man, took the truck out into the gloomy morning light, turned left and went around the storage depot. He fell in behind the stolen car the Garrands were in, and they all left the premises at a sedate pace.

When it was Hope's turn for a cup of tea, she decided she really wanted milk.

'Dad, I'll pop to the shop for some milk,' she called.

'No, you won't. I'll go.'

'I'll just be two minutes on my bike.'

Cindy had wandered through, placing her tray in the kitchen. 'I go with her, Michael. We go on the bikes, then I shower when I get back.'

'If you're sure, baby.'

Cindy put on some trousers, her boots and a jacket, and went off happily with Hope, taking the bikes down the stairs.

It was starting to rain.

'Oh, so bad for the Christening,' said Cindy, looking to the skies. 'Maybe it brighten up by later.'

They cycled off towards the High street. Hope was in front, chatting over her shoulder. Cindy didn't catch most of it, but she laughed and called back. At the Spar shop Cindy bought milk and a variety of sweets, prompted by Hope.

'Let us hurry,' said Cindy, as they headed back in the worsening rain. They got as far as the corner where they turned back towards Michael's building, Hope riding on the pavement. Cindy didn't hear anything coming, what with the rain, until suddenly there was a truck where the last house should have been, one side of it up in the air, steam and smoke billowing into the downpour, bricks and white plaster everywhere. Cindy screamed and got off her bike as quickly as possible. Two women rushed from a neighbouring property, one immediately on her mobile phone, dialling 999. A passing car had stopped, and the elderly male driver grabbed Cindy and kept her from jumping into the terrible scene. There was no fire but bricks were still tumbling down.

'Were you with someone, love?' asked the woman who was not on the phone.

'Yes! A young girl on a bike. Please!'

Both the women tried to look under the wagon, but there were hundreds of catalogue parcels dumped on the road.

More people were rushing to the scene. There were cries of "Oh my God" and more calls to the emergency services. Of course, some people were filming on their phones.

Cindy broke free of the old man. Clearing smoke had shown her that she could squeeze between the cab of the cock-eyed wagon and the wall on the other side of the road. Two younger men went with her. Instantly they were faced with the horrible sight of the wagon driver hanging by his legs, backwards from the shattered windscreen. He was almost decapitated. One of the men held his mouth to keep from vomiting, while the other swore.

'Fucking hell, that's old Lionel Rimmer.'

Cindy was screaming for Hope, engulfed with panic. Two

more men arrived; Stephen and Alfie Garrand, although Cindy didn't know them. She saw the bike first, mangled, sticking out from under one of the massive wheels. Then parts of Hope became visible to her through the terrible conditions of fallen bricks and masonry. 'Hope!' She turned to the men. 'The little girl! Help the little girl!'

50

ELISE

Michael finally found a space to park his car in Warrington Hospital's main car-park and paid at the machine. It was two days after the accident, and he had just been home to shower and have a change of clothes. He slung a bag over his shoulder and headed in. Suddenly drained, he took a moment at the entranceway, leaning on a wall to watch the world pass him by. Ambulances were arriving and departing, the public streamed in and out (some complaining bitterly about the parking fees), an obese couple took the length of Michael's stay to get from the public phones to the waiting taxi, a drunk woman lolled out of a wheelchair, bemoaning her lost love. Michael took a deep breath and entered the building.

Cindy met him on the children's ward, standing to embrace him, before they sat close together, holding hands.

'They're with her now,' said Cindy, 'ask me to walk outside room.'

'It's okay, baby. Tony's on his way soon, to take you home again. You must get some sleep.'

'No, I stay, Michael. I stay.'

'We'll see.' He caressed her cheek. 'How are you?'

'No matter me.'

They waited in silence, watching people and staff pass by. They read all the posters on the wall for the umpteenth time. At last, the senior nurse, who had been doing a great job of looking after them, came out.

'We're done,' she said. 'You can go back in now.'

'Thank you very much,' said Michael.

They went through, as quietly as possible. They found Hope awake, bandaged heavily around the head and connected up to several machines, but smiling at them without showing her teeth (she had lost one at the front). Her right leg was in full plaster and slightly elevated.

'Hello, darling,' said Michael.

Cindy took the only seat, close to Hope's side. Cindy had been mortified to have almost lost the child; now she didn't want to let her out of her sight. Michael gently kissed Hope's left cheek.

'I've brought you some stuff,' he said, 'your Gameboy, your favourite teddy. I'll ask the nurse when you can have them.'

'Thanks, mister,' she whispered.

He looked up as Cindy regained her feet.

'Loo,' she explained, pulling a face. She blew Hope a kiss and left the room.

Michael was grateful to take the chair.

'Everyone's been asking after you,' he said. He tried to remember the names, 'Errm, Aimee, Lily, the famous Jack P. have all been round, according to Gloria; she's holding the fort. The press keep ringing the buzzer, newspapers and local TV. Hey, I'm supposed to be the famous one.'

She giggled.

'I've left another message for your mum,' he continued. 'She must be travelling, or something. How are you feeling?'

'Not too bad. I just feel weird.'

'That'll be the drugs. You're starting early. Sorry, I shouldn't make you laugh. You lie quietly.'

Michael sat there, still feeling the shock and stress wash over him. In the last forty-eight hours he had only drunk bottled water and eaten a couple of sandwiches. He took a deep breath; surely the adrenalin would level out soon, now that the tragedy had settled down into a scare.

It had been the Prince of Darkness who had come for him in a terrible panic, after stumbling upon the incident and realising that Cindy was distraught over Hope being involved. Michael would never forget that immediate feeling of total despair, followed by the mad rush to the scene. Police cars and Fire engines were all over the place, but the ambulance had already taken Hope and Cindy away.

Apparently, the Garrand brothers had helped to remove rubble off Hope's unconscious form – and it was Rimski, the driver, dead at the scene; that would be looked into fully when

Hope was safe and sound, he was sure about that.

Thankfully, Hope had been hit by the falling wall of the side of the house, and not by the out of control truck, and she had been wearing her cycle helmet. Thank God for that, Michael thought again. There was the broken leg, lacerations to her neck and shoulders, and serious blood loss which had been superbly dealt with by one of the paramedics. Suddenly Michael felt like crying; he had almost lost his baby.

'Dad, it's okay.'

'I know it is, sweetheart.' He tried to smile. 'Everything's just brilliant.'

A nurse came in, did a nursey thing at one of the monitors, then left again. Michael stood, looking out of the window.

'Awful view you've got. You're not missing much.'

'Did Jack say anything in particular?'

'I don't know, darling. Shall I make something up for you.'

She giggled again. 'No, don't. Dad, how long do I have to stay here?'

A doctor popped his head in and requested Michael's company.

'I'll ask now. I'll just be outside, okay.'

Michael went for a chat with the specialist. It was all positive and the man gave the impression that everything was progressing in a routine fashion. That conversation certainly levelled out Michael's adrenalin levels, and he came back in and retook his seat.

'He couldn't say how long, sweetheart,' he said. 'They'll

keep you as long as necessary. And we won't leave you for a minute.'

Michael scanned the austere room, coming to a stop on a bunch of flowers near the television.

'Those are nice,' he said. 'Where are they from?'

'The lady who helped me brought them in. The doctor in the ambulance.'

'Oh, you mean the paramedic.' Michael was suddenly extraordinarily touched. 'That's wonderful, Hope. I'm going to make sure to say nice things about her to her bosses. Is there a card attached?'

'No, I don't think so. But she signed my leg.'

Michael laughed. 'What, even before Jack P has been there?' He stood up to look along the Plaster of Paris. He found a small, feminine signature. He had to crane his neck to read it:

Get well soon,
ELISE

www.ingramcontent.com/pod-product-compliance
Lightning Source LLC
Chambersburg PA
CBHW031246170626
46807CB00001B/4